A Tale of Two Cities

GLOBE BOOK COMPANY, INC.

New York/Chicago/Cleveland

A Tale of Two Cities

CHARLES DICKENS

Adapted by
Mabel Dodge Holmes

Reading Consultant
M. Jerry Weiss

An
Adapted
Classic

Mable Dodge Holmes
formerly Head of the English Department
Kensington High School
Philadelphia, Pennsylvania

M. Jerry Weiss
Distinguished Service Professor of Communication
Jersey City State College
Jersey City, New Jersey

ISBN: 0-87065-007-6

ABOUT THE AUTHOR

Charles Dickens was born the second of eight children in England in 1812. He was taught by his mother, and went to school for only a short time. The Dickens family moved to London when Charles was about nine. Since they were very poor, Charles was sent to work in a factory when he was only ten. Later, after the family had inherited some money, Charles went to boarding school for two years. Dickens became a clerk to a lawyer, then a court reporter. At 19 he became a reporter in Parliament.

In 1836 Dickens began writing a story called *Pickwick Papers*. This book was a great success and made him famous. For the rest of his life Dickens continued to write. He created many famous characters, including David Copperfield, Oliver Twist, and Scrooge. Dickens often used his own unhappy, poor childhood as a model in his novels.

Besides writing novels, Dickens also managed a theater company, started a weekly journal, and lectured widely. He toured America twice and visited Europe often.

Charles Dickens died in 1870. He was buried in Westminster Abbey, in London, with many of England's greatest citizens. Among his most famous books are: *Pickwick Papers, Oliver Twist, A Christmas Carol, David Copperfield, Bleak House, A Tale of Two Cities,* and *Great Expectations.*

PREFACE

The book you are about to read was written over 100 years ago. The story brings to life events that changed the course of world history. More than any other story, A TALE OF TWO CITIES makes the events of the French Revolution come alive.

In the following pages you will meet the golden-haired Lucie, the brave old banker who was her friend, and the sinister Madame Defarge who was her enemy. You will meet nobles, peasants, spies, and revolutionists.

A TALE OF TWO CITIES shows people at their best and at their worst. Hatred, cruelty, treachery, and revenge are pitted against courage, love, loyalty, and self-sacrifice.

Styles of clothing, buildings, and even food have changed since the events in this book took place. But the impulses and feelings that make people act the way they do remain the same.

CAST OF CHARACTERS

(In the order of their appearance)

Mr. Jarvis Lorry	An officer of Tellson's Bank
Jerry Cruncher	A messenger for Tellson's Bank
Lucie Manette	A ward of Tellson's
Miss Pross	Lucie's nurse and housekeeper
Ernest Defarge	The owner, with his wife, of a wine shop
Madame Defarge	The owner, with her husband, of a wine shop
Dr. Manette	A French doctor
Charles Darnay	A Frenchman of noble family
Mr. Stryver	A successful lawyer
John Barsad	A spy
Roger Cly	A spy
Sydney Carton	An unsuccessful lawyer
The Marquis	Charles Darnay's uncle
Gabelle	Manager of the Marquis' estate
The Road Mender	Worker on the Marquis' estate: later a woodsawyer in Paris

FACT AND FICTION

EVENTS IN HISTORY		EVENTS IN THE STORY
The American Revolution begins. France and England are not on friendly terms.	1775	A TALE OF TWO CITIES begins. Lucie Manette and Mr. Lorry travel to Paris.
France is at war with England because the French helped the American colonies rebel against England.	1780	Charles Darnay is tried for treason in London.
The American Revolution ends. Revolutionary ideas are spreading among the French people.	1783	Lucie Darnay is born.
The French Revolution begins. The Bastille is captured.	1789	The Defarges take part in the capture of the Bastille.
The French king and queen are prisoners of the French Republic. All nobles who had not left France are in prison or have been put to death. A law forbidding nobles who had left France to return or be put to death is passed.	1792	Charles Darnay goes to Paris in the autumn of this year.
This is the year of the Reign of Terror in Paris. It begins late in 1792 with the murder of the imprisoned nobles.	1793	In winter of this year A TALE OF TWO CITIES ends.

CONTENTS

Book One—Recalled to Life

1. The Mail Coach 3
2. Ma'mselle 8
3. The Wine Shop 16
4. The Shoemaker 25

Book Two—The Golden Thread

1. Five Years Later 37
2. The Trial for Treason 41
3. Charles Darnay and His Double 54
4. Hundreds of People 62
5. The Marquis in Paris 71
6. The Marquis in the Country 76
7. Two Unselfish Lovers 89
8. Knitting 96
9. Eight Years 110
10. Echoing Footsteps 121
11. Fire Rises 128
12. For the Honor of a Noble Name 135

Book Three—The Track of a Storm

1. In Secret 145

2. The Grindstone 155

3. The Shadow 161

4. The Woodsawyer 168

5. A Knock at the Door 173

6. A Hand at Cards 180

7. The Game Made 188

8. The Substance of the Shadow 196

9. Farewell in the Darkness 207

10. Fifty-Two 218

11. The Knitting Done 230

12. "Greater Love Hath No Man" 238

    Reviewing Your Reading 245

A Tale of Two Cities

Book 1

Recalled to Life

1 The Mail Coach

On a Friday night late in November, 1775, the stagecoach that carried passengers and mail from London to Dover was toiling slowly up Shooter's Hill, just outside of London. The hill was steep and the road was muddy, and even though the three passengers had alighted from the coach to lessen its load, the horses had several times stopped as if refusing to go farther. A steaming mist, cold and clammy, shut out from the coach lamps everything but a few yards of road.

The passengers plodding up the hill by the side of the coach had nothing to say to each other. Their faces were hidden by hats and mufflers; their high boots squashed through the mire. In those days, travelers were shy of chance acquaintances, for the roads were beset with highwaymen, and anyone might be a robber or in league with robbers. Because of this, the guard of the mail coach was sharply alert, as he stood on his perch at the rear, with eyes straining into the fog, and hand ready to seize a weapon from the chest of pistols and cutlasses beside him.

Whenever the coach stopped, the passengers stopped also. If one of the three had dared to propose to another to walk a little ahead into the mist and darkness, he would probably have been shot instantly as a highwayman.

At last the top of the hill was reached, and the

guard got down to open the coach door to let the passengers in.

"Tst! Joe!" cried the coachman, in a warning voice, looking down from his box.

"What do you say, Tom?"

They both listened.

"I say a horse at a canter coming up, Joe."

"*I* say a horse at a gallop, Tom," returned the guard, leaving his hold of the door, and mounting nimbly to his place. "Gentlemen! In the king's name, all of you!"

With this hurried command, he cocked his pistol and stood ready for an attack.

One passenger was on the step, getting in; the other two were behind him. They remained in these positions, looking suspiciously at each other, at the guard, and at the coachman. All five men listened; even the horses listened.

The sound of a horse at a gallop came fast and furiously up the hill.

"So-ho!" the guard sang out, as loud as he could roar. "Yo there! Stand! I shall fire!"

The pace was suddenly checked, and, with much splashing and floundering, a man's voice called from the mist, "Is that the Dover mail?"

"Never you mind what it is," the guard retorted. "What are you?"

"*Is* that the Dover mail?"

"Why do you want to know?"

"I want a passenger, if it is."

"What passenger?"

"Mr. Jarvis Lorry."

The passenger who stood on the step started at the sound of his name.

"Keep where you are," the guard called to the voice in the mist. "Gentleman of the name of Lorry, answer straight."

"What is the matter?" asked the passenger mildly. "Who wants me? Is it Jerry?"

"Yes, Mr. Lorry."

"What is the matter?"

"A note sent after you from the bank—some news just received."

"I know this messenger, guard," said Mr. Lorry, getting down into the road. "He may come close; there's nothing wrong."

"I hope there ain't," said the guard gruffly. "Hallo you!"

"Well, and hallo you!" said Jerry.

"Come on at a footpace; d'ye mind me? And if you've got pistols in that saddle o' yourn, don't let me see your hand go nigh 'em. So now let's look at you."

The mud-covered figures of a horse and rider came slowly through the eddying mist and reached the side of the coach where the passenger stood. Casting up his eyes at the guard, the rider handed the passenger a small folded paper.

"Guard," said the passenger in a tone of quiet business confidence, "there is nothing to fear. I am an officer of Tellson's Bank. You must know Tellson's Bank in London. I am going to Paris on business. I may read this?"

"If so be as you're quick, sir."

He opened it in the light of the coach lamp on that side, and read—first to himself and then aloud: " 'Wait at Dover for Mam'selle.' It's not long, you see, guard. Jerry, say that my answer was, RECALLED TO LIFE."

Jerry started in his saddle. "That's a blazing strange answer, too," said he.

"Take that message back, and they will know that I received this, as well as if I wrote. Make the best of your way. Good night."

With those words the passenger opened the coach door and got in, as his fellow passengers had already done, and the coach lumbered on again. As it jolted, rattled, and bumped upon its tedious way, Mr. Jarvis Lorry, trust officer of Tellson's Bank, nodded in his place with half-shut eyes. His bank was a reliable institution with offices in both London and Paris, and he had grave responsibilities in taking charge of trust funds for its clients. But his half-waking dreams had little to do with his daytime activities. All night it seemed to him that he was on his way to dig someone out of a grave. This person appeared to be a man of forty-five years, with hair turned white before its time. In his dream, a hundred times the dozing passenger inquired of this figure,

"Buried how long?"

The answer was always the same: "Almost eighteen years."

"You had abandoned all hope of being dug out?"

"Long ago."

"You know that you are recalled to life?"

"They tell me so."

"I hope you care to live?"

"I can't say."

Over and over the fancied conversation repeated itself in his mind, until when he opened the window he found that the shadows of the night were gone. Beyond a ploughed field and a quiet wood the sun was rising, bright and beautiful.

"Eighteen years!" said the passenger, looking at the sun. "Gracious Creator of Day! To be buried alive for eighteen years!"

2 *Ma'mselle*

By the middle of the morning, Mr. Jarvis Lorry was seated at his breakfast in the coffee-room of the Royal George Hotel in Dover. In bright daylight and relieved of his traveler's wrappings, he proved to be a neat, dignified gentleman of some sixty years of age, carefully dressed in brown and wearing an odd, sleek little flaxen wig.

After breakfast, having left orders for a room to be made ready for a young lady who was to arrive that day, Mr. Lorry went out for a stroll on the beach. It was not until late in the afternoon, when he sat again by the coffee-room fire, that the waiter announced the arrival of Miss Manette from London. Following the waiter to a large, dark room, he saw standing there to receive him a young lady of not more than seventeen, in a riding-cloak, holding her straw traveling-hat by its ribbon in her hand. His eyes rested on a short, slight, pretty figure, a quantity of golden hair, and a pair of blue eyes that met his own with an inquiring look. A sudden vivid likeness passed before him of a child whom he had held in his arms on the passage across the English Channel, one cold time, when the hail drifted heavily and the sea ran high.

"Pray take a seat, sir," said a very clear and pleasant young voice, a little foreign in its accent.

"I kiss your hand, miss," said Mr. Lorry, as he made his formal bow.

8

"I received a letter from the bank, sir, yesterday, informing me that some discovery respecting the small property of my poor father whom I never saw—so long dead—made it necessary that I should go to Paris, where I would find a gentleman from the bank, so good as to have traveled to Paris to help me."

"Myself."

"As I was prepared to hear, sir." She curtseyed to him, as if to show that she felt he was older and wiser than she. He made her another bow.

"I replied to the bank, sir, that as I am an orphan and have no friend who could go with me, I should be glad if I might be permitted to make the journey under that worthy gentleman's protection. The gentleman had left London, but the bank sent a messenger after him to beg the favor of his waiting for me here."

"I was happy," said Mr. Lorry, "to be entrusted with the charge. I shall be more happy to execute it."

"Sir, I thank you indeed. I thank you very gratefully. It was told me by the bank that the gentleman would explain to me the details of the business, and that I must prepare myself to find them surprising. I naturally have a strong and eager interest to know what they are."

"Naturally," said Mr. Lorry. "Yes—I—I find it very difficult to begin."

He did not begin, but looked at her uncertainly. Her brows were knit in a puzzled frown.

"Are you quite a stranger to me, sir?" she asked.

"Am I not?" Mr. Lorry opened his hands and extended them outward with a smile.

Not apparently convinced, she took her seat thoughtfully. Mr. Lorry drew a chair up beside her.

"Miss Manette," began the bank officer, "I am a man of business. I have a business charge to carry out.

As you listen, don't heed me any more than if I was a speaking machine—truly, I am not much else. I will, with your leave, relate to you, miss, the story of one of our customers. He was a French gentleman; a scientific gentleman; a man of great acquirements—a doctor."

"Not of Beauvais?"

"Why, yes, of Beauvais. Like Monsieur Manette, your father, the gentleman was of Beauvais. Like Monsieur Manette, your father, the gentleman was well known in Paris. I had the honor of knowing him there. Our relations were business relations, but confidential. I was at that time in our French house, and had been— oh! twenty years."

"At that time—may I ask, at what time, sir?"

"I speak, miss, of twenty years ago. He married—an English lady. His affairs, like the affairs of many other French gentlemen and French families, were entirely in Tellson's hands. I was trustee for him, as I have been for scores of our customers."

"But this is my father's story, sir; and I begin to think that, when I was left an orphan by my mother's death two years after my father's, it was you who brought me to England. I am almost sure it was you."

Mr. Lorry took the hesitating little hand that confidingly advanced to take his, and he put it with some ceremony to his lips. "Miss Manette," he said, "it *was* I. But I have never seen you since, though you have been the ward of Tellson's Bank. But to go on. So far, miss, as you say, this is the story of your regretted father. Now comes the difference. If your father had not died when he did—Don't be frightened! How you start!"

She caught his wrist with both her hands.

"Pray," said Mr. Lorry, in a soothing tone, "pray control your agitation—a matter of business. As I was saying—if Monsieur Manette had not died; if he had suddenly and silently disappeared; if he had been spirited away to a dreadful place, whose name we guessed; if this had been done by an enemy who had the privilege of filling up a blank form, already signed by the king, condemning the man whom he hated to prison for any length of time; if his wife had implored the king, the clergy, the courts, for news of him, but in vain—if these things had been true, then the history of your father would have been the history of this unfortunate gentleman, the doctor of Beauvais."

"I entreat you to tell me, sir."

"I will. I am going to. You can bear it?"

"I can bear anything but the uncertainty you leave me in at this moment."

"A matter of business. Regard it as a matter of business—business that must be done. Now, if this doctor's wife, though a lady of great courage and spirit, had suffered so intensely from this cause before her little child was born—"

"The little child was a daughter, sir."

"A daughter. A—a—matter of business—don't be distressed. Miss, if the poor lady had suffered so intensely before her little child was born, that she resolved to spare the poor child the agony she had known, by rearing her in the belief that her father was dead—No, don't kneel! In Heaven's name why should you kneel to me!"

"For the truth. O dear, good, kind sir, for the truth!"

"A—a matter of business. You confuse me, and how can I transact business if I am confused? Let us be clearheaded."

She sat so still when he had gently raised her, and her hands were so much steadier that Mr. Lorry felt it safe to go on.

"That's right, that's right. Courage! Business! You have business before you; useful business. Miss Manette, your mother took this course with you. And when she died—I believe broken-hearted—having never stopped her vain search for your father, she left you, at two years old, to grow to be blooming, beautiful, and happy, without the dark cloud upon you of your father's fate.

"You know that your parents had no great possession, and that what they had was secured to your mother and to you. There has been no new discovery, of money, or of any other property; but—he has been—been found. He is alive. Greatly changed, it is too probable; almost a wreck, it is possible; though we will hope the best. Still, alive. Your father has been taken to the house of an old servant in Paris, and we are going there: I, to identify him if I can; you, to restore him to life, love, duty, rest, comfort."

A shiver ran through her frame. She said, in a low, distinct, awe-stricken voice, as if she were saying it in a dream,

"I am going to see his ghost! It will be his ghost—not him!"

Mr. Lorry quietly chafed the hands that held his arm. "There, there, there! See now, see now! The best and the worst are known to you now. You are well on your way to the poor wronged gentleman, and, with a fair sea voyage and a fair land journey, you will be soon at his dear side."

She repeated in the same tone, sunk to a whisper, "I have been free, I have been happy, yet his ghost has never haunted me!"

"Only one thing more," said Mr. Lorry. "He has been found under another name, his own having been long forgotten or long concealed. It is worse than useless—indeed, it would be dangerous—to inquire now whether he has been for years overlooked or intentionally kept a prisoner. It will be better to say nothing, now that for some reason—perhaps because the charges against him have been forgotten—he has been released. Even I, safe because I am an Englishman, carry not a scrap of writing referring to the matter. Whatever message has to be sent is expressed in the words, 'Recalled to Life.' It is a secret service altogether. It will be best to remove him from France, and then—but she doesn't hear a word I'm saying!"

For she sat there perfectly still and silent, and utterly unconscious, still holding tightly to his wrist. Frightened, he called loudly for help.

A wild-looking, red-haired woman came running into the room, ahead of the inn servants, and promptly pushed Mr. Lorry out of the way.

"Why, look at you all!" bawled this figure, addressing the inn servants. "Why don't you go and fetch things, instead of standing there staring at me? Bring smelling salts, cold water, and vinegar, quick!"

Then, as the servants hurried to obey, she softly laid the patient on a sofa, and tended her with great skill and gentleness, calling her "my precious!" and "my bird!" and spreading her golden hair aside over her shoulders with great pride and care.

"And you in brown!" she said, indignantly turning to Mr. Lorry; "couldn't you tell her what you had to tell her, without frightening her to death? Look at her, with her pretty pale face and her cold hands. Do you call *that* being a banker?"

Mr. Lorry could only look on with sympathy and humility, while the strong woman revived the young lady.

"I hope she will do well now," said Mr. Lorry.

"No thanks to you in brown, if she does. My darling pretty!"

"I hope," said Mr. Lorry, after another pause, "that you accompany Miss Manette to France?"

"A likely thing, too!" replied the strong woman. "If it was ever intended that I should go across salt water, do you suppose Providence would have cast my lot in an island?"

This being another question hard to answer, Mr. Jarvis Lorry withdrew to consider it.

3 *The Wine Shop*

In a narrow street in a poor quarter of Paris, a large cask of wine had been dropped and broken on the rough, irregular stones of the pavement. In being taken from a cart, the cask had tumbled out, the hoops had burst, and it lay on the stones just outside the door of the wine shop, shattered like a walnut shell. All the people within reach had left their work or their idleness to run to the spot and drink the wine. It lay in little pools, each surrounded by its own jostling group. So poor were these people that they seldom tasted wine, and they could not let this be wasted. Some men kneeled, made scoops of their hands, and sipped, or tried to help the women beside them to sip, before the wine had all run out between their fingers. Others dipped in the puddles with little mugs; others made small banks of mud, to stop the wine as it ran; still others darted here and there to cut off little streams of wine that started away in new directions.

A shrill sound of laughter and of amused voices sounded in the street while this wine game lasted. There was little roughness in the sport, and much playfulness, frolicsome embraces, drinking of healths, shaking of hands, and even joining of hands and dancing. When the wine was gone, the merriment ceased as suddenly as it had broken out. The man who had left his saw sticking in the firewood he was cutting set it in motion again. The woman who had left on a doorstep a little pot of hot ashes, at which she had been trying to warm her starved fingers and toes, returned to it. Men with bare arms, matted locks, and haggard faces, who had emerged into the winter light from cellars, moved away to descend again. A gloom gathered on the scene that appeared more natural to it than sunshine.

The wine was red wine, and had stained the ground of the narrow street. It had stained many hands, too, and many faces, and many naked feet, and many wooden shoes. One tall joker scrawled upon the wall with his finger dipped in wine-reddened mud the word— BLOOD.

The time was to come when that wine too would be spilled on the street stones, and when the stain of it would be red upon many there.

The street was in a quarter of Paris that had once been outside the city wall, and was therefore still called a suburb—the Suburb Saint Antoine. People oppressed by cold, dirt, sickness, ignorance, and poverty shivered at every corner, passed in and out at every doorway, looked from every window. The children had old faces and grave voices; and upon them and upon the grown faces was the sign, Hunger. Everywhere that sign could be seen: in the wretched clothing that hung on lines from the windows of tall houses; in the windows patched with straw and rag and paper; in the bits of firewood that the man sawed off; in the smokeless chimneys. Hunger was written on the baker's shelves, on every small loaf of his scanty stock of bad bread; it rattled its dry bones among the roasting chestnuts; it waited at the sausage shop.

In the hunted air of the people of this narrow street there was yet some look of the wild beast at bay. Sad and slinking though they were, eyes of fire were not wanting among them, nor compressed, white lips, nor knitted, thoughtful brows.

There were no sidewalks in the street; the cobblestones reached to the doors, and the gutter ran down the middle of the rough pavement. Here and there, far apart, clumsy lamps were hung, lighted each night by a lamplighter, who raised and lowered them by a pulley.

The wine shop was a corner shop, more prosperous-looking than the other shops. Its owner had stood at the door, in a yellow waistcoat and green breeches, looking on at the struggle for the lost wine. He was a bull-necked, good-humored looking man of about thirty, Ernest Defarge by name. His hair was short, dark, and crisply curling; his eyes were good, with a good bold breadth between them; his expression showed strong resolution and the set purpose of a man who would not easily be turned aside from his chosen course. He wore no coat; his shirt-sleeves were rolled up, and his brown arms were bare to the elbows.

Noticing the tall joker writing up his joke, Defarge called to him across the way,

"Say, then, my Gaspard, what do you do there? Are you a subject for the mad hospital?" He crossed the road and smeared over the word with a handful of mud. "Call wine, wine," he said, "and finish there." With that advice, he recrossed the road and entered his wine shop.

Madame Defarge, his wife, sat in the shop behind the counter. She was a handsome woman of about his own age, with a watchful eye that seldom seemed to look at anything, a large hand heavily ringed, a steady face, strong features, and a very calm manner. Gold hoops hung from her ears, and about her head a bright scarf was wound. Her knitting lay before her on the counter.

A little cough and a slight lifting of her dark eyebrows warned her husband, as he came in, to look about the shop for new customers.

Two men were playing cards, two playing dominoes, and three standing by the counter drinking. These were all the usual frequenters of the shop. But in a corner sat an elderly gentleman and a young lady. These were strangers. Defarge wondered what they were doing there. However, he appeared not to notice them, but began to talk with the three men at the counter.

"How goes it, Jacques?" said one of the three to Monsieur Defarge. "Is all the spilt wine swallowed?"

"Every drop, Jacques," answered Monsieur Defarge.

As if struck by the likeness of the names exchanged, Madame Defarge gave another little cough, and raised her eyebrows by the breadth of another line.

"It is not often," said the second of the three, addressing Monsieur Defarge, "that many of these miserable beasts know the taste of wine, or of anything but black bread and death. Is it not so, Jacques?"

"It is so, Jacques," Monsieur Defarge returned.

Once more, at the exchange of the same name, Madame Defarge coughed; again she raised her eyebrows. Her husband seemed not to notice her signal.

The last of the three now said his say, as he put down his empty drinking vessel and smacked his lips in apparent satisfaction.

"Ah! So much the worse! A bitter taste it is that such poor cattle always have in their mouths, and hard lives they live, Jacques. Am I right, Jacques?"

"You are right, Jacques," was the response of Monsieur Defarge.

The use of the name Jacques was evidently a password or signal, for at its third interchange Madame Defarge slightly rustled in her seat.

"Hold then! True!" muttered her husband. "Gentlemen—my wife!"

The three customers pulled off their hats to Madame Defarge, with three flourishes. She acknowledged their salute by bending her head and giving them a quick look. Then she glanced in a casual manner round the wine shop and calmly took up her knitting.

"Gentlemen," said her husband, "the furnished room that you wished to see is on the fifth floor. The doorway of the staircase opens on the little courtyard just outside my shop. But, now that I remember, one of you has already been there and can show the way. Gentlemen, adieu!"

As they paid for their wine and left the place, the elderly gentleman stepped from his corner and begged the favor of a word.

"Willingly, sir," said Monsieur Defarge, and quietly stepped with him to the door.

Their conversation was short but decided. Almost at the first word, Monsieur Defarge started and became deeply attentive. After a moment, he nodded and went out. The gentleman then beckoned to the young lady, and they, too, went out. Madame Defarge knitted with nimble fingers and steady eyebrows, and saw nothing.

Mr. Jarvis Lorry and Miss Manette, emerging from the wine shop thus, joined Monsieur Defarge in the doorway to which he had directed his other company just before.

A remarkable change had come over the wine shop keeper. His face was no longer open and good-humored; he had become a secret, angry, dangerous man.

"It is very high; it is a little difficult. Better to begin

slowly," said Monsieur Defarge in a stern voice to Mr. Lorry, as they began mounting the stairs.

"Is he alone?" the latter whispered.

"Alone! God help him, who should be with him!" said the other, in the same low voice.

"Is he always alone, then?"

"Yes."

"Of his own desire?"

"Of his own necessity. He is as he was when I first saw him, some days ago. That was after they found me and asked if I would take him—warning me, at my peril, to be careful in speaking of the matter."

"He is greatly changed?"

"Changed!"

The keeper of the wine shop stopped to strike the wall with his hand and mutter a curse. No direct answer could have been half so forcible. Mr. Lorry's spirits grew heavier and heavier, as he and his two companions climbed higher and higher.

At last the top of the staircase was reached. Defarge stopped and took a key from his pocket.

"The door is locked then, my friend?" said Mr. Lorry, surprised.

"Ay. Yes," was the grim reply.

"You think it necessary to keep the unfortunate gentleman so retired?"

"I think it necessary to turn the key." Monsieur Defarge whispered it closer in his ear, and frowned heavily.

"Why?"

"Why! Because he has lived so long, locked up, that he would be frightened—rave—tear himself to pieces—die—come to I know not what harm—if his door were left open."

"Is it possible!" exclaimed Mr. Lorry.

"Is it possible!" repeated Defarge, bitterly. "Yes. And a beautiful world we live in, when it *is* possible, and when many other such things are possible."

By this time the young lady showed in her face such dread and terror that Mr. Lorry felt he must encourage her.

"Courage, dear miss," he urged. "Courage! Business! The worst will be over in a moment. Then think what relief and happiness you will bring to him. Come, now. Business, business!"

As they turned the corner of the garret passage, they came in sight of three men, bent down, looking intently through some chinks in a door into the room beyond it. On hearing footsteps, they turned, and proved to be the three men named Jacques who had been drinking in the wine shop.

"Leave us, good boys; we have business here," said Monsieur Defarge.

The three glided by and went silently down. Defarge approached the door.

"Do you then make a show of Monsieur Manette?" asked Mr Lorry in some anger.

"I show him, in the way you have seen, to a chosen few."

"Is that well?"

"*I* think it is well."

"Who are the few? How do you choose them?"

"I choose them as real men, of my name,—Jacques is my name,—to whom the sight is likely to do good."

Pausing no longer, the wine shop keeper struck twice upon the door, evidently only in order to make a noise there. With the same intention, he drew the key

across it, three or four times, before he put it clumsily
into the lock, and turned it as heavily as he could.

The door slowly opened inward under his hand, and
he looked into the room and said something. A faint
voice answered something. He looked back over his
shoulder and beckoned them to enter. With his arm
around the daughter's waist, Mr. Lorry drew her forward, though she hung back, shuddering, whispering, "I
am afraid!" Just within the door of the room he paused
and held her, clinging to him.

Defarge closed the door, locked it on the inside, and drew out the key again, all as noisily as possible. Finally, he walked with heavy tread across to the window, stopped there, and faced around. The garret was so dim and dark that upon first coming in it was difficult to see anything. But as their eyes became adjusted to the half-light, they saw a figure seated with his back to the door and his face toward the window. It was the figure of a white-haired man who sat on a low bench, stooping forward and very busy, making shoes.

The Shoemaker

"Good day!" said Monsieur Defarge, looking down at the bent white head.

A very faint voice replied to the greeting.

"You are still hard at work, I see?"

After a long silence, the head was lifted for a moment, and the voice replied, "Yes, I am working," while a pair of haggard eyes looked at the questioner. The faintness of the voice was like the last feeble echo of a sound made long and long ago.

"I want," said Defarge, "to let in a little more light here. You can bear a little more?"

"What did you say?" came the faint voice.

"You can bear a little more light?"

"I *must* bear it, if you let it in."

The shutter was opened a little further. A broad ray of light showed the workman with an unfinished shoe upon his lap, pausing in his labor. His few common tools and various scraps of leather were at his feet and on his bench. He had a white beard, raggedly cut, but not very long, a hollow face, and exceedingly bright eyes. His yellow rags of shirt lay open at the throat and showed his body to be withered and worn. He had put up a hand between his eyes and the light, and the very bones of it seemed transparent. So he sat, looking blankly before him, pausing in his work.

"Are you going to finish that pair of shoes today?"

asked Defarge, motioning to Mr. Lorry to come forward. "What did you say?"

"Do you mean to finish that pair of shoes today?"

"I can't say that I mean to. I suppose so. I don't know."

But the question reminded him of his work, and he bent over it again.

Mr. Lorry came silently forward, leaving the daughter by the door. When he had stood for a minute or two by the side of Defarge, the shoemaker looked up. He showed no surprise at seeing another figure, but once more bent over the shoe.

"You have a visitor, you see," said Monsieur Defarge.

"What did you say?"

"Here is a visitor."

The shoemaker looked up as before.

"Come!" said Defarge. "Here is monsieur, who knows a well-made shoe when he sees one. Show him that shoe you are working at. Take it, monsieur."

Mr. Lorry took it in his hand.

"Tell monsieur what kind of shoe it is, and the maker's name."

There was a longer pause than usual, before the shoemaker replied,

"I forget what it was you asked me. What did you say?"

"I said, couldn't you describe the kind of shoe, for monsieur's information?"

"It is a lady's shoe. It is a young lady's walking shoe. It is in the present mode. I never saw the mode. I have had a pattern in my hand." He glanced at the shoe, with some little passing touch of pride.

"And the maker's name?" said Defarge.

Now that he had no work to hold, he laid the

knuckles of the right hand in the hollow of the left, and then the knuckles of the left hand in the hollow of the right, and then passed a hand across his bearded chin, and so on in regular changes.

"Did you ask me for my name?"

"Certainly I did."

"One Hundred and Five, North Tower."

"Is that all?"

"One Hundred and Five, North Tower."

With a weary sound that was not a sigh nor a groan, he bent to work again, until the silence was again broken.

"You are not a shoemaker by trade?" said Mr. Lorry, looking steadfastly at him.

His haggard eyes turned to Defarge, then back on the questioner.

"I am not a shoemaker by trade? No, I was not a shoemaker by trade. I—I learnt it here. I taught myself. I asked leave to—"

He lapsed away, even for minutes; then he went on, in the manner of a sleeper just awakened, "I asked leave to teach myself, and I got it with much difficulty after a long while, and I have made shoes ever since." He reached out his hand for the shoe which had been taken from him; his fingers closed and unclosed nervously.

Mr. Lorry looked steadfastly in his face. "Monsieur Manette," he said, "do you remember nothing of me?"

The shoe dropped to the ground, and the shoemaker sat looking fixedly at the questioner.

Mr. Lorry laid his hand upon Defarge's arm. "Do you remember nothing of this man?" he asked. "Look at him. Look at me. Is there no old banker, no old business, no old servant, no old time, rising in your mind, Monsieur Manette?"

As the captive of many years looked at them fixedly, his forehead knit in a frown—an expression showing an effort at thought, at recollection; an expression that showed a faint survival of what had once been an active intelligence. The mind was not wholly a wreck; its broken pieces might, with time and care, be built again into a sound structure. The shoemaking had been his salvation, as he must have foreseen when, feeling his mind breaking, he had asked to learn it.

The thoughtful frown faded; he looked at the two less and less attentively. Finally, with a deep, long sigh, he took the shoe up and resumed his work.

"Have you recognized him, monsieur?" whispered Defarge.

"Yes. At first I thought it quite hopeless, but I have seen for a moment the face that I once knew well."

During this time the daughter had not remained standing by the door. She had crept along the wall to where she could see the shoemaker, and stood looking at him. Now, with hands stretched toward him, she moved from the wall close to the bench on which he sat.

"Hush!" said Mr. Lorry to Defarge. "Let us draw further back."

Not a word more was spoken; not a sound was made. She stood like a spirit beside him, and he bent over his work.

At length, as he reached for his sharp shoemaker's knife, his eye caught the skirt of her dress. He looked up and saw her face. In fear of his striking at her with the knife, the two spectators started forward, but she, fearless now, stopped them with a motion of her hand.

He stared at her with a frightened look; then, between quick, hard breaths, he muttered, "What is this!"

With the tears streaming down her face, she put

her two hands to her lips and kissed them to him; then clasped them on her breast.

"You are not the jailer's daughter?"

"No," she sighed.

"Who are you?"

Not yet trusting the sound of her voice, she sat down on the bench beside him and laid her hand upon his arm. A thrill passed over him, and he laid the knife down softly. Her golden hair, which she wore in long curls, had fallen forward over her neck. Timidly he put out his hand, took up a curl, and looked at it. Then he put his hand to his neck and took off a blackened string with a scrap of folded rag attached to it. He opened this carefully on his knee, and it contained a very little quantity of hair; not more than one or two long golden hairs, which he had in some old day wound off upon his finger and kept carefully as a treasure.

He took her hair into his hand again, and looked closely at it. "It is the same. How can it be! When was it! How was it!"

As the thoughtful frown appeared again on his brow, he seemed to see the same expression on hers. He turned her full to the light and looked hard at her.

"She had laid her head upon my shoulder, that night when I was summoned out—she had a fear of my going, though I had none—and when I was brought to the North Tower they found these upon my sleeve. 'You will leave me them? They can never help me to escape in the body, though they may in the spirit.' Those were the words I said. I remember them very well."

He paused; then suddenly cried out sharply,

"How was this?—*Was it you?*"

Once more, the two spectators started, as he turned upon her with a frightful suddenness. But she sat per-

fectly still in his grasp, and only said, in a low voice, "I entreat you, good gentlemen, do not come near us, do not speak, do not move!"

"Hark!" he exclaimed. "Whose voice was that?"

His hands released her as he uttered this cry, and went up to his white hair, which they tore in a frenzy. Then his passion died, and he gloomily shook his head. "No, no, no; you are too young, too blooming. It can't be. See what the prisoner is. These are not the hands she knew, this is not the face she knew, this is not a voice she ever heard. No, no. She was—and he was —before the slow years of the North Tower—ages ago. What is your name, my gentle angel?"

Hailing his softened tone and manner, his daughter fell upon her knees before him with her appealing hands upon his breast.

"O, sir, at another time you shall know my name, and who my mother was, and who my father, and how I never knew their hard, hard history. But I cannot tell you at this time, and I cannot tell you here. Only I pray to you to touch me and to bless me. Kiss me, kiss me! O my dear, my dear!"

His cold white head mingled with her radiant hair as he drooped against her shoulder.

"If my voice is like one that was once sweet music in your ears; if my hair recalls a beloved head that once lay upon your breast when you were young and free, weep for it, weep for it! If, when I tell you of a home where I will be true to you and love you, you remember a home long deserted, while your poor heart pined away, weep for it. Dearest dear, your agony is over. I have come to take you from it to England, to be at peace and at rest. And if, when I shall tell you of my name, you learn that I must implore my father's pardon because I have not worked and prayed and wept for his sake, because the love of my poor mother hid his torture from me, weep for her, then, and for me!"

His face had sunk upon her breast and her arms were round him. "Good gentlemen," she cried to her companions, "thank God for us! I feel his tears upon my face, and his sobs strike against my heart."

When the storm of weeping that had roused the captive from his dazed hopelessness was passed, Mr. Lorry and Defarge came forward. The father had drooped to the floor and lay there in a stupor of exhaustion; the daughter sat beside him, his head upon her lap and his thin hand clasped in hers.

"If, without disturbing him," she said softly to Mr. Lorry, "all could be arranged for our leaving Paris at once, so that from this very door he could be taken away—"

"But is he fit for the journey?" asked Mr. Lorry.

"More fit for that than to remain in this city, so dreadful to him."

"It is true," said Defarge. "Monsieur Manette is for all reasons best out of France. Say, shall I hire a carriage and posthorses?"

"That's business," said Mr. Lorry, "and if business is to be done, I had better do it."

"Then be so kind," urged Miss Manette, "as to leave us here. You see how calm he has become, and you cannot be afraid to leave him with me now. Why should you be? If you will lock the door, I do not doubt that you will find him, when you come back, as quiet as you leave him. In any case, I will take care of him until you return, and then we will remove him straight."

Both Mr. Lorry and Defarge were rather against this course, and in favor of one of them remaining. But, as there were not only carriage and horses to be seen to, but traveling papers, and as it was late in the afternoon, they divided between them the work that had to be done and hurried away to do it.

It was dark when they returned, lighted by a lamp and bringing traveling garments for the captive, as well as bread and meat, wine, and hot coffee. With a scared, blank wonder in his face, and often clasping his head in his hands in a wild, lost manner, he ate and drank what they gave him to eat and drink, and put on the cloak and other wrappings that they gave him to wear. Then, with his arm drawn through his daughter's, and with Defarge going ahead with the lamp and Mr. Lorry bringing up the rear, the little procession started down the stairs.

"You remember the place, my father? You remember coming up here?"

"Remember? No, I don't remember. It was so very long ago."

It was clear that he did not recall having been brought from his prison to this house. He looked about him for the strong fortress walls which had long shut him in; and when, at the door, he saw the carriage waiting in the open street, he clasped his head again in bewilderment.

No crowd was about the door; no people were at any of the windows; not even a chance passer-by was in the street. Only one soul was to be seen, and that was Madame Defarge, who leaned against the doorpost knitting, and saw nothing.

The prisoner had got into the coach and his daughter had followed him when he asked, miserably, for his shoemaking tools and the unfinished shoes. Madame Defarge quickly went and brought them—and immediately afterwards leaned against the doorpost, knitting, and saw nothing.

Defarge climbed upon the coachman's box and gave the word, "To the city gate!" The postboy cracked his whip and they clattered away. At the guardhouse were soldiers with lanterns, demanding passports. Defarge got down from the box to answer their inquiries.

"See here then, Monsieur the Officer," said he, "these are the papers of monsieur inside, with the white head. They were turned over to me at the—" He dropped his voice, and the officer peered into the coach to look with amazement at monsieur with the white head.

"It is well. You may proceed," he then declared.

"Adieu!" cried Defarge.

So out under the lamps they passed, out into the night under a great arch of stars.

Book 2

The Golden Thread

1 Five Years Later

Tellson's Bank by Temple Bar on Fleet Street, London, was an old-fashioned place, even in the year 1780. It was very small, very dark, very ugly. All its clerks were very old. Its door was down two steps, and inside were two little counters, under the dingiest of iron-barred windows. The depositors' money came out of or went into wormy old wooden drawers, and the bank notes had a musty odor.

Outside Tellson's, seated upon a wooden stool, was an odd-job-man, often used as a porter and messenger. He was never absent during business hours except upon an errand. His name was Jerry Cruncher, and he was well known to Fleet Street.

On a windy March morning, soon after Jerry arrived at his post, a head was put through the door of Tellson's and a voice called, "Porter wanted!"

Jerry presented himself before one of the old clerks.

"You know the Old Bailey courtroom well, my man, no doubt?"

"Yes, sir, I do know the Bailey," replied Jerry.

"And you know Mr. Lorry?"

"Yes, sir."

"Very well. Find the door where the witnesses go in, and show the doorkeeper this note for Mr. Lorry. He will then let you in."

"Into the court, sir?"

"Into the court. The doorkeeper will pass the note to Mr. Lorry, and you must make some motion that will attract Mr. Lorry's attention and show him where you stand. Then remain there until he wants you."

"Is that all, sir?"

"That is all. He wishes to have a messenger at hand. This is to tell him you are there."

Jerry took the letter, made his bow, and went his way.

The Old Bailey was famous as a criminal court, in which were tried the prisoners confined in the Old Bailey prison, most of them on capital charges, for many crimes were in those days punishable by death.

Making his way through the crowd which always filled the approach to the court, the messenger found the door he sought and handed in his letter. After some delay, he was allowed to squeeze himself through.

"What's coming on?" he asked in a whisper of the man he found himself next to.

"The treason case."

"That's hanging, eh?"

"He'll be hanged, drawn, and quartered," said the man. "That's the sentence for treason."

"If he's found guilty, you mean to say," Jerry added.

"Oh, they'll find him guilty," said the other. "Don't you be afraid of that."

Mr. Cruncher's attention was here turned to the doorkeeper, whom he saw making his way to Mr. Lorry with the note in his hand. Mr. Lorry sat at a table with the gentlemen in wigs, who, Jerry knew, were lawyers. One wigged gentleman who had a great pile of papers before him turned out later to be the lawyer for the defense. Opposite Mr. Lorry was another wigged gentleman with his hands in his pockets, whose whole attention seemed to be fixed on the ceiling.

Mr. Lorry, receiving the note, stood up to look for Jerry, who raised his hand as a signal. Presently the judge entered, and two jailers went out and brought in the prisoner. He was a well-built, handsome young gentleman of about twenty-five, with a sunburnt cheek and a dark eye. He was plainly dressed in black, and his hair, which was long and dark, was gathered in a ribbon at the back of his neck. Though pale, he was calm and self-controlled.

Silence in the court! Charles Darnay, it was announced, had yesterday pleaded not guilty to the charge that he was a traitor to King George. It was claimed that he had at various times and in various ways assisted Louis, the French king, in his wars against Great Britain. It was said that he had traveled back and forth between the two countries, and had wickedly revealed to the French what forces his Majesty King George was preparing to send to North America, where the rebellious colonies had four years before declared their independence.

The prisoner stood quietly at the bar, watching the proceedings with a grave interest. Over his head there was a mirror, to throw the light down upon him. As it cast a bar of light across his face, he looked up, flushing when he saw the glass. He turned to that side of the court which was on his left. About on a level with his eyes sat two persons upon whom his look rested. They were a young lady of about twenty years, and a gentleman who was evidently her father. He was a man remarkable for the perfect whiteness of his hair, and for his intense expression. When his face was quiet, he looked as if he were old; but when he spoke, he became a handsome man, not past the prime of life.

His daughter had drawn close to him, with her hand through his arm. Her expression showed both dread of the scene and great pity for the prisoner.

"Who are they?" whispered Jerry.

"Witnesses against the prisoner."

Just then the Attorney General rose to present the case for the prosecution.

2 The Trial for Treason

"My lord, and gentlemen of the jury," began the Attorney General, "it is my duty to inform you that the prisoner before you, though young in years, is old in treasonable practices. His correspondence with the public enemy is not a matter of today, or of yesterday, or even of last year or of the year before. It is certain that for longer than that the prisoner has been in the habit of passing to and fro between France and England on secret business of which he can give no honest account. His guilt might have remained undiscovered if a fearless and honorable citizen had not ferreted out his schemes. This patriotic citizen will be produced before you to tell his own story.

"He was once the prisoner's friend; but when he discovered his guilt he could no longer hold him dear. He resolved to disclose the prisoner's treachery to the government. Led by this patriotic example, the prisoner's servant examined his master's table drawers and pockets. The evidence of these two witnesses and the papers which they discovered will prove to you that the prisoner has obtained and handed over to the enemy lists of his Majesty's forces and of their positions and preparation, both by sea and land.

"The lists, indeed, cannot be proved to be in the prisoner's handwriting; but that fact only increases his guilt, as showing how artful he has been in his precautions. The proof will go back five years, and will show the prisoner already engaged in these missions within a few weeks of the date of the very first battle between British and American troops.

"For these reasons, gentlemen of the jury, I cannot doubt that you will find the prisoner guilty of treason."

When the Attorney General ceased, the patriotic witness was summoned to the witness-box. His name was John Barsad, and he told his story exactly—perhaps a little too exactly—as the Attorney General had said he would. Thereupon the wigged gentleman beside Mr. Lorry begged leave to cross-examine. The wigged gentleman opposite still looked at the ceiling. The cross-examiner's name was Stryver.

"Were you ever a spy yourself?" inquired Mr. Stryver mildly, receiving for answer a scornful denial. "What do you live on?" he asked then.

"My property."

"Where is your property?"

"I don't remember precisely."

"What is this property?"

The witness said that that was his business and nobody else's.

"Did you inherit it?"

"Yes, I did."

"From whom?"

"From a distant relative."

Mr. Stryver changed the subject. "Have you ever been in prison?"

"Certainly not."

"Never in a debtors' prison?"

The witness muttered sulkily that he didn't see what that had to do with it, but on being pressed a second and a third time for an answer, admitted that he had been in prison for debt, not once, but several times. "What is your profession?" then smoothly asked the lawyer.

"Gentleman."

"Have you ever been kicked downstairs?" The question seemed abrupt and rude, but the witness agreed that he had once received a kick at the top of a staircase and had then fallen down the stairs of his own accord.

"On that occasion were you kicked for cheating at dice?"

"No! The man who kicked me said so, but he lied."

"You swear it was not true?"

"Positively."

"Do you ever live by cheating at cards?" This question being firmly denied, Mr. Stryver changed it. "Do you ever live by gambling?" he inquired.

"Not more than other gentlemen do."

"Did you ever borrow money of the prisoner?"

"Yes."

"Did you ever pay him?"

"No," reluctantly.

"Was not your friendship with the prisoner really a slight acquaintance, which you forced upon him in coaches, inns, and boats?"

"Not at all."

"Are you sure you saw the prisoner with these lists?"

The witness was sure of that, but he knew no more about the lists; and he asserted vigorously that he had not, as was suggested, written them himself. Nor did he, so he swore, expect to receive any reward for his evidence.

"You are not in regular government pay and employment, to spy and to lay traps?"

"Most certainly not." And with the witness's declaration of his patriotic motives he was allowed to stand down. It was evident that Mr. Stryver had somewhat shaken the jury's belief in the noble character of Mr. Barsad, and had suggested a possible motive for his wishing to harm the prisoner.

The virtuous servant, Roger Cly, was next called as witness. He had taken service with the prisoner, so he said, four years ago. On the boat from Calais he had asked Mr. Darnay if he wanted a valet, and had thereupon been engaged. Soon afterwards he began to have suspicions of the prisoner, and to keep an eye upon him. In arranging his clothes, while traveling, he had over and over again seen in the prisoner's pockets lists similar to the lists produced in court, which he himself had taken from the prisoner's desk. He had seen the prisoner show them to French gentlemen both at Boulogne and at Calais. His love of England had thereupon compelled him to give information.

Mr. Cly's character also suffered somewhat under cross-examination. He denied that he had asked the prisoner to employ him as an act of charity; he denied that he had put the lists into the desk before he found them there. But he had to admit that he had once been accused of stealing a silver teapot, which—though it didn't matter to him, as he hadn't stolen it—turned out to be only plated.

"How long have you known the last witness?" now asked Mr. Stryver.

"Seven or eight years; but that is only a coincidence."

"Don't you think that is a particularly curious coincidence?"

"No. Most coincidences are curious."

"Then you don't think it a curious coincidence that your only motive, like his, was patriotism?"

"No, I don't. I'm a true Briton, I am, and I hope there's many like me."

The virtuous servant left the box, and Mr. Lorry was called. Having verified the fact that he was an officer of Tellson's Bank, the Attorney General continued:

"On a certain Friday night in November, 1775, did business cause you to travel to Dover by the mail coach?"

"It did."

"Were there other passengers in the coach?"

"Two."

"Did they alight on the road in the course of the night?"

"They did."

"Mr. Lorry, look upon the prisoner. Was he one of those two passengers?"

"I cannot undertake to say that he was."

"Does he resemble either of these two passengers?"

"Both were so wrapped up, and the night was so dark, and we were all so reserved, that I cannot undertake to say even that."

"Mr. Lorry, look again upon the prisoner. Supposing him wrapped up as those two passengers were, is there anything in his size and build to make it unlikely that he was one of them?"

"No."

"You will not swear, Mr. Lorry, that he was not one of them?"

"No."

"So at least you say he may have been one of them?"

"Yes."

"Mr. Lorry, look upon the prisoner once more. Have you seen him, to your certain knowledge, before?"

"I have."

"When?"

"I was returning from France a few days afterwards, and, at Calais, the prisoner came on board the ship in which I returned and made the voyage with me."

"At what hour did he come on board?"

"At a little after midnight."

"In the dead of the night. Was he the only passenger who came on board at that late hour?"

"He was."

"Were you traveling alone, Mr. Lorry, or with any companion?"

"With two companions. A gentleman and a lady. They are here."

"Had you any conversation with the prisoner?"

"Hardly any. The weather was stormy, and the passage long and rough, and I lay on a sofa almost from shore to shore."

"Miss Manette!"

The young lady stood up where she had sat. Her father rose with her and kept her hand drawn through his arm.

"Miss Manette, look upon the prisoner. Have you seen the prisoner before?"

"Yes, sir."

"Where?"

"On board the ship just now referred to, sir, and on the same occasion."

"You are the young lady just now referred to?"

"Oh! most unhappily, I am!"

"Answer the questions put to you," interrupted the judge sharply, "and make no remark upon them."

The prosecutor went on, "Miss Manette, had you any conversation with the prisoner on that passage across the Channel?" and when she assented, he requested her to describe it.

"When the gentleman came on board," she began, but was interrupted again by the judge.

"Do you mean the prisoner?" he asked gruffly.

"Yes, my Lord."

"Then say the prisoner."

"When the prisoner came on board," she began again, "he noticed that my father was very ill. I was afraid to take him out of the air, and I had made a bed for him on the deck near the cabin steps, and I sat on the deck at his side to take care of him. There were no other passengers that night, but we four. The prisoner was so good as to advise me how I could shelter my father from the wind and weather better than I had done. He expressed great gentleness and kindness for my father's state, and I am sure he felt it. That was the manner of our beginning to speak together."

"Let me interrupt you for a moment. Had he come on board alone?"

"No, two French gentlemen were with him."

"Did they talk together?"

"Yes, till the last moment, when the French gentlemen had to go ashore."

"Were any papers handed about among them, similar to these lists?"

"Yes, there were some papers, but I don't know what papers."

"Like these in size and shape?"

"Possibly, but indeed I don't know. They were very near me, but the light was dim, and they spoke very low. I did not hear what they said, and saw only that they looked at papers."

"Now, to the prisoner's conversation, Miss Manette."

"The prisoner was as open in all he said to me as he was kind and good and helpful to my father. I hope," bursting into tears, "I may not repay him by doing him harm today."

"Miss Manette, we all, including the prisoner, perfectly understand that you give most unwillingly the evidence which it is your duty to give. Please to go on."

"He told me that he was traveling on business of a private and difficult nature, which might get people into trouble. He was therefore using an alias. He said that this business caused him frequently to go back and forth between England and France."

"Did he say anything about America, Miss Manette?"

"At my request, he tried to explain to me how that quarrel had arisen, but that was all."

The young lady was dismissed, and her father was called for.

"Doctor Manette, look upon the prisoner," said the prosecutor. "Can you identify him as your fellow passenger that night on the boat?"

"Sir, I cannot."

"Is there any special reason why you cannot?"

He answered in a low voice, "There is."

"Was it your misfortune to suffer a long imprisonment in your native country?"

"A long imprisonment," he answered in a tone that went to every heart.

"Were you newly released on the night in question?"

"They tell me so."

"Have you no remembrance of the occasion?"

"None. My mind is a blank, from some time—I cannot even say what time—when I employed myself, in my captivity, in making shoes, to the time when I found myself living in London with my dear daughter here. She had become familiar to me, when a gracious God restored my mental powers; but I am quite unable even to say how she had become familiar. I have no remembrance of the process."

After the father and daughter had sat down, a curious circumstance arose. The object in hand was to show that the prisoner went down in the Dover mail that November night five years ago, and got out of the coach in the night, as a blind, at a place where he did not remain. It was said that he traveled back a dozen miles or more to a town where there were a military post and a dockyard, and there collected information. A witness was called to identify him as having been in the coffee room of a hotel in that town.

Mr. Stryver was cross-examining this witness with little result in the prisoner's favor, when the gentleman who had been looking at the ceiling, where he could see his own face reflected in the mirror above the prisoner's head, wrote a word or two on a little piece of paper, screwed it up, and tossed it to the lawyer for the defense. Having opened and read the message, Mr. Stryver looked with great attention at the prisoner, and resumed:

"You say again that you are quite sure that it *was* the prisoner?"

"Quite sure."

"Did you ever see anybody very like the prisoner?"

"Not so alike that I could be mistaken."

"Look well upon that gentleman, my learned friend there," pointing to him who had tossed the note, "and then look well upon the prisoner. How say you? Are they very like each other?"

Allowing for the wigged gentleman's careless and slovenly appearance, they were enough like each other to surprise, not only the witness, but everybody present. By request, the judge rather ungraciously bade the lawyer lay aside his wig, and then the likeness was more striking.

"Do I understand," inquired the judge of Mr. Stryver, "that we are next to try Mr. Carton for treason?"

"No, my Lord," replied the delighted Stryver, "but I will ask the witness to say whether what has happened once might have happened twice; whether it is possible to swear certainly to an identity when two men look so much alike that one might be mistaken for the other; and whether he would have been so confident had he seen this likeness sooner. And I will ask the jury," he continued, as the crushed witness slunk from the box, "whether it is just to condemn a man to death on the basis of so uncertain an identification."

There followed now the summing up by both lawyers and the final review of the case by the judge. Then at last the jury turned to consider. The lawyers whispered to each other; the spectators moved about; even the judge walked up and down his platform. But all this time Mr. Carton still sat looking at the ceiling. His torn gown was off at one shoulder, his wig was crooked, his hands were in his pockets. Something reckless in his manner lessened his strong resemblance to the prisoner.

Yet it was Mr. Carton who, for all his seeming indifference, noticed when Miss Manette, overcome by the excitement, dropped her head upon her father's shoulder. "Officer!" he called, "look to that young lady. Help the gentleman to take her out. Don't you see she is fainting?"

There was much pity for her as she was removed, and much sympathy with her father. It had evidently been a great distress to him to have the days of his imprisonment recalled. That brooding look which made him old had been upon him like a heavy cloud ever since.

As the Manettes left the courtroom, the foreman of

the jury spoke. They were not agreed, and wished to re-
tire. The judge, somewhat surprised, gave permission.
The trial had lasted all day, and the lamps were being
lighted. The spectators drifted off in search of supper,
and the prisoner sat down at the back of the dock.

Jerry, who all this time had been an interested
spectator, approached to speak to Mr. Lorry. As he
turned away, he was close beside Mr. Carton, who had
come over to the dock and was talking with the prisoner.

"You will naturally be anxious to hear of the witness, Miss Manette," he heard Carton say. "Mr. Lorry
tells me that she is much better now that she is out of
court."

"I am deeply sorry to have caused her so much
distress," said Darnay. "Could you tell her so for me,
with my warm thanks?"

"Surely I can, and will," said Carton, lounging carelessly with his elbow against the bar. "What," he went
on, "do you expect, Mr. Darnay?"

"The worst."

"It is the wisest thing to expect, and the likeliest.
But I think their withdrawing is in your favor."

Jerry heard no more, being on his way to find some
supper. He left them—so like each other in feature, so
unlike in manner—standing side by side, both reflected
in the glass above them.

An hour and a half had passed before Jerry, struggling to get back to the courtroom through an excited
mob of people, heard Mr. Lorry calling him.

"Here, sir! It's a fight to get back again. Here I am,
sir!"

Mr. Lorry handed him a paper. "Quick! Have you
got it?"

"Yes, sir."

Hastily written on the paper was the word "Ac-QUITTED."

"If you had sent the message, 'Recalled to Life,' again," muttered Jerry, as he turned, "I should have known what you meant, this time."

3 Charles Darnay and His Double

In the dimly lighted passage of the court, Mr. Lorry, the Manettes, and Mr. Stryver stood gathered around Charles Darnay, congratulating him on his escape from death and receiving his thanks. The lawyer, a stout, loud, red-faced man in his thirties, was especially pleased with himself for his performance, and had a little too much to say about it quite to suit Mr. Lorry, who did not like his pushing manner.

"Miss Lucie," said the banker at last, "do you not think we should go home? Mr. Darnay has had a terrible day, you and I are weary, and your father," with a pointed glance at him, "looks ill."

Doctor Manette's face, indeed, had become fixed in a very strange look at Darnay. It was an intent look, deepening into a frown of dislike and distrust, not unmixed with fear. His thoughts were evidently far away.

"My father," said Lucie softly, laying her hand on his, "shall we go home?"

He slowly shook the shadow off and turned to her, answering, "Yes," with a long sigh.

Saying farewell to Mr. Stryver, the little group passed out into the open air, and a hackney coach * was called. While Charles Darnay stood looking after it, Sydney Carton, who had been watching the group from

* A carriage for hire, like a modern taxicab.

a little distance, stepped up to him. No one had made any mention of Mr. Carton's part in the day's events, for nobody except the prisoner had realized the importance of the note he had tossed to Stryver, if, indeed, anyone else had noticed it.

"It is a strange chance that throws you and me together," he said now to Darnay. "This must be a strange night to you, standing here alone with your double."

"I hardly seem yet," said Darnay, "to belong to this world again."

"I don't wonder. It's not long since you were well on your way to another. But you speak faintly."

"I suppose I am hungry; I've not eaten since early morning."

"Then why don't you dine? I did, while the jury was out. Let me show you the nearest tavern where you can dine well."

Walking down to Fleet Street, they turned up a covered way to the Cheshire Cheese Tavern.* Here Charles Darnay was soon seated at a good plain dinner with good wine, while Carton sat opposite him with a bottle of port before him.

"Do you feel now that you belong to this earth again, Mr. Darnay?"

"I am still somewhat confused, but I begin to realize that much."

"It must be a great satisfaction," said Carton bitterly, filling his glass again. "As for me, I should like to forget that I belong to it. It has no good in it for me, nor I for it. So you and I are not much alike after all."

Confused by the day's experiences, Charles Darnay

---

* A favorite haunt of Dickens, often visited by tourists in London, where the table occupied by Carton and Darnay is indicated by an inscription on a brass plate.

did not answer. The rude manner of this man who in outward appearance was almost his double was making him regret that so disagreeable a fellow looked so much like him.

"Now that your dinner is done," said Carton presently, "why don't you call a toast, Mr. Darnay?"

"What toast?"

"Why, it's on the tip of your tongue. It must be!"

"Miss Manette, then!"

"Miss Manette, then!" echoed Carton. Looking his companion full in the face while he drank the toast, he flung his glass over his shoulder against the wall, where it shattered to pieces. Then he rang the bell and ordered another. It was as if he were resolved that the glass should not be used again for a less lofty purpose than the health just drunk.

"That's a fair young lady to hand to a coach in the dark, Mr. Darnay," he said, filling his new goblet. "That's a fair young lady to be pitied by and wept for by! How does it feel? Is it worth being tried for one's life, to be the object of such sympathy?"

Again Darnay made no answer.

"She was mightily pleased to have your message, when I gave it to her."

The allusion reminded Darnay that this disagreeable companion had been of service to him in the dangers of the day. Changing the subject, he thanked him.

"I don't want thanks," answered Carton carelessly. "It was nothing to do."

The waiter brought the bill at this moment, and Darnay rose to go. Carton rose too. "A last word, Mr. Darnay; you think I am drunk?"

"I think you have been drinking, Mr. Carton."

"I will tell you why. I am a disappointed drudge,

sir. I care for no man on earth, and no man cares for me."

"Much to be regretted. You might have used your talents better."

"Maybe so, Mr. Darnay; maybe not. Good night!"

When he was left alone, Carton called for another bottle of wine, and asked the waiter to come and wake him at ten. Then he took up a candle, and by its light looked at himself closely in a mirror on the wall. "Do you particularly like the man?" he muttered. "Why should you particularly like a man who resembles you? There is nothing in you to like. You know that. A good reason for liking a man, that you see in him what you might have been and aren't! Change places with him, and would you have been looked at by those blue eyes as he was? Come on, and have it out in plain words! You hate the fellow!"

He turned to his pint of wine for comfort, drank it all in a few minutes, and fell asleep on his arms, with his hair straggling over the table. So he remained until the waiter roused him at ten o'clock, when he rose, tossed on his hat, and started for the lodgings of his employer, Mr. Stryver.

The successful lawyer and the unsuccessful one had known each other since their schooldays. But Stryver was full of push and energy, a good speaker, clever in dealing with witnesses, and easily able to persuade a jury. Carton had neither the easy manner nor the silvery tongue that were necessary to win him clients. Nor had he the ambition which Stryver possessed. He was, however, by far the more clever of the two in thinking out the main points of a case and in planning how it might be won. Carton could outline but not plead a case; Stryver was an orator with little gift for thinking. So in Stryver's cases, of which he had plenty, Carton did the preparatory brainwork, behind the scenes, while Stryver made a splendid court appearance and won the glory. As today, however, Carton was usually present in court and often useful.

Tonight Stryver came to the door in dressing gown and slippers to answer his assistant's knock. They went into a dingy room lined with books and littered with papers. There was a blazing fire with a kettle steaming over it. In the midst of the papers on a table were bottles of wine and brandy and rum, and sugar, and lemons.

"You have had your bottle, I see, Sydney," observed Stryver.

"Two of them. I have been dining with the day's client, or rather watching him dine."

"That was a clever point that you made about the identification. How did you happen to think of it?"

"I saw his face and mine together in the mirror, and I thought I might have been as handsome as he, if I had had any luck."

Stryver laughed. "You and your luck, Sydney! Get to work, get to work."

Sullenly Carton removed his coat and loosened his neckcloth. From the next room he brought a large jug of cold water, a basin, and a towel or two. Soaking a towel in water and partially wringing it out, he folded it on his head, sat down at the paper-strewn table, and announced, "Now I am ready!"

"Not much boiling down to be done tonight," said Stryver gaily, as he looked among his papers. "Only two sets of them."

"Give me the worst first."

"There they are, Sydney. Fire away!"

With that the employer stretched himself on his

back on the sofa. The table with the papers, the bottles, and the glasses was between them. So the night passed, with Stryver reclining comfortably, glass in hand, looking at the fire. Carton, with knitted brows and intent face, was deep in the task before him. Now and then he reached out his hand for his glass; now and then he changed the wet towel on his head.

When the first set of papers was finished, the brief for that case was handed to Stryver, who set to work to study it, that he might have it ready for court next day. At three o'clock in the morning the second case was finished. Carton removed the towel from his head, stretched, yawned, and shivered.

"You were very sound, Sydney, in the matter of those witnesses today. Every question told."

"I always am sound, am I not?"

"I don't deny it. What has roughened your temper? You're still the old Sydney Carton of Shrewsbury School—the old seesaw Sydney, up one minute and down the next!"

"Ah!" returned the other, sighing, "yes! The same Sydney, with the same luck. Even then I did exercises for other boys, and seldom did my own."

"And why not?"

"God knows. It was my way, I suppose."

He sat with his hands in his pockets and his legs stretched out before him, looking at the fire.

"Carton," said his friend, "your way is and always was a lame one. You have no energy and purpose. Look at me. How have I done what I have done? How do I do what I do?"

"Partly through paying me to help you, I suppose. But you were always in the front rank; I was always behind."

"I had to get into the front rank; I was not born there, was I?"

"I was not present at the ceremony; but my opinion is you were," said Carton. At this they both laughed.

"Before Shrewsbury, and at Shrewsbury, and ever since Shrewsbury," pursued Carton, "you have fallen into your rank, and I have fallen into mine. Even when we were fellow students in the student quarter of Paris, picking up French and French law, you were always somewhere, and I was always—nowhere. But it's a gloomy thing to talk about one's own past, with the day breaking. Turn me in some other direction before I go."

"Well then! Pledge me to the pretty witness," said Stryver, holding up his glass. "Are you turned in a pleasant direction?"

Apparently not, for he became gloomy again.

"Pretty witness," he muttered, looking down into his glass. "I have had enough of witnesses today and tonight. Who's your pretty witness?"

"The doctor's daughter, Miss Manette."

"*She* pretty?"

"Why, man alive, she was the admiration of the whole court!"

"Who made the Old Bailey a judge of beauty? She was a golden-haired doll!"

"Do you know, Sydney," said Stryver, looking at him shrewdly, "I rather thought, at the time, that you sympathized with the golden-haired doll, and were quick to see what happened to her."

"Quick to see! If a girl, doll or no doll, faints within a yard or two of a man's nose, he can see it without a magnifying glass. And now I'll have no more drink; I'll get to bed."

When his host followed him out on the staircase

with a candle to light him down the stairs, the day was coldly looking in through grimy windows. When he got out of the house, the air was cold and sad, the dull sky overcast, the river dark and dim, and wreaths of dust were spinning round and round before the morning breeze.

Carton stood still a moment on a silent terrace, seeing around him a scene like a lifeless desert. He saw for a moment, lying before him in the gray dawn, a vision of honorable ambition, self-denial, and perseverance. A moment, and it was gone, leaving only his sense of the wasted powers within him. Climbing to a lonely room high in a gloomy lodging house, he threw himself down in his clothes upon a neglected bed and fell into a drunken sleep.

Sadly, sadly the sun rose. It rose upon no sadder sight than this man of good abilities and good impulses. He was unable to direct their use, unable to live wisely or to win happiness, because of the weakness of will that lay like a disease upon him.

4 Hundreds of People

Doctor Manette and his daughter lived on a quiet street corner in London not far from Soho Square. The place had been found by Lucie not long after their return from France; and in it, with Miss Pross to keep the house and make them comfortable, she had nursed her father back to health and helped him to recover his mental powers.

The corner was at the end of a pleasant, quaint little street that led at no great distance to open fields where wild flowers blossomed. Bright and sunny in the morning, the house lay in shadow later in the day. It was a large, dignified, and cheerful house. The top floor was let to a lodger, and the family occupied the other floors, the kitchens being in the basement. One room was used as an office where Doctor Manette received his patients, for he had taken up again his practice of medicine and was becoming known as a skilled physician.

It was hard to realize that this distinguished-looking white-haired gentleman, intellectual of face and erect in bearing, was the shoemaker of the garret in Paris. Yet his low, grave voice was mournful, and gloom often overclouded him. Only his daughter had the power to charm away these black, brooding moods. She was the golden thread that united him to a past beyond his misery and to a present beyond his misery. The sound of her voice, the light of her face, the touch of her hand always comforted him.

On a pleasant Sunday afternoon, four months after the trial for treason, Mr. Jarvis Lorry, as usual on Sunday, was on his way to Soho to dine with the doctor, now his very good friend. He arrived while Lucie and her father were still out on their Sunday walk; so he made himself at home, walking about the rooms, of which there were three on a floor, opening into each other. The first was the living room, and in it were Lucie's birds and flowers and books and desk and worktable and box of watercolors. The second was the doctor's office, used also as a dining room; the third, which looked out upon a plane tree in the garden, was the doctor's bedroom. There, in a corner, stood the unused shoemaker's bench and tray of tools.

"I wonder," said Mr. Lorry aloud to himself, "that he keeps that reminder of his sufferings by him!"

"And why wonder at that?" came the abrupt question from behind him. Miss Pross had entered the room.

"I should have thought—" Mr. Lorry began.

"Pooh! *You'd* have thought!" said Miss Pross. Mr. Lorry left off the subject, and instead inquired after Miss Pross's health.

"Nothing to boast of," said that lady. "I am very much put out about my Ladybird."

"May I ask the cause?" inquired Mr. Lorry meekly.

"I don't want dozens of people who are not at all worthy of Ladybird to come here looking after her."

"*Do* dozens come for that purpose?"

"Hundreds," said Miss Pross.

"Dear me!" said Mr. Lorry, as the safest remark he could think of.

"I have lived with the darling and taken care of

her since she was ten years old, and it's really very hard to see all sorts of people, not in the least degree worthy of my pet, always turning up. When you began it—"

"*I* began it, Miss Pross?"

"Didn't you? Who brought her father to life?"

"Oh! If *that* was beginning it—"

"It wasn't ending it, I suppose? I say, when you began it, it was hard enough; not that I have any fault to find with Doctor Manette, except that he is not worthy of such a daughter. But it really is doubly hard to have crowds and multitudes of people turning up, besides him, to take my Ladybird's affections away from me."

Mr. Lorry knew Miss Pross to be very jealous, but he also knew her to be utterly unselfish and devoted; and he realized that there is nothing better in the world than the faithful service of the heart. So he did not offer to disagree with her.

"There never was, nor will be, but one man worthy of Ladybird," went on Miss Pross; "and that was my brother Solomon, if he hadn't made a mistake in life."

Mr. Lorry made no comment on this statement. His inquiries into Miss Pross's background, at the time when Tellson's Bank had engaged her as a guardian for Lucie, had revealed the fact that her brother Solomon was a heartless rascal. He had robbed her of everything she possessed, gambled with it, lost it, and left her in her poverty. But Mr. Lorry thought all the better of her for her faithfulness.

"As we happen to be alone for the moment," he said, when they had sat down together in the living room, "let me ask you this. Does the doctor, in talking with Lucie, never refer to the shoemaking time?"

"Never."

"Do you believe that he thinks of it much?"

"I do," said Miss Pross.

"Do you suppose that he has any theory of his own about the cause of his imprisonment, or the name of the person who brought it about?"

"Ladybird thinks he has."

"Then is it not remarkable that, innocent as he is of any crime, he should never touch upon the question? I will not say with me, good friends though we are; but with his fair daughter, since they are so devoted to each other."

"Well, to the best of my understanding," said Miss Pross, "he is afraid of the whole subject."

"Afraid?"

"It's plain enough, I should think, why he may be. It's a dreadful remembrance. Besides that, his loss of himself grew out of it. Not knowing how he lost himself, or how he recovered himself, he may never feel certain of not losing himself again. That alone wouldn't make the subject pleasant, I should think."

It was a wiser remark than Mr. Lorry had looked for.

"True," said he, "and fearful to reflect upon. But I wonder, Miss Pross, whether it is good for Doctor Manette to have such thoughts always shut up within him."

"Can't be helped," said Miss Pross, shaking her head. "Touch that string, and he instantly changes for the worse. Better leave it alone. Sometimes he gets up in the dead of the night, and from upstairs we hear him walking up and down in his room. Ladybird has learnt to know then that his mind is walking up and down, walking up and down in his old prison. She hurries to him, and they go on together, walking up and down, walking up and down together, until her love and company have brought him to himself. But here they are," she said, rising, "and now we shall have hundreds of people pretty soon."

The corner where the Manettes' house stood was a wonderful corner for echoes. When no one was in sight in the street, the footsteps of people walking in neighboring streets could be heard as plainly as thought a great crowd were approaching. Such echoes sounded now, as Mr. Lorry stood at the open window, but only the father and daughter appeared. Miss Pross was at the street door to receive them, but no hundreds of people followed.

Dinner time came, and still no hundreds of people. It was a very warm day, and after dinner Lucie proposed that the gentlemen should have their wine sitting under the plane tree in the garden. While they sat there talking, the tree whispered to them in its own way above their heads. But still the hundreds of people did not appear. Mr. Darnay presented himself while they sat under the plane tree, but he was only one.

Doctor Manette received him kindly, and so did Lucie, though Miss Pross went abruptly into the house and stayed there until tea time. Even then no hundreds of people had arrived. Mr. Carton lounged in, when Miss Pross appeared with the tea things, but he made only two.

The doctor was in his best condition, looking so young that the resemblance between him and Lucie was very marked. He talked in lively fashion on many subjects and at last the talk turned to the old buildings of London, which Darnay had been exploring.

"Pray, Doctor Manette," said he, "have you seen much of the Tower?"

"Lucie and I have been there, but we have seen only enough of it to know that it is full of interest."

"I have been there, you remember," said Darnay with a smile, "but not as a visitor. I had no chance to see much of it. But I remember one curious thing they told me."

"What was that?" asked Lucie.

"In making some alterations, the workmen came upon an old dungeon, which had been for many years built up and forgotten. Every stone of its inner wall was covered by inscriptions which had been carved by prisoners—dates, names, complaints, and prayers. Upon a corner stone in an angle of the wall, one prisoner, who seemed to have gone to execution, had cut his last work, three letters. They were done with some very poor instrument, and hurriedly, with an unsteady hand. The letters proved to be, not initials, but the complete word, DIG. The floor below was examined carefully. In the earth beneath a stone were found the crumbled remnants of a paper, mingled with the shreds of a small leather case. What the unknown prisoner had written will never be read, but he had written something, and hidden it away to keep it from the jailer."

"My father," exclaimed Lucie, "you are ill!"

He had suddenly started up, with his hand to his head. His manner and look quite terrified them all.

"No, my dear, not ill. There are large drops of rain falling, and they made me start. We had better go in."

He recovered himself almost instantly. Rain was really falling in large drops. But as they went into the house, Mr. Lorry fancied he saw on his face, as he turned toward Charles Darnay, the same strange look that had been upon it when he saw him in the passage of the courthouse.

The night was so sultry that at dusk, when a breeze

blew up, they moved to one of the windows and looked out into the heavy twilight. Lucie sat beween her father and Darnay; Carton lounged on the wide window sill in his usual careless fashion.

"The raindrops are still falling, large, heavy, and few," said Doctor Manette. "It comes slowly."

"It comes surely," said Carton.

There was a great hurry in the streets, of people speeding to get shelter before the storm broke. The corner resounded with the echoes of footsteps coming and going, yet not a footstep was there.

"A multitude of people, and yet a solitude!" said Darnay.

"Is it not impressive, Mr. Darnay?" asked Lucie. "Sometimes I have sat here alone of an evening, until I fancied the echoes to be those of all the footsteps that are coming by-and-by into our lives."

"There is a great crowd coming one day into our lives, if that be so," Sydney Carton struck in, in his moody way.

The footsteps never ceased, and the hurry of them became more and more rapid. The corner echoed and reechoed with the tread of feet; some, as it seemed, under the windows; some coming, some going, some stopping altogether; all in the distant streets, and not one within sight.

"Are all these footsteps meant to come to all of us, Miss Manette, or are we to divide them among us?"

"I don't know, Mr. Darnay; I told you it was a foolish fancy. When I have been alone, I have imagined them the footsteps of the people who are to come into my life and my father's."

"I take them into mine!" said Carton. "There is a great crowd bearing down upon us, Miss Manette. I see them by the lightning." He added the last words after a vivid flash which had shown him lounging in the window.

"And I hear them!" he added again, after a peal of thunder. "Here they come, fast, fierce, and furious!"

The rush and roar of rain stopped him, for no voice could be heard in it. A memorable storm of thunder and lightning broke, which lasted until after the moon rose at midnight.

It was one o'clock when the three gentlemen set forth from the Soho corner. Jerry Cruncher, high-booted and carrying a lantern, had come as bodyguard for Mr. Lorry.

"Good night," said that gentleman to his companions. "What a night it has been! Shall we ever see such a night again, together?"

Perhaps. Perhaps see the great crowd of people with its rush and roar, bearing down upon them, too.

5 *The Marquis in Paris*

On a sunshiny day later in this same July, a carriage and four horses, with coachman and footman whose livery showed that they were in the service of a nobleman, waited in the courtyard of the palace of one of the great lords of the French court. It was the last of many carriages, the others having already driven away; for this was one of the days when the duke held a reception, and it paid his admirers to be in attendance there. Dukes must be cringed to and flattered; their favor or disfavor could make or break those of lower station.

Presently the owner of the carriage appeared, coming down the stairway into the courtyard, with his hat under his arm and his snuffbox in his hand. Evidently his treatment by the duke had not pleased him, for his face showed that he was in an evil temper. He was a man of about sixty, handsomely dressed, with a face like a fine mask. It was a pale face, with clearly defined features, wearing one set expression. The line of the mouth was much too straight and thin, and could be cruel. Still, the face was a handsome face, and a remarkable one.

He turned at the foot of the stairway and shook a pinch of snuff from his fingers. "I devote you," he said, probably to the duke who had treated him coldly, "to the Devil!" With that he entered his carriage and was driven away.

With the memory of slights still upon him, it was rather agreeable to him to see the common people scatter before his horses, often barely escaping from being run down. His man drove as if he were charging an enemy, but his recklessness was not checked by his master. With a wild rattle and clatter, the carriage dashed through streets and swept round corners, with women screaming before it and men clutching children out of its way. At last, swooping at a street corner by a fountain, one of its wheels came to a sickening little jolt. There was a loud cry from a number of voices,

and the horses reared and plunged. The frightened valet got down in a hurry, and there were twenty hands at the horses' bridles.

"What has gone wrong?" said the gentleman, calmly looking out.

A tall man had caught up a bundle from among the feet of the horses. He had laid it on the base of the fountain and was down in the mud and wet, howling over it like a wild animal.

"Pardon, Monsieur the Marquis," said a ragged and respectful man, "it is a child."

"Why does he make that abominable noise? Is it his child?"

"Excuse me, Monsieur the Marquis—it is a pity—yes."

The fountain was a little removed; for the street opened, where it was, into a space some ten or twelve yards square. As the tall man suddenly got up from the ground and came running at the carriage, the Marquis clapped his hand for an instant on his sword hilt.

"Killed!" shrieked the man wildly, waving both arms above his head. "Dead!"

The people closed round and looked at the Marquis. There was nothing in their gaze but watchfulness and eagerness; there was no threat or anger. They said nothing; after the first cry they had been silent. The Marquis ran his eyes over them all, as if they had been mere rats come out of their holes.

He took out his purse.

"It is extraordinary to me," said he, "that you people cannot take care of yourselves and your children. One or the other of you is forever in the way. How do I know what injury you have done my horses? See! Give him that."

He threw out a gold coin for the valet to pick up, and all the heads craned forward that all the eyes might look down at it as it fell. The tall man called out again with a most unearthly cry, "Dead!"

He was stopped by the quick arrival of another man, for whom the rest made way. On seeing him, the miserable creature fell upon his shoulder, sobbing and crying, and pointing to the fountain, where some silent women were stooping over the motionless bundle and moving gently about it.

"I know all, I know all," said the last comer. "Be a brave man, my Gaspard! It is better for the poor little thing to die so, than to live. It has died in a moment without pain. Could it have lived an hour as happily?"

"You are a philosopher, you there," said the Marquis, smiling. "How do they call you?"

"They call me Defarge."

"Of what trade?"

"Monsieur the Marquis, seller of wine."

"Pick up that, philosopher and seller of wine," said the Marquis, throwing him another gold coin, "and spend it as you will. The horses there; are they right?"

The Marquis leaned back in his seat with the air of a gentleman who had accidentally broken some common thing, and had paid for it, and could afford to pay for it. His ease was suddenly disturbed by a coin flying into his carriage, and ringing on its floor.

"Hold!" said the Marquis. "Hold the horses! Who threw that?"

He looked to the spot where Defarge had stood a moment before; but the wretched father had taken up his pitiful bundle and disappeared, and the figure that remained was that of a dark, handsome woman, knitting, who saw nothing.

"You dogs!" said the Marquis smoothly, "I would ride over any or all of you very willingly. If I knew which rascal threw at the carriage, and the wretch were near enough, he should be crushed under the wheels."

So well did they know what such a man could do to them that not a voice, or a hand, or even an eye was raised. Among the men, not one. But the woman who stood knitting looked up steadily and looked the Marquis in the face. It was not for his dignity to notice it; his scornful eyes passed over her and over all the other rats. He leaned back in his seat again and gave the word, "Go on!"

The woman who stood knitting still knitted on with the steadfastness of Fate. She seemed to see nothing; but it might be that she had seen a tall, thin figure creep out of a cellar and start at a loping run along the street in the direction where the carriage of the Marquis was disappearing.

6 The Marquis in the Country

The sun of the next day was setting as the traveling carriage of the Marquis dragged up a steep hill to the west of Paris. The landscape, though beautiful, showed scanty crops—wheat bright but not abundant, patches of poor rye where wheat should have been, patches of poor peas and beans, patches of coarse vegetable substitutes for wheat.

At the top of the hill the carriage stopped while the coachman fastened to the wheel a heavy, curved wooden block that acted as a brake for the descent. This drag, as it was called, hung when not in use by a chain below the body of the carriage. The sunset struck so brilliantly into the carriage while it stopped that the Marquis was drenched in crimson. "It will die out directly," said he.

In fact, as the carriage slid downhill in a cloud of dust, the red glow departed quickly. The road led now through a broken country, bold and open, to a little village at the bottom of the hill, with a broad sweep and rise beyond it, a church tower, a windmill, a forest for hunting, and a crag with a fortress on it used as a prison. Round upon all these objects, darkening as the night drew on, the Marquis looked, with the air of one who was coming near home.

The village had its one poor street, with its poor brewery, poor tannery, poor tavern, poor stable yard, poor fountain. It had its poor people, too. All its people were poor, and many of them were sitting at their doors, shredding spare onions and the like for supper. Many were at the fountain, washing leaves, and grasses, and any small green things that could be eaten. Placards showing what made them poor were posted on many of the walls—the tax for the state, the tax for the church, the tax for the lord, tax general and tax local. So many were the taxes, to be paid here and to be paid there, that the wonder was there was any village left. Few children were to be seen, and no dogs; these things were luxuries.

The Marquis drew up in his carriage at the post house gate. It was near the fountain, and the peasants paused in their work to look at him. He cast his eyes over the patient faces that drooped before him, till he saw among them that of a gray-haired mender of roads.

"Bring me hither that fellow!" said the Marquis.

The fellow was brought, blue cap in hand, and the other fellows closed round to look and listen.

"I passed you on the road?"

"Monseigneur,* it is true. I had the honor of being passed on the road."

"Coming up the hill, and at the top of the hill, both?"

"Monseigneur, it is true."

"What did you look at, so fixedly?"

"Monseigneur, I looked at the man." He stooped a little, and with his tattered blue cap pointed under the carriage.

"What man, pig? And why look there?"

* French equivalent of "My lord."

"Pardon, Monseigneur; he swung by the chain of the drag."

"Who?" demanded the traveler.

"Monseigneur, the man."

"May the Devil carry away these idiots! How do you call the man? You know all the men of this part of the country. Who was he?"

"Your pardon, Monseigneur! He was not of this part of the country. Of all the days of my life, I never saw him."

"Swinging by the chain? To be suffocated?"

"With your gracious permission, that was the wonder of it, Monseigneur."

"What was he like?"

"Monseigneur, he was whiter than the miller. All covered with dust, white as a ghost, tall as a ghost!"

"Truly you did well," said the Marquis, "to see a thief accompanying my carriage, and not open that great mouth of yours. Bah! Put him aside, Monsieur Gabelle!"

Monsieur Gabelle was the master of the post house,* and the tax collector, and in general took care of the Marquis's interests in the village. He had been holding the road mender by the arm in an official manner. "Bah! Go aside!" he now said, letting go of him.

"And, Gabelle, if this ghost seeks to lodge in your village tonight, lay hands on him."

"Monseigneur, I am flattered to devote myself to your orders."

"One thing more, fellow!" The roadmaster paused in his departure. "Did the man run away when we stopped for the drag?"

---

* The office where the mail coaches stopped to change horses and to leave or take on mail, parcels, and passengers.

"Monseigneur, he flung himself over the hillside head first, as one plunges into the river."

"See to it, Gabelle. Drive on!"

The burst of speed with which the carriage started out of the village and up the rise beyond was soon checked by the steepness of the hill. Gradually it slowed to a footpace, lumbering upward in the twilight among the many sweet scents of a summer night. If a tall figure, white as a ghost, skulked along the hedges by the roadside, the coachman, walking beside his horses, did not see it. And the Marquis looked neither to right nor left.

At the top of the hill there was a little burial ground, with a wayside shrine where a woman was kneeling. She rose quickly as the carriage came up to her, and presented herself at the door.

"Monseigneur, a petition!" she cried.

With an exclamation of impatience, the Marquis looked out at her.

"How, then! What is it? Always petitions!"

"Monseigneur! For the love of the great God! My husband, the forester."

"What of your husband, the forester? Always the same with you people. He cannot pay something?"

"He has paid all, Monseigneur. He is dead."

"Well! He is quiet. Can I restore him to you?"

"Alas, no, Monseigneur! But he lies yonder, under a little heap of poor grass."

"Well?"

"Monseigneur, there are so many little heaps of poor grass."

"Again, well?"

She looked an old woman, but was young. Her manner was one of passionate grief; she clasped her veined and knotted hands together with wild energy.

"Monseigneur, hear me! Monseigneur, hear my petition! My husband died of hunger; so many die, so many more will die of hunger."

"Again, well? Can I feed them?"

"Monseigneur, the good God knows; but I don't ask it. My petition is, that a morsel of stone or wood, with my husband's name, may be placed over him to show where he lies. Otherwise, the place will be quickly forgotten, it will never be found when I am dead, I shall be laid under some other heap of poor grass. Monseigneur, they are so many, they increase so fast. Monseigneur, Monseigneur!"

The valet put her away from the door, the horses broke into a brisk trot, and she was left far behind. If a tall, dust-covered figure was also left behind, losing sight of the carriage which he had trailed from Paris, it did not matter. The castle was in sight to which the carriage had journeyed.

By the light of a torch the great gate of the large, high-roofed house was opened to Monsieur the Marquis, and he stepped inside.

"Monsieur Charles, whom I expect—is he arrived from England?"

"Monseigneur, not yet."

Lighted by the torchbearer, the Marquis mounted a broad flight of shallow steps and crossed a large stone courtyard to where two stone staircases met in a stone terrace before the principal door. All about were heavy stone railings, and stone urns, and stone flowers, and carved about the eaves stone faces of men and lions—a stony business altogether, but perhaps no more so than the heart of the owner of the building.

The great door clanged behind him, and he crossed a hall grim with old armor and weapons. Avoiding the larger rooms, which were dark and closed for the night, he mounted to a door in the upper corridor, which admitted him to his own private apartment of three rooms, his bedchamber and two others. They were high, vaulted rooms with cool, uncarpeted floors and wide hearths for winter fires; and they were furnished with all the luxuries of a nobleman in an extravagant and luxurious age and country.

In the third room, a round room in one of the castle's four round towers, a supper table was set for two persons.

"They said my nephew had not arrived," commented the Marquis, glancing at the two places on the table.

"That is true; but he was expected with Monseigneur."

"I see. It is not probable he will arrive tonight; nevertheless, leave the table as it is."

In a quarter of an hour, the Marquis sat down to his supper. His chair was opposite to the window, which was open, with its slate-gray Venetian blind lowered. Beyond it the dark night showed in horizontal lines of black.

He had taken his soup, and was raising his wine glass to his lips when he suddenly put it down.

"What is that?" he calmly asked, looking with attention at the horizontal stripes of black and gray.

"Monseigneur? That?"

"Outside the blinds. Open the blinds."

It was done.

"Well?"

"Monseigneur, it is nothing. The trees and the night are all that are here."

The servant who spoke had drawn up the blinds and looked out into the vacant darkness. If a gray shadow had for a moment flitted past across the stripes of black, it was gone now; only the leaves of the vine that climbed the tower fluttered in a faint breeze.

"Good," said the master. "Close the blinds again."

That was done too, and the Marquis went on with his supper. He was halfway through it, when he heard the sound of wheels. It came on briskly, and came up to the front of the castle.

"Ask who is arrived."

It was the nephew of Monseigneur.

"Tell him," said the Marquis, "that supper awaits him, and ask him to come in."

In a little while he came. He had been known in England as Charles Darnay. His uncle received him in a courtly manner, but they did not shake hands.

"You left Paris yesterday, sir?" the nephew inquired as he took his seat at table.

"Yesterday. And you?"

"I come direct from London."

"You have been a long time intending the journey."

"I have been detained by various business," said the nephew.

"Without doubt," said the polished uncle.

So long as a servant was present, no other words passed between them. When coffee had been served and they were alone together, the nephew opened a conversation.

"I have come back, sir, as you suppose, pursuing the same purpose that took me away. It carried me into great danger, but I should have had no regrets even if it had carried me to death."

"Not to death," said the uncle. "It is not necessary to say to death."

"I doubt, sir," returned the nephew, "whether you would have tried to save me, even at the very brink of death."

The uncle made a graceful gesture of protest.

"Indeed, sir," went on the nephew, "I feel that you may yourself have tried to add to the suspicious circumstances that caused my arrest for treason. It would have been an easy way to get rid of me, to have me put to death in England."

"No, no, no," said the uncle pleasantly.

"However that may be, I know that you would use any means to stop me from carrying out my dead mother's wish, and seeking to right the wrongs done by my family for generations."

"My friend, I told you so, long ago. It is useless now to discuss the question. We have already lost so many privileges that it is difficult enough to assert our station, without your making it more so."

"We have so asserted our station," said the nephew gloomily, "that I believe our name to be more hated than any other name in France. There is not a face I see, in all this country round about us, that looks at me with any expression but one of fear."

"A compliment," said the Marquis, "to the grandeur of the family. Fear, my friend, will keep the dogs obedient to the whip as long as this roof shuts out the sky."

That might not be so long as the Marquis supposed.

"Meanwhile," continued the Marquis, "I will preserve the honor of the family, if you will not. Shall we end our conversation?"

"In a moment. Sir, we have done wrong, and we shall reap the fruits of wrong."

"*We* have done wrong?" repeated the Marquis with an inquiring smile.

"Our family; our honorable family; my father; you, his twin brother, heir to his title and estate." He paused, adding sadly, "I am bound to a system that is frightful to me. Unwillingly I am responsible for it, while I seek in vain for help to right the wrongs of the wretched peasants who cry to us for mercy."

"Seeking help from me, my nephew, you will ever seek in vain. I will die upholding the system under which I have lived." He rang a small bell on the table. "But you are lost, Monsieur Charles, I see. It is useless to try to persuade you that you are wrong."

"This property and France are lost to me," said the nephew gloomily. "I renounce them."

"Are they both yours to renounce? France may be; but is the property?"

"I had no intention to claim it yet. If it passed to

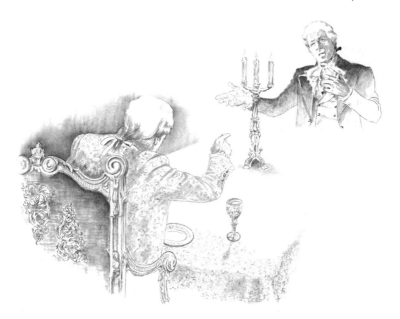

me from you tomorrow, or twenty years hence, I would abandon it, and live otherwise and elsewhere. It is little to give up. What is it but a wilderness of misery and ruin?"

The Marquis glanced around the luxurious room, as if to say he differed with his nephew's choice of words.

"Oh, yes, it is fair enough to the eye. Nevertheless, beneath the surface, it is a crumbling tower of waste, cruelty, oppression, debt, hunger, nakedness, and suffering. If it ever becomes mine, I shall have it managed so that the miserable people shall suffer less. But not one penny of income will I ever draw from it. There is a curse on it."

"And you?" said the uncle. "Forgive my curiosity, but how, then, do you intend to live?"

"I must do, to live, what others of my countrymen, even noblemen, may have to do some day—work."

"In England, for example?"

"Yes. The family honor, sir, is safe in this country in your hands. And it will not suffer in England, for I do not use the family name there."

At the ringing of the bell, the adjoining chamber had been lighted up. The Marquis looked that way.

"England is very attractive to you," he observed, "in spite of your hardships there."

"I have already said that for those hardships I feel I may thank you, sir. For the rest, it is my refuge."

"The English boast that it is the refuge of many. You know another Frenchman who has found a refuge there? A doctor, with a daughter?"

"Yes."

"Yes," repeated the Marquis. "You are weary. Good night! I look to the pleasure of seeing you again in the morning. A doctor with a daughter; yes. Good repose! Light Monsieur my nephew to his bedroom."

After his valet had come and gone, the Marquis walked to and fro in his loose robe, to prepare himself gently for sleep, that hot, still night. Rustling on softly slippered feet, he moved like a refined tiger, from end to end of the luxurious room.

"I am cool now," he said at last, "and may go to bed."

So, leaving only one light burning, he let his thin gauze curtains fall around him.

The stone faces on the outer walls stared blindly at the black night for three heavy hours. Dead darkness lay on all the landscape. If a tall shadow moved among the vines outside the window of the Marquis, there was no one but the owl to see. In the village, taxers and taxed were fast asleep. The fountain flowed unseen and un-heard through three dark hours. Then the gray water began to be ghostly in the light, and the eyes of the stone faces of the castle were opened.

Lighter and lighter, until at last the sun touched the tops of the still trees, and poured its radiance over the hill. The carol of the birds was loud and high, and, on the sill of the great window of the bedchamber of the Marquis, one little bird sang its sweetest song with all its might. Now the sun was fully up, and the toil of the day began in the village. The castle awoke later, but awoke gradually and surely. Doors and windows were thrown open. Horses in their stables looked round over their shoulders. Dogs pulled hard at their chains, asking to be loosed.

But what could be the reason for the ringing of the great bell of the castle, for the running up and down the stairs, for the hurried figures on the terrace, for the quick saddling of horses and riding away? All the people of the village gathered at the fountain, whispering low, showing only grim curiosity and surprise. Some of the servants from the castle were grouped on the other side of the street, together with the officials of the village.

What did all this mean? And why was Monsieur Gabelle so quickly hoisted up on horseback behind a servant and carried away toward the castle?

It meant that there was one stone face too many, up at the castle. A stone face had been added, during the night, for which the castle had waited through about two hundred years.

It lay back on the pillow of the Marquis. It was like a fine mask, suddenly startled, made angry, and hardened. Driven home into the heart of the stone figure attached to it was a knife, which until yesterday had been thrust through the belt of a tall, dust-covered ghost whose name was Gaspard. Round the hilt was a frill of paper, on which was scrawled:

"*Drive him fast to his tomb. This, from* JACQUES."

7 Two Unselfish Lovers

Charles Darnay was true to his word. After the murder of his uncle the Marquis, he left France, instructing the agents in charge of his estate to use the income from it for the benefit of the oppressed and poverty-stricken peasants on his lands. The pursuit of the murderer he left to the governmental authorities. By the time a year had passed, he was becoming well known in London and at the University of Cambridge as a successful tutor of the French language and literature, and as a translator of French books into elegant English.

During the part of each week that he spent in London, Darnay passed his happiest hours at the house on the quiet corner of Soho. He had loved Lucie Manette from the hour of his danger at the trial. He had never heard a sound so sweet and dear as the sound of her voice. He had never seen a face so tenderly beautiful as hers when he beheld it from the edge of the grave that had been dug for him. But he had not yet spoken to her on the subject; for, according to the custom of the time, he felt that he must first ask her father's permission.

He chose a summer afternoon, when he knew that Lucie and Miss Pross were out of the house, to make his call upon the doctor. The young man found some difficulty in approaching the subject near his heart, for the doctor's manner was distant and strained, as if he feared he would have to listen to words that would disturb him. However, once the topic of his love for Lucie had been introduced, Darnay spoke eloquently, assuring Doctor Manette that he understood the devotion between him and his daughter, and that he would never do anything to separate them from each other.

"Like you, I am an exile from France," he said. "Like you, I was driven from it by its madness, its oppression, its misery. I look only to sharing your fortunes, sharing your life and home, and being faithful to you and to Lucie until death."

Doctor Manette was looking at him with that dark look of doubt and dread that Mr. Lorry had twice noticed.

"Have you any reason to believe that Lucie loves you?" he asked.

"None, as yet."

"Do you wish any help from me?"

"None, sir. I know that if you should speak in my behalf, your wish would be enough to decide her. For that reason, I would rather that you did not speak. I want her answer to be of her own free will. But may I ask that, if she loves me, you will not use your influence against me?"

"That I promise you," said the doctor. "If she ever tells me that you are necessary to her happiness, I will give her to you."

The two men clasped hands as Darnay continued, "Your confidence in me ought to be returned with full confidence on my part. My present name, though but slightly changed from my mother's, is not, as you will remember, my own. I wish to tell you what it is, and why I am in England."

"Stop!" said the doctor.

"I wish it, that I may the better deserve your confidence, and have no secret from you."

"Stop!"

For an instant, the doctor even had his two hands at his ears; for another instant, even had his two hands laid on Darnay's lips. "Tell me when I ask you, not now. If your suit should prosper, if Lucie should love you, you shall tell me on your marriage morning. Do you promise?"

"Willingly."

"Give me your hand. She will be home directly, and it is better she should not see us together tonight. Go! God bless you!"

When Lucie came home, an hour later, she was surprised to find her father's reading chair empty.

"My father!" she called to him. "Father dear!"

There was no answer, but she heard a low, hammering sound in his bedroom. As she looked in at his door, her blood chilled, and she whispered to herself, "What shall I do?" But her uncertainty lasted only a moment; then she tapped at the door and softly called to him. The noise ceased at the sound of her voice, and he presently came out to her, and they walked up and down together for a long time.

She came down from her bed to look at him in his sleep that night. He slept heavily, and his tray of shoe-making tools and his old unfinished work were all as usual.

Not long after this, Lucie was surprised by a day-time call from Sydney Carton. He came often to the house, and she knew that he admired her. But if he ever shone anywhere, he certainly never shone in the house of Doctor Manette. He was always the same moody and unhappy lounger, though when he cared to talk, he talked well. Only the streets outside knew how much he cared for the house and its occupants. Many a night he wandered there, watching the lights go out in the windows. Many a daybreak showed his solitary figure lingering there.

On the day in question, Sydney arrived to find Lucie at her needlework, alone. She had never been quite at her ease with him, and was a little embarrassed. But looking up at his face, she saw a change in it.

"I fear you are not well, Mr. Carton!"

"No. But the life I lead, Miss Manette, is not good for one's health."

"Is it not—forgive me—a pity to live no better life?"

"God knows it is a shame!"

"Then why not change it?"

Looking gently at him again, she was surprised and saddened to see that there were tears in his eyes. There were tears in his voice too, as he answered,

"It is too late for that. I shall never be better than I am. I shall sink lower, and be worse."

He leaned an elbow on her table, and covered his eyes with his hand.

She had never seen him softened and was much distressed.

"Pray forgive me, Miss Manette," he said. "I break down before the knowledge of what I want to say to you. Will you hear me?"

"If it will make you any happier, Mr. Carton, I shall be very glad!"

"God bless you for your sweet compassion!"

He unshaded his face after a little while and spoke steadily.

"If it had been possible that you could have returned my love—poor, wasted, drunken creature as you know me to be—I would have known, in spite of my happiness, that I would bring you to misery, disgrace, and sorrow; that I would pull you down with me. So, even had it been possible, I would not have asked it. As it is, I know well that you can have no tenderness for me. I deserve none and I ask for none."

"Without it, can I not save you, Mr. Carton? I know you would say these things to no one else. Cannot I repay your trust in me by helping you to some better course?"

He shook his head.

"No, Miss Manette, to none. If you will hear me a little longer, all you can ever do for me is done. I wish you to know that you have been the last dream of my soul. Since I knew you, I have been troubled by a remorse that I thought would never reproach me again. I have had vague ideas of striving afresh, beginning anew, and fighting out the abandoned fight. A dream, all a dream, that vanishes in the cold light of reality and ends in nothing; but I wish you to know that you inspired it."

"Will nothing of it remain? Oh, Mr. Carton, think again! Try again!"

"No, Miss Manette; all through it, I have known myself to be quite undeserving. And yet I wish you to know with what a sudden mastery you kindled me, heap of ashes that I am, into fire."

"Since it is my misfortune, Mr. Carton, to have made you more unhappy than you were before you knew me—"

"Don't say that, Miss Manette, for you would have saved me, if anything could. You will not be the cause of my becoming worse."

"But can I use no influence to serve you? Have I no power for good with you at all?"

"Only this—let me carry the memory that I opened my heart to you, last of all the world, and that there was something left in me which you could pity."

"I entreat you to believe yourself capable of better things!"

"No; I have proved myself, and I know better. But I distress you; I draw fast to an end. Will you let me believe, when I recall this day, that the last confidence of my life was reposed in you, and that it will be shared by no one?"

"If that will be a consolation to you, yes."

"Not even by the dearest one ever to be known to you?"

"Mr. Carton," she answered, "the secret is yours, not mine. I promise to respect it."

"Thank you. And again, God bless you."

He put her hand to his lips, and moved towards the door.

"Do not fear that I shall ever resume this conversation. I will never refer to it again. But in the hour of my death, I shall hold sacred the memory that my last confession was made to you, and that my name, and faults, and miseries, were gently carried in your heart. May it otherwise be light and happy!"

He was so unlike what he had ever shown himself to be, and it was so sad to think how much he had thrown away, that Lucie wept mournfully for him as he stood looking back at her.

"Be comforted!" he said. "I am not worth such feeling, Miss Manette. Be comforted! Within myself I shall always be toward you what I am now, though outwardly

I shall be what you have heretofore seen me. Believe this of me."

"I will, Mr. Carton."

"My last plea of all is this. It is useless to say it, I know, but it rises out of my soul. For you, and for any dear to you, I would do anything. If my career were such as to give opportunity for sacrifice, I would make any sacrifice for you and for those dear to you. The time will not be long in coming when you will form new ties, the dearest ties that will ever grace and gladden you. O Miss Manette, when the little picture of a happy father's face looks up in yours, when you see your own bright beauty springing up anew at your feet, think now and then that there is a man who would give his life, to keep a life you love beside you!"

He said, "Farewell!" Said, "A last God bless you!" and left her.

8 *Knitting*

On a hot morning in August, Madame Defarge sat calmly knitting at her counter in the wine shop in Saint Antoine, as usual seeming to see nothing. She might, however, have observed that the shop was unusually full of people, a few of them drinking but more of them seeming restless, as if waiting for something to happen. What they were waiting for became clear at noon, when two dusty, thirsty men entered the shop. One was Ernest Defarge, returned after three days' absence from Paris; the other was a mender of roads in a blue cap.

An exchange of greetings and a comment on the weather by Defarge were followed by a silence, in which every man looked at his neighbor and then cast down his eyes. One man got up and went out.

"My wife," said Defarge then, "I have traveled a long way with this good mender of roads, called Jacques."

A second man got up and went out.

"I met him," went on Defarge, "by accident, a day and a half's journey out of Paris. He is a good child, this mender of roads, called Jacques."

A third man got up and went out. As six years before, the name Jacques seemed to represent some sort of code signal.

The road mender took off his blue cap to the company and drank the wine set before him, munching with it some coarse dark bread which he took from his pocket.

When he had finished, Defarge led him to the door, out into a courtyard, and up a steep staircase into a garret— the garret where a white-haired man had sat on a low bench, busily making shoes.

The three men were there who had one by one gone out of the wine shop. Two sat on the old pallet bed; the third knelt behind them. And between them and the white-haired man afar off was the one small link, that they had once looked in at him through the chinks in the wall.

Defarge closed the door carefully, and spoke in a low voice.

"Jacques One, Jacques Two, Jacques Three! This is the witness met by appointment, by me, Jacques Four. He will tell you all. Speak, Jacques Five!"

The mender of roads, blue cap in hand, wiped his forehead with it, and said, "Where shall I commence, monsieur?"

"Commence," was Monsieur Defarge's not unreasonable reply, "at the commencement."

The commencement was, of course, the story of how the mender of roads had first seen the tall man, Gaspard of Saint Antoine, hanging by the chain under the coach of the Marquis. So often in the past year had he retold his story for the entertainment of his village that it needed no effort of memory. He went on to describe his second meeting with Gaspard, who, after a search of many months, had at last been captured.

"I am again at work on the hillside," said the road mender, "and the sun is again about to go to bed. I am collecting my tools to go home, when I raise my eyes and see coming over the hill six soldiers. In their midst is a tall man with his arms bound to his sides.

"I stand aside by my heap of stones to watch them

pass. At first I see no more than that they are six soldiers and a prisoner, covered with dust. But when they
come quite near to me, I recognize the tall man and he
recognizes me. But we do not let the soldiers see this
recognition. 'Come on!' says the chief soldier, pointing
to the village; 'bring him fast to his tomb!' and they
bring him faster. I follow. His arms are swelled because
of being bound so tight, his wooden shoes are large and
clumsy, and he is lame. Because he cannot go fast
enough, they drive him with their guns, and as they race
down the hill, he falls. They laugh and pick him up
again. They bring him into the village; they take him
past the mill and up to the prison. All the village sees
the prison gate open in the darkness of the night and
swallow him!"

The mender of roads lowered his voice as he went on. "All the village whispers by the fountain. All the village dreams of that unhappy one within the locks and bars of the prison on the crag. In the morning, on my way to work, I pass by the prison. There I see him, high up, behind the bars of a lofty iron cage, bloody and dusty as last night. He has no hand free to wave to me. I dare not call to him. He looks at me like a dead man."

Defarge and the other three glanced darkly at one another. Their looks were dark, stern, and revengeful as they listened to the countryman's story. They had the air of a rough court of justice.

"Go on, Jacques," said Defarge.

"He remains up there in his iron cage for some days. The village is afraid. In the evening when the folk gather to gossip at the fountain, they whisper that although he is condemned to death, he will not be executed. They say that petitions have been presented in Paris, showing that he was enraged and made mad by the death of his child. They say that a petition has been presented to the king himself. It is possible. Perhaps yes, perhaps no."

"Listen then," Jacques One sternly interrupted. "A petition *was* presented to the king and queen. We four saw the king take it, in his carriage in the street, sitting beside the queen. It was Defarge here who, at the risk of his life, darted out before the horses with the petition in his hand."

"And once again listen," said the kneeling Jacques Three. "The guard surrounded the petitioner, Defarge here, and struck him blows. You hear?"

"I hear, Monsieur."

"Go on, Jacques Five," said Defarge.

"Some whisper this, some that. They speak of nothing else. Even the fountain appears to fall to that tune. At length, on Sunday night when all the village is asleep, come soldiers, winding down from the prison. Workmen dig, workmen hammer, soldiers laugh and sing. In the morning there stands by the fountain a gallows forty feet high, poisoning the water. At noon is heard the roll of drums, and the captive is brought in the midst of many soldiers. He is bound as before, and in his mouth there is a gag. At the top of the gallows is fixed the knife, with its point in the air. He is hanged there, forty feet high; and is left hanging, poisoning the water."

He paused to wipe the sweat from his face with his blue cap.

"It is frightful, my friends. How can the women and children draw water? Who can gossip of an evening, under that shadow? Under it, have I said? When I left the village, Monday evening as the sun was going to bed, and looked back from the hill, the shadow struck across the church, across the mill, across the prison— seemed to strike across the earth to where the sky rests upon it!"

He stopped abruptly, as if horrified at his own tale. "That's all, sirs," he then concluded. "I left at sunset, as I had been told to do, and I walked on, that night and half next day, until I met, as I had been told I should, this comrade. With him I came the rest of the journey, and here you see me!"

After a gloomy silence, the first Jacques said, "Good. You have told your story faithfully. Will you wait for us a little, outside the door?"

Defarge escorted the stranger to the top of the stairs, and leaving him seated there, returned.

The three were standing when he entered the garret. "How say you, Jacques?" demanded Number One. "Shall vengeance be taken for Gaspard?"

"To be registered?" asked Number Two.

"To be registered as doomed to destruction," answered Defarge.

"Magnificent!" croaked Jacques Three.

"The castle and all the family?" inquired the first.

"The castle and all the family," replied Defarge. "Extermination."

They did not know that one of the doomed family, an exile far away in London, sat at that hour with the white-haired man whom once they had watched in that garret. Nor did Charles Darnay dream, in peaceful England, that at that hour his fate was being decided by men whom he had never seen.

"Are you sure," asked Jacques Two of Defarge, "that no trouble can arise from our manner of keeping the register? To have our decisions woven into the knitting of Madame Defarge is without doubt safe, for no one but ourselves can read her code. But shall we always be able to read it? Or, I ought to say, will she?"

"Jacques," returned Defarge, drawing himself up, "if madame my wife undertook to keep the register in her memory alone, she would not lose a word of it—not a syllable of it. Knitted in her own stitches and her own symbols, it will always be as plain to her as the sun. Trust Madame Defarge. It would be easier for a man to erase himself from existence than to erase one letter of his name or crimes from the knitted register of Madame Defarge."

There was a murmur of approval. Then Jacques Three inquired, "Is this peasant to be sent home soon? I hope so. He is very simple; is he not a little dangerous?"

"He knows nothing of our affairs," said Defarge. "I

charge myself with him; let him remain with me. I will take care of him and set him on his road. He wishes to see the fine world—the king, the queen, the court. Let him see them."

"Is it a good sign," exclaimed Jacques Two, "that he wishes to see royalty and nobility?"

"Show a cat milk," said Defarge, "if you wish her to thirst for it. Show a dog his natural prey, if you wish him to hunt it down. We shall send this peasant home to tell his village of his hate for those he has seen lapped in luxury while he hungers in poverty."

Accordingly, the mender of roads spent several agreeable days in this Paris that he had never seen before. The visit was concluded with a trip on Sunday to Versailles to see the court ride out in all its splendor. Thence he set out upon his homeward way, a speck in a blue cap toiling through the darkness, while Madame Defarge and her husband returned to Saint Antoine. At the gate of Paris they stopped for the usual inquiries made of all persons entering the city, and Monsieur Defarge alighted for a few moments from the coach to talk with a friend of his among the police in the guardhouse.

As they walked from the coach to their house, Madame Defarge spoke to her husband.

"Say then, my friend; what did Jacques of the police tell thee?"

"Very little tonight, but all he knows. There is another spy commissioned for our quarter."

"Eh, well!" said Madame Defarge, raising her eyebrows. "It is necessary to register him. How do they call that man?"

"He is English."

"So much the better. His name?"

"John Barsad."

"Good. His appearance—is it known?"

"Age, about forty years; height, about five feet nine; black hair and dark complexion; eyes dark; face long, thin, and sallow, with a Roman nose that bends slightly toward the left cheek."

"Eh, my faith, it is a portrait!" said madame, laughing. "He shall be knitted into the register tomorrow."

They reached the shop, and went about the work of closing it for the night.

"You seem low of spirit," commented Madame Defarge with a glance at her husband, who with a sigh had laid down his half-smoked pipe.

"A little, truly," he answered. "Vengeance is long in coming."

"Vengeance requires a long time; it is the rule."

"It does not take a long time to strike a man with lightning."

"How long," demanded madame, "does it take to make and store the lightning? But it is always preparing, though it is not seen or heard. Look at the world around us. Look at the rage and discontent that are increasing. Can such things last?"

"My brave wife," returned Defarge, "I do not question all this. But you know well that it is possible that the change may not come during our lives. We may not see the triumph of the liberty we strive for."

"We shall have helped it," answered madame. "Nothing that we do is done in vain. Come, then. We must sleep. There is another day tomorrow."

Next noonday saw Madame Defarge in her usual place in the wine shop, knitting away busily. A rose lay beside her. There were a few customers sprinkled about. A figure entering at the door threw a shadow on her

work, and she glanced sidelong from narrowed eyes. She laid down her knitting and began to pin the rose in her headdress. This had a curious effect. The moment Madame Defarge took up the rose, the customers stopped talking and began gradually to drop out of the shop.

"Good day, madame," said the newcomer.

"Good day, monsieur," she replied, adding to herself as she resumed her knitting, "Hah! Age about forty, black hair, eyes dark, long, sallow face—good day, one and all!"

"Have the goodness to give me a little glass of old brandy, madame."

Madame obeyed politely.

"Marvellous brandy this, madame!"

It was the first time it had ever been so complimented, and Madame Defarge knew better.

"You knit with great skill, madame."

"I am accustomed to it."

"A pretty pattern too!"

"*You* think so?" said madame, looking at him with a smile.

"Decidedly. May one ask what it is for?"

"Pastime," said madame, still looking at him with a smile, while her fingers moved nimbly.

"Not for use?"

"That depends. I may find a use for it one day."

The customers seemed to dislike madame's wearing a rose in her headdress. Two men had entered separately and had been about to order drink when, catching sight of the rose, they had hesitated, pretended to be looking about for someone who was not there, and gone away. Of those who had been there when the visitor entered, there was not one left. They had all dropped off, lounging away in an accidental manner.

" 'JOHN,' " thought madame, as her fingers knitted and her eyes looked at the stranger. "Stay long enough, and I shall knit 'BARSAD' before you go."

"You have a husband, madame?"

"I have."

"Children?"

"No children."

"Business seems bad?"

"Business is very bad. The people are so poor."

"Ah, the unfortunate, miserable people! So oppressed, too—as you say."

"As *you* say," madame retorted, correcting him.

"Pardon me. Certainly it was I who said so, but you naturally think so. Of course."

"*I* think?" returned madame. "I and my husband have enough to do to keep this wine shop open, without thinking. All we think, here, is, how to live. That gives us enough to think about. *I* think for others? No, no."

The spy, who was there to pick up any crumbs he could find or make, stood leaning his elbow on the little counter and sipping his brandy.

"A bad business, this, of Gaspard's execution. Ah, the poor Gaspard!"

"My faith!" returned madame, coolly and lightly, "if people use knives for such purposes, they have to pay for it. He knew beforehand what the price of his luxury was; he has paid the price."

"I believe," said the spy, "there is much anger about it in this neighborhood?"

"Is there?" asked madame vacantly.

"Is there not?"

"—Here is my husband!" said Madame Defarge.

As the keeper of the wine shop entered at the door, the spy saluted him by touching his hat and saying, with an engaging smile, "Good day, Jacques!" Defarge stopped short and stared at him.

"Good day, Jacques!" the spy repeated, with not quite so much confidence or quite so easy a smile under the stare.

"You deceive yourself, monsieur," returned the keeper of the wine shop. "You mistake me for another. That is not my name. I am Ernest Defarge."

"It is all the same," said the spy, airily. "I was saying to madame that they tell me there is much sympathy and anger among the people for the unjust and unhappy fate of poor Gaspard."

"No one has told me so," said Defarge, shaking his head. "I know nothing of it."

The spy, well used to his business, drained his glass and asked for another. Madame Defarge hummed a little song over her knitting.

"The pleasure of conversing with you, Monsieur

Defarge, recalls to me," pursued the spy, "that I have some interesting associations with your name."

"Indeed!" said Defarge, with indifference.

"Yes, indeed. When Dr. Manette was released, you, his old servant, had charge of him, I know."

"Such is the fact, certainly," said Defarge.

"It was to you," said the spy, "that his daughter came; and it was from your care that his daughter took him, accompanied by a neat brown monsieur—in a little wig—Lorry—of the bank of Tellson and Company."

"Such is the fact," repeated Defarge.

"Very interesting memories!" said the spy. "I have known Dr. Manette and his daughter, in England."

"Yes?" said Defarge.

"You don't hear much about them now?" said the spy.

"No," said Defarge.

"In effect," madame struck in, "we never hear about them. We received the news of their safe arrival, and perhaps another letter, or perhaps two; but since then we have held no correspondence."

"Perfectly so, madame," replied the spy. "She is going to be married."

"Going?" echoed madame. "She was pretty enough to have been married long ago. You English are cold, it seems to me."

"Oh! You know I am English."

"I perceive your tongue is," returned madame; "and what the tongue is, I suppose the man is."

The spy made the best of the identification. "Yes," he resumed, "Miss Manette is going to be married; and, strangely enough, to the nephew of Monsieur the Marquis, for whom poor Gaspard was so unjustly executed. He is, of course, the present Marquis, but that is not known in England. He is no Marquis there. He goes by the name of Charles Darnay. D'Aulnais was his mother's name."

Madame Defarge knitted steadily, but the spy would have been no spy if he had not noticed that her husband's hand trembled as he lighted his pipe. So, having made at least this one hit, though he had gained little information of the sort for which he had come, Mr. Barsad paid for what he had drunk and took his leave courteously expressing the hope that he might sometime return.

"Can it be true," said Defarge in a low voice, "what he has said of Ma'amselle Manette?"

"As he has said it, it is probably false. But it may be true."

"If it is—" he paused, his face troubled; "if it is, I hope, for her sake, fate will keep her husband out of France."

"Her husband's fate," said his wife, unmoved, "will take him where he is to go and will lead him to the end that is to end him. That is all I know."

"But is it not strange that after all our sympathy for her father and herself, her husband's name should be knitted into the register under your hand at this moment, by the side of that traitorous dog's who has just left us?"

"Stranger things than that may happen," answered madame, rolling up her knitting.

In a moment she took the rose out of her headdress. The customers strolled back, and the wine shop took on its usual appearance.

In the evening, when people sat on doorsteps and window ledges, Madame Defarge, with her work in her hand, passed from place to place and from group to group. All the women knitted. When their bony fingers were busy, their stomachs were less hungry.

But as the fingers moved, the eyes moved, and the thoughts. And as Madame Defarge passed from group to group, all three moved quicker and fiercer among every little knot of women that she had spoken with and left behind. Darkness closed around, and then came the ringing of church bells and the distant roll of drums as the women sat knitting, knitting. Another darkness was closing in as surely, when the church bells should be melted into thundering cannon, and when the drums should roll to drown out cries of pain and terror. In that darkness these women would still sit knitting, knitting, counting dropping heads.

9 *Eight Years*

John Barsad had been right in his statement to the Defarges regarding Lucie's engagement to Charles Darnay. She had loved him long, as he learned when he asked her for her hand. Doctor Manette was cheerful about the matter. He knew it was for Lucie's happiness, and she had convinced him no new ties could make any change in her tender devotion to him. The marriage was to make no change in the Manettes' place of residence. They had merely added to the size of their home by renting for themselves the rooms on the top floor that had previously been let to another lodger.

The sun of Lucie's marriage morning was shining brightly, and she, with Mr. Lorry and Miss Pross, was waiting, ready to start for the church, when the door of her father's room opened and he came out with Charles Darnay, with whom he had been talking privately; for this was the occasion on which Charles had agreed to tell the doctor his real name. The doctor's face was deadly pale, but the calmness of his manner was unchanged. The shrewd glance of Mr. Lorry, however, saw a shadow of that old look of dislike and dread.

Two carriages were waiting, in which the party rode to a neighboring church where, without other guests, the marriage took place. They returned home for the wedding breakfast, and all went well until Lucie parted from her father on the threshold, to drive away with her husband in the chaise that was to take them for their honeymoon in Warwickshire. Mr. Lorry had promised that he and Miss Pross would take the greatest care of Doctor Manette while the others were away. The plan was that after two weeks the doctor should join his daughter and son-in-law for another two weeks in Wales. When the two gentlemen, with Miss Pross, turned back into the house, Mr. Lorry saw that a great change had come over the doctor. The old scared, lost look was in his face; and when they went upstairs, he clasped his head absently and kept drearily wandering away into his own room. Stirred by anxiety, Mr. Lorry suggested to Miss Pross that they should leave the doctor to himself, without speaking to him or disturbing him.

"I must look in at Tellson's," he said. "Then I will come back and we will take him for a ride into the country and dine there."

Two hours later, when the banker returned, he went straight upstairs to the doctor's room. The door was closed, but from within he could hear a low sound of knocking.

"Good God!" he said, with a start. "What's that?" Miss Pross, with a terrified face, was at his ear. "Oh me, O me! All is lost!" cried she, wringing her hands. "What is to be told to Ladybird? He doesn't know me, and is making shoes!"

Mr. Lorry said what he could to calm her, and went himself into the doctor's room. The bench was turned towards the light, as it had been when he had seen the shoemaker at his work before, and his head was bent down, and he was very busy.

"Doctor Manette. My dear friend, Doctor Manette!"

The doctor looked at him half inquiringly, half angrily, and bent over his work again. He had laid aside his coat and vest, his shirt was open at the throat, and the old haggard expression had returned. He worked hard, impatiently, as if with some feeling of having been interrupted.

Mr. Lorry glanced at the work in his hand, and observed that it was a shoe of the old size and shape. He took up another that was lying by him, and asked what it was.

"A young lady's walking shoe," he muttered, without looking up. "It ought to have been finished long ago. Let it be."

"But, Doctor Manette. Look at me!"

He obeyed without pausing in his work.

"You know me, my dear friend? Think again. This is not your proper occupation. Think, dear friend!"

Nothing would induce him to speak more. He worked, and worked, and worked, in silence.

Two things struck Mr. Lorry at once: the first, that this must be kept secret from Lucie; the second, that it must be kept secret from all the doctor's acquaintances and patients. He at once gave out the news that the doctor was not well, and needed a few days of complete rest. Miss Pross, meanwhile, wrote Lucie that her father had been called away professionally in a great hurry, adding that he himself was writing a few lines by the same post. This note would later be said to have been lost.

Hoping that Doctor Manette would come to himself in a few days, Mr. Lorry made arrangements to be absent from Tellson's for the first time in his life, and took his post by the window in the doctor's room. There he sat, not trying to speak to his friend, but reading or writing, showing in as many natural and pleasant ways as he could that it was a free place.

The doctor took what was given him to eat and drink, and worked on, that first day, until it was too dark to see. When he put his tools aside, Mr. Lorry rose and said to him, "Will you go out?"

He looked up in the old vague manner, and repeated in the old low voice, "Out?"

"Yes; for a walk with me. Why not?"

There was no answer, but Mr. Lorry thought he saw, as he leaned forward on his bench in the dusk, that he was in some misty way asking himself, "Why not?" The wisdom of the man of business perceived an improvement here.

He and Miss Pross divided the night between them, keeping watch from the next room. The doctor paced up and down for a long time, but, when he finally lay down, he fell asleep. In the morning, he was up early, and went straight to his bench and to work.

On this second day, Mr. Lorry called him cheerfully by his name, and spoke to him on topics that had been of late familiar to them. He returned no reply, but it was evident that he heard what was said, and that he thought about it, however confusedly. This encouraged Mr. Lorry to have Miss Pross in with her work, several times during the day. At those times, they quietly spoke of Lucie, and of her father, as though there were nothing wrong.

When it fell dark again, Mr. Lorry asked him, as before, "Dear Doctor, will you go out?

As before, he repeated, "Out?"

"Yes; for a walk with me. Why not?"

This time Mr. Lorry pretended to go out and after an hour returned. The doctor had moved to the seat in the window and sat there looking down at the plane tree; but on Mr. Lorry's return, he slipped back to his bench.

The time went very slowly on, and Mr. Lorry's hope darkened, and his heart grew heavier and heavier every day. The third day came and went, the fourth, the fifth. Five days, six days, seven days, eight days, nine days.

With a hope ever darkening, and with a heart always growing heavier and heavier, Mr. Lorry passed through this anxious time. The secret was well kept, and Lucie was unconscious and happy; but he could not fail to observe that the shoemaker, whose hand had been a little out at first, was growing dreadfully skillful. He had never been so intent on his work, and his hands had never been so nimble and expert, as in the dusk of the ninth evening.

That night, worn out by anxious watching, Mr. Lorry fell asleep at his post. On the tenth morning, he was awakened by the shining of the sun into the room. He rubbed his eyes and roused himself, becoming immediately aware that the sound of hammering in the next room had ceased. Going to the door and looking in, he saw that the bench and tools were put aside, and that the doctor, in his usual morning dress, sat reading by the window.

Making no sound, Mr. Lorry sought out Miss Pross. They decided to wait until the regular breakfast hour, and then meet the doctor as if nothing unusual had occurred. This was done. The doctor was summoned to his breakfast in the usual way. It was soon evident that he thought his daughter's marriage had taken place only yesterday. A mention of the day of the week and then of the day of the month set him thinking and counting uneasily. Otherwise, however, he was entirely himself.

Mr. Lorry had all along been planning that, when the doctor came to himself, he would ask his opinion as to the best treatment for a patient mentally affected as he had been. He knew of no more skilled physician than Doctor Manette; and he remembered that his own prescription of shoemaking, made for himself when he felt his reason going, had probably saved him from complete insanity. So, after breakfast, he presented to the doctor the case of a friend of his who had suffered a mental shock. When he mentioned this friend's daughter, he saw that Doctor Manette understood of whom he was speaking.

"Unfortunately," he concluded, with a deep breath, for here was the danger spot, "there has been a slight relapse."

"How long did it last?" asked the doctor in a low voice.

"Nine days and nights."

As he had done several times before, the doctor glanced at his hands, which were discolored by the work he had been doing.

"I infer that the relapse made him take up again an old pursuit connected with the shock?"

"That is the fact."

"Now, did you ever see him engaged in that pursuit originally?"

"Once."

"And in the relapse was he in most ways as he was before?"

"I think in every way."

"You spoke of his daughter. Does she know of the relapse?"

"No. It has been kept from her. It is known only to myself and one other, who may be trusted."

"That was very kind," murmured the doctor. "That was very thoughtful."

Mr. Lorry went on to explain that he wanted advice from the doctor, as an expert on mental ailments, as to what was best to do to help his friend. "What can have caused such a relapse?" he asked.

After a long silence, the doctor said with an effort, "I think it probable that the relapse was not quite unexpected by your friend."

"Was it dreaded by him?"

"Very much. I believe that something had brought freshly to mind the events that were the first cause of the trouble. Distressing memories must have been aroused. Perhaps he had long feared that on a certain occasion those memories would be recalled. He had tried to prepare himself, but in vain."

"Would he remember what took place in the relapse?" inquired Mr. Lorry.

The doctor looked forlornly round the room, shook his head and answered sadly, "Not at all."

"Now, as to the future," pursued Mr. Lorry. "Would it not be better if these tools were put out of his way altogether? Are they not a constant reminder of the past? He used to work at—let us say—a little forge. Is it not a pity that he should keep it by him?"

The doctor shaded his eyes with his hand and beat his foot nervously on the floor.

"He has always kept it by him," said Mr. Lorry. "Would it not be better that he should let it go?"

"I suppose," said the doctor slowly, "that he cannot bear the thought of putting it quite out of reach, for fear he might need it again. To feel that he might need it and not find it gives him a sudden sense of terror like that of a lost child."

"But if the things were gone, my dear Manette, might not the fear go with it?"

"You see," said the doctor, "it is such an old companion."

"I would not keep it," said Mr. Lorry, shaking his head. "I am sure it does no good. Come! Give me your sanction—for his daughter's sake, my dear Manette!"

"In her name, then, let it be done. But I would not take it away while he was present. Let it be removed when he is not there. Let him miss his old companion after an absence."

Mr. Lorry readily promised that. They passed the day in the country, and the doctor seemed perfectly well again, and remained so for the three following days. On the fourteenth day, he went away to join Lucie and her husband.

On the night of that day, Mr. Lorry went into the doctor's room with a hatchet, saw, chisel, and hammer, attended by Miss Pross carrying a light. There, with closed doors and in a mysterious and guilty manner, the banker hacked the shoemaker's bench to pieces,

while Miss Pross held the candle as if she were assisting at a murder. The two looked and felt almost like partners in a horrible crime, as they burned the wooden fragments in the kitchen stove and buried the tools, shoes, and leather in the garden.

When the travelers came home, Doctor Manette made no reference to the absence of the workbench, though its disappearance made it necessary for Miss Pross to tell Lucie of the relapse. For a few days she watched over her father anxiously. But Mr. Lorry's judgment proved to have been good. In the years that followed Lucie's marriage, her father was calmer, more normal, less often gloomy than she had ever known him.

When the newly married pair came home, the first person who appeared to offer his congratulations was Sydney Carton. He was not improved in habits, or in looks, or in manner; but there was a certain rugged air of truth about him which Charles Darnay had not noticed before.

As soon as he could, Carton drew Darnay aside into a window for a talk. The conversation that followed removed the barrier of unspoken unfriendliness that had existed between the two young men ever since the evening at the Cheshire Cheese. Carton apologized for his rudeness on the night after the trial, and asked that Darnay might be willing to have him continue his visits to the home in Soho.

"If you could bear," he said, "to have a worthless fellow with a doubtful reputation coming and going at odd times, I should ask that I might be permitted to come and go as a privileged person here. Regard me as a useless piece of furniture, kept for the sake of its old service and taken no notice of. I should not abuse the permission. I doubt if you would see me four times in a year."

Darnay was cordial and gracious in his welcome to Carton to come as often as he wished. When, later, Lucie asked for his special generosity for Carton, he was ready to promise that, too.

"I would ask you to believe," she said, "that he has a heart he very seldom reveals, and that there are deep wounds in it. My dear, I have seen it bleeding."

"I regret deeply," said Charles, "that I should have misjudged him. I never thought this of him."

"But it is so. I fear there is scarcely a hope that his character or fortunes can now be changed for the better. But I am sure that he is capable of good, gentle, even noble things."

So it came about that Carton was established as friend of the family, although, as he had foretold, he came to see them but a few times each year. Strangely enough, when little Lucie and little Charles became members of the family, it was to Carton that they turned with special affection. He was the first stranger to whom little Lucie held out her chubby arms, and he kept his place with her as she grew. When the little boy lay dying, he spoke of Carton almost at the last.

A wonderful corner for echoes, it has been said, was that corner where the doctor lived. Ever busily winding the golden thread which bound her husband and her father and her children and herself in a life of quiet happiness, Lucie sat in the still house at the echoing corner, listening to the echoing footsteps of the years. She heard the strong and prosperous footstep of her husband, the firm tread of her father, the patter of little Lucie's feet. Even when sounds of sorrow came, they were not harsh or cruel. Even when her golden-haired little son was snatched away from her arms, it was the rustling of an angel's wings that mingled with the earthly echoes.

Her home was directed with wise and elegant thrift. Her father had told her many times that he found her more devoted to him married than single. Her husband asked her often, "What is the magic secret by which you are everything to all of us, and yet never seem to be hurried or to have too much to do?"

But there were other echoes, from a distance, that rumbled threateningly in the corner all through these years. And it was about little Lucie's sixth birthday, in the year 1789, that they began to have an awful sound, as of a great storm in France, with a dreadful sea rising.

10 *Echoing Footsteps*

One night in mid-July, 1789, Mr. Lorry came in late from Tellson's and sat down by Lucie and her husband in the dark window. It was a hot, wild night.

"I began to think," said Mr. Lorry, "that I should have to pass the night at Tellson's. We have been so busy all day that we have not known what to do first. There is such unrest in Paris that our customers over there cannot seem to send their property to us in England fast enough."

"That has a bad look," said Darnay.

"Yes, but what reason is there in it? I'm tired and cross. Where is Manette?"

"Here he is!" said the doctor, entering.

"I am glad you are at home, for the hurries and worries of this day have made me nervous. Is the tea tray still there, Lucie?"

"Of course. It has been kept for you."

"Thank you, my dear. I have been so put out all day, and I'm not as young as I was! Now come," he added, as Lucie handed him his tea, "and let us sit quietly and hear the echoes about which you have your theory."

"Not a theory. It was only a fancy."

"A fancy, then," said Mr. Lorry, patting her hand. "They are very numerous and very loud, though, are they not? Only hear them!"

Headlong, mad, and dangerous footsteps to force their way into anybody's life, were the footsteps raging in Saint Antoine afar off, as the little group sat in the dark London window.

Saint Antoine had been, that morning, a vast dusky mass of scarecrows heaving to and fro, with gleams of light where steel blades and bayonets shone in the sun. A great roar arose from the throat of Saint Antoine, and naked arms struggled in the air, the hands clutching at every weapon thrust within their grasp. Muskets were being distributed, as well as bullets and gunpowder, bars of iron and wood, knives, axes, and pikes. People who could lay hold of nothing else forced stones and bricks out of the walls. Every pulse and heart in Saint Antoine was at high fever heat. The day for which the Defarges had waited, for which the Jacques had been preparing, had arrived.

Before Defarge's wine shop stood Defarge himself, black with gunpowder and sweat. In the thickest of the uproar he labored and strove, giving out arms, issuing orders.

"Keep near to me, Jacques Three," he cried. "Jacques One and Two, separate and put yourselves at the head of as many of these patriots as you can. Where is my wife?"

"Eh, well! Here you see me!" said madame, calm as ever, but not knitting today. Her right hand was occupied with an ax, and in her belt were a pistol and a cruel knife.

"Where do you go, my wife?"

"I go," said madame, "with you at present. You shall see me at the head of women, by and by."

"Come then!" cried Defarge. "Patriots and friends, we are ready! The Bastille!"

With a roar the living sea rose, wave on wave, depth on depth, and overflowed the city to the place, not far from Saint Antoine, where stood the prison most feared and hated in all France. It was a military fortress where for centuries political prisoners had been confined, with or without trial. Into it had been thrown, never to be heard of again, persons who had given offense to kings or nobles, or whom these personages feared. To the people of Paris, the Bastille was a symbol of tyranny, injustice, and oppression. Now that the time had come for them to rise, their first attack would be against that symbol. Alarm bells ringing, drums beating, the sea raging and thundering, the attack began.

Deep ditches, double drawbridge, massive stone walls, eight great towers, cannon, muskets, fire, and smoke. In the fire and in the smoke, Defarge of the wine shop worked manfully as gunner of a cannon, two fierce hours. "Work, comrades, work all!" he kept crying to the struggling mob around him. "In the name of all the angels or all the devils—whichever you prefer—work!"

"To me, women!" cried madame his wife. "We can kill as well as the men, when the place is taken!" And to her, with a shrill, thirsty cry, trooped women, armed in hunger and revenge.

Cannon, muskets, fire, and smoke. One drawbridge was taken. But still there remained a deep ditch, another drawbridge, the massive stone walls, the eight great towers. Falling wounded, flashing weapons, blazing torches, shrieks, volleys, curses, bravery without end, boom, smash, rattle, and the furious sounding of the living sea. But still the deep ditch, and the drawbridge, and the massive stone walls, and the eight great towers, and still Defarge of the wine shop at his gun, grown hot by the service of four fierce hours.

At last a white flag from within the fortress! Suddenly the sea rose wider and higher and swept Defarge of the wine shop over the lowered drawbridge, past the massive stone outer walls, in among the eight great towers surrendered!

To draw his breath or turn his head was impossible until he was landed in an angle of a wall. Jacques Three was beside him; Madame Defarge, still heading some of her women, could be seen crossing the courtyard, and her knife was in her hand. Everywhere was tumult, rejoicing, the noise of many voices.

"The prisoners!"

"The records!"

"The secret cells—the instruments of torture!"

"The prisoners!" This last was the cry most taken up by voices of the people rushing in like the sea, bearing along the prison officers. Defarge laid his strong hand on the breast of one of these officers, a jailer with a gray head, who had a lighted torch in his hand.

"Show me the North Tower!" said Defarge. "Quick!"

"I will faithfully," replied the man, "if you will come with me. But there is no one there. There are only seven prisoners in the whole fortress."

"What is the meaning of One Hundred and Five, North Tower?" asked Defarge. "Quick!"

"Monsieur, it is a cell."

"Show it me!"

"Pass this way, then!"

Jacques Three held Defarge's arm as Defarge held the jailer's. Through gloomy vaults where the light of day had never shone, past hideous doors of dark dens and cages, down flights of steps, and again up steep rugged ascents of stone and brick, these three, linked hand in arm, went with all the speed they could make. At last they were winding and climbing up a tower, alone, with the mob left far behind.

The jailer stopped at a low door, put a key in a clashing lock, swung the door slowly open, and said, as they all bent their heads and passed in:

"One hundred and five, North Tower!"

Defarge looked in at the cell where for eighteen years his old master had been buried alive. There was a small, barred, unglazed window high in the wall. On the hearth of a small chimney lay a heap of old, feathery wood ashes. There were a stool, and a table, and a straw bed. There were the four blackened walls, and a rusted iron ring in one of them.

"Pass that torch slowly along the walls, that I may see them," said Defarge to the jailer.

The man obeyed, and Defarge followed the light closely with his eyes.

"Stop!—Look here, Jacques!"

"A. M.!" croaked Jacques Three, as he read greedily.

"Alexandre Manette," said Defarge in his ear. "And here he wrote 'a poor physician.' And it was he, without doubt, who scratched a calendar on this stone. What is that in your hand? A crowbar? Give it me!"

Turning on the worm-eaten stool and table, he beat them to pieces in a few blows.

"Hold the light higher!" he said wrathfully to the jailer. "Look among those fragments with care, Jacques. And see! Here is my knife," throwing it to him; "rip open that bed, and search the straw. Hold the light higher, you!"

Crawling upon the hearth and peering up the chimney, he struck at its sides with the crowbar and worked at the iron grating across it. Some mortar and dust came dropping down. In this and in the old wood ashes and in a crevice in the chimney into which his tool had slipped, he groped with a cautious touch.

"Nothing in the wood, and nothing in the straw, Jacques?"

"Nothing."

"Let us collect them together, in the middle of the cell. So! Light them, you!"

The jailer fired the little pile, which blazed high and hot. Stooping again to come out at the low-arched door, they retraced their way to the courtyard, where they were in the raging flood once more.

They found it surging and tossing in search of Defarge himself. Saint Antoine was demanding that its wine shop keeper be foremost in the guard upon the governor of the prison, who had defended it and shot the people. Otherwise, the governor would not be marched to the City Hall for judgment; otherwise, the governor would escape the vengeance of the people. Faithful to his duty, the grim old officer stood conspicuous in his gray coat and red decoration. Around him surged a howling tumult, in the midst of which one steady figure stood her ground. "See, there is my husband!" she cried. "See Defarge!" She stood close to the grim old officer, and remained close to him as Defarge and the rest bore him along through the streets. Remained close to him when he was near his destination and began to be struck at from behind. Remained close to him when the rain of stabs and blows fell heavy and when he dropped dead under it.

The hour was come that began the horrible fashion of hanging men from the iron brackets that held the swinging lamps. On the steps of the City Hall the governor's body lay. One of his little garrison stood near. "Lower the lamp iron yonder!" was the cry now raised. "Here is one of his soldiers to be left on guard!" The swinging sentry was posted, and the sea rushed on—the angry sea of swaying shapes, voices of vengeance, and faces hardened in the fires of suffering.

So do the loudly echoing footsteps press through the Paris streets in mid-July. Now Heaven defeat the fancy of Lucie Darnay and keep these feet far out of her life! For they are headlong, mad, and dangerous.

11 *Fire Rises*

A week after the capture of the Bastille, Madame Defarge sat in the sunshine outside her door, looking at the shop and the street. It had been a week of rejoicing. Even the loungers, ragged and miserable, seemed to stretch their lean, bare arms with a sense of power. The fingers of the knitting women were vicious, having learned that they could tear as well as knit.

As his wife sat in the pleasant morning light, Defarge appeared, breathless, around a corner. He pulled off a red cap he wore, such as many of the men had begun to wear, soon to be known as a "Liberty Cap." He stood, panting, as neighbors rushed up and grouped around him to hear the news he brought.

"Does everyone here," he cried, "recall old Foulon, who told the starving people that they might eat grass? Well, he has been found hiding in the country. I saw him just now, on his way to the City Hall, a prisoner."

There was a moment's deep silence. Then cries arose. "Villain Foulon taken!" "Foulon a prisoner!" "At the City Hall for trial!" "But he may be loosed!"

The last cry was taken up by many voices. "Foulon, who told my old father, who told my dead baby, that they might eat grass—this Foulon may be loosed! That must not be!"

A deep note came from the drum that lay at the feet of one of the knitting women. Defarge and his wife looked steadfastly at each other.

"Patriots!" he said in a determined voice, "are we ready?"

Instantly Madame Defarge's knife was in her belt, and the drum was beating in the streets. In the houses the men caught up what arms they had and came pouring out. Women ran out with streaming hair and wild cries of fury, to join the growing mob, which passed from mouth to mouth the word of the savage errand on which they were bent.

In the City Hall, the ugly and wicked old man stood trial for his life. He was bound with ropes, and upon his back was tied a bunch of grass. But the trial dragged on too long for the patience of the mob. After three hours of waiting, they swooped upon the prisoner like birds of prey, snatched him from the safety of the courtroom, hauled him, pleading for mercy, to the nearest street corner where a lamp swung. There could be no mercy for Foulon. Soon his head, with grass stuffed in the mouth, was upon a pike, with the rejoicing mob dancing about it. In the wine shop of Saint Antoine, it was almost morning before the last rejoicing customers departed.

Amid such scenes as this the weeks and months passed, while an assembly strove, with the usual slowness of lawmakers everywhere, to arrive at some arrangement for a free government, and to frame a democratic constitution for France. While they debated, the people seized the freedom which they had never had before, for which they were not educated, and which, therefore, they often misused to unjust and cruel ends. Yet the disasters which fell upon the nobles of France, most of them had earned by their selfish oppression of the people.

Not only in Paris had the temper of the people changed from submission to violence. A change had come, too, in the village where the road mender lived, and in all the villages like it. The officers in the prison on the crag were no longer feared; they were not sure of obedience even from their own soldiers. The nobleman who owned the castle was far away. In the road mender's village matters for the last few years had improved a little. The owner paid wages, through his agent, Monsieur Gabelle, to those villagers who worked for him, and had refused to receive from them either rent or taxes more than enough to keep their houses in repair. But all the other taxes were still enough to keep them ground down in poverty.

Far and wide lay a ruined country. Every green leaf, every blade of grass and stalk of grain was as shrivelled and poor as the miserable people. Everything was bowed down, dejected, oppressed, and broken. And yet into the eyes of these wretched beings had come a new light, as they spoke, not quite in whispers now, of vengeance. Strange faces appeared from time to time; faces of shaggy-haired men in clumsy wooden shoes; faces grim, rough, and soiled with the mud and dust of many highways. These went about the countryside carrying the message of liberty and equality.

As the mender of roads sat at noonday on a heap of stones under a bank, there came to him such a man.

"How goes it, Jacques?" said the stranger.

"All well, Jacques."

"Touch, then!"

They joined hands, and the man sat down on the heap of stones.

"No dinner?"

"Nothing but supper now," said the mender of roads, with a hungry face.

"It is the fashion," growled the man. "I meet no dinner anywhere."

He took out a blackened pipe, filled and lighted it, pulled at it until it was in a bright glow; then suddenly held it from him and dropped something into it that blazed and went out in a puff of smoke.

"Touch, then," said the mender of roads. "Tonight?"

"Tonight," said the man, putting his pipe in his mouth.

"Where?"

"Here."

They sat on the heap of stones looking silently at one another. At last the traveler rose and moved to the brow of the hill. "Show me!" he said.

"See!" returned the mender of roads, pointing. "About two leagues beyond the top of that hill above the village."

"Good! I will sleep now. I have walked two nights without resting. Wake me when you stop your work."

He lay down on the heap of stones and was fast asleep in a moment. The road mender, who wore a red cap now in place of his blue one, looked often, as he worked, at the sleeping figure. The bronzed face, the shaggy black hair and beard, the coarse woollen red cap, the rough homespun clothing, the sullen pressing together of the lips, all filled the countryman with awe. The stranger had traveled far, and his feet were sore and his ankles chafed and bleeding from the rubbing of his great shoes, stuffed with leaves and grass.

The man slept on until the sun was low in the west.

Then, roused by the mender of roads, he went his way. Going home to his village, the road mender whispered here and there among the people. When the village had taken its poor supper, it did not creep to bed, as usual, but came out of doors again and remained there. When it gathered together at the fountain in the dark, it looked expectantly at the sky in one direction only.

Monsieur Gabelle became uneasy. He went out on his housetop alone and looked in the same direction as the villagers.

The night deepened. The trees around the lonely old castle moved in a rising wind. The rain beat at the great door. From east, west, north, and south, through the woods, four heavy-treading, ragged figures came striding on cautiously, to meet in the castle courtyard. Four lights flared there, and moved away in different directions, and all was black again.

But not for long. Presently the castle began to grow strangely visible. A flickering streak played across the front. It soared higher and grew broader and brighter. Soon, from a dozen of the great windows, flames burst forth, and the stone faces, awakened, stared out of fire.

A faint sound of voices arose about the house from the few caretakers who were left there. Someone saddled a horse and rode away. Presently the horse in a foam stood at Monsieur Gabelle's door. "Help, Gabelle! Help, everyone!" The church bell rang impatiently, but help there was none. The villagers stood with folded arms at the fountain, looking at the pillar of fire in the sky. "It must be forty feet high," they said grimly, thinking of Gaspard.

The rider from the castle clattered away through the village and up the stony steep to the prison on the crag. At the gate, a group of officers were looking at the fire; at some distance from them stood a group of soldiers. "Help, gentlemen officers! The castle is on fire! Help, help!" The officers looked toward the soldiers, who looked at the fire and never moved. The captain answered, "It must burn."

So the castle was left to itself, amid the roaring and raging of the fire. With the rising and falling of the blaze, the stone faces showed as if they were in torment. When great masses of stone and timber fell, one face struggled out of the smoke as if it were the face of the cruel Marquis, burning at the stake.

The castle burned; the nearest trees, laid hold of by the fire, scorched and shrivelled. Four fierce figures trudged away—east, west, north, south—along the dark roads, towards their next mission. The villagers had seized hold of the church bell and were ringing it for joy; candles gleamed in every little window.

Now only that; but the village, remembering that Monsieur Gabelle had to do with the collection of rent and taxes—though lately he had collected few taxes and no rent at all—became impatient for an interview with him. Surrounding his house, they called to him to come out. Gabelle barred his door and again withdrew himself to his housetop behind his stack of chimneys. He passed a long night up there, with the distant castle for fire and candle, and the beating at his door, combined with the joyful church bell, for music.

But the friendly dawn appeared at last, and the people happily departed. Monsieur Gabelle came down, bringing his life with him for that while.

12 For the Honor of a Noble Name

In such risings of fire and risings of sea, three years of tempest were passed. Little Lucie was nine years old. Many a night and many a day had her parents listened with failing hearts to the echoes at their corner. The footsteps that they heard seemed the footsteps of a people changed into wild beasts.

The nobles had fled from France; their property had all been seized by the republican government. Those who had left that dangerous land were called by a new name, emigrants. The royal court was gone, with all its splendors. At the latest news, royalty itself was gone; the king and queen had been besieged in their palace of the Tuileries. August, 1792, had come.

The French nobles in London used as their meeting place and headquarters Tellson's Bank, which had taken care of their property and which still guarded the possessions which they had been able to save. The bank was the place to which the most reliable French news came most quickly.

On a misty afternoon, Charles Darnay stood talking with Mr. Lorry, who sat at his desk.

"Of course, you are the youngest man that ever lived," said Darnay, "but still—"

"I understand. You think me too old?" said Mr. Lorry.

"Unsettled weather, a long journey, uncertain means of traveling, a city that is almost certainly unsafe for you—these are great risks to take."

"My dear Charles," said Mr. Lorry with cheerful confidence, "you give some of the reasons for my going, not for my staying away. Paris is safe enough for me. Nobody will bother an old fellow of almost eighty when there are so many people better worth interfering with. And if the city were not in confusion, there would be no need for anyone to go. I know the business, and I know Paris as well. If I can't do that much for Tellson's, what use am I?"

"I wish I were going myself," said Charles Darnay restlessly.

"Indeed! You are a pretty fellow to object and advise!" exclaimed Mr. Lorry. "You wish you were going yourself—and you a Frenchman born!"

"It is because I am a Frenchman born that the thought has passed my mind often. I have had sympathy for the miserable people; I have given up much for their sake. I can't help thinking that they might listen to me, that I might persuade them to be less violent. However," as Mr. Lorry shook his head, "I am not going. It is more to the purpose that you say you are."

"Yes, I am. The truth is, my dear Charles, you can have no idea of the peril in which our books and papers over yonder are involved. The Lord above knows what the results would be to numbers of people, if some of our documents were seized or destroyed. That might happen at any time, for who can say that Paris will not be set afire today or sacked tomorrow! No one knows so well as I how to deal with matters over there. And shall I hang back because I am a little stiff in the joints?"

"I admire the gallantry of your youthful spirit, Mr. Lorry. Do you really go tonight?"

"Tonight. The case is too pressing to allow more delay."

"And do you take no one with you?"

"I intend to take Jerry. He has been my bodyguard in the evenings for so long that I am used to him. Nobody will suspect Jerry of being anything but an English bulldog, ready to fly at anyone who touched his master."

The bank, while this dialogue was taking place, was full of French noblemen, talking of the Revolution as if they and their ancestors had been in no way to blame for it. As Darnay turned to leave Mr. Lorry, one of the heads of the bank approached and laid a soiled and unopened letter before the old gentleman. Darnay could not avoid seeing the direction on the envelope, the more quickly because it was his own right name—the name which no one in London knew except Doctor Manette. The address, turned into English, ran: "Very pressing. To Monsieur heretofore the Marquis St. Evrémonde, of France. Confided to the cares of Messrs. Tellson and Co."

"Have you found any trace of the person addressed?" inquired the banker of Mr. Lorry.

"Not yet. I think I have asked everyone now here, and no one can tell me where this gentleman is to be found."

He spoke loudly and held the letter out inquiringly before the French gentlemen nearest his desk. All had something uncomplimentary to say about the Marquis who was not to be found.

"Nephew, I believe—but in any case unworthy successor—of the polished Marquis who was murdered," said one. "Happy to say I never knew him."

"A coward who deserted his post," said another, who had lately escaped from Paris in a load of hay. "He left France some years ago."

"Touched with the new doctrines of freedom and equality," said a third. "He set himself in opposition to the last Marquis, gave up the estates when he inherited them, and left them to the ruffians. They will reward him now, I hope, as he deserves."

Darnay controlled his feelings until the talkative crowd gradually drifted out. Then he said quietly to Mr. Lorry, "I know the gentleman."

"Will you take charge of the letter, then? Do you know where to deliver it?"

"I do, and I will. Do you start for Paris from here?"

"From here, at eight."

"I will come back to see you off."

Across Fleet Street from Tellson's was the entrance of the Temple, the quiet, old-fashioned enclosure where many lawyers and writers had their lodgings. In the lovely garden of this peaceful retreat, Charles Darnay opened the letter. It was from his agent, Gabelle; it was dated in June, and written from the Abbaye Prison in Paris.

"MONSIEUR HERETOFORE THE MARQUIS," it began.

"After having long been in danger of my life at the hands of the village, I have been seized, with great violence, and brought a long journey on foot to Paris. On the road I have suffered a great deal. Nor is that all; my house has been destroyed.

"The crime for which I am imprisoned, Monsieur heretofore the Marquis, and for which I shall be summoned before the tribunal* and shall lose my life (without your so generous help), is, they tell me, treason against the majesty of the people, in that I have acted

* Name for a Revolutionary court.

against them for an emigrant. It is in vain I say that I have acted for them, and not against, according to your commands. It is in vain I say that, long before the seizure of emigrant property, I had collected no rent and no taxes; that I have, according to your wishes, used the income of the estate to feed and clothe the needy. The only response is that I have acted for an emigrant, and where is that emigrant?

"Ah! most gracious Monsieur heretofore the Marquis, where is that emigrant! I cry in my sleep where is he! I demand of Heaven, will he not come to deliver me! No answer. Ah, Monsieur heretofore the Marquis, I send my desolate cry across the sea, hoping it may perhaps reach your ears through the great bank of Tilson known at Paris!

"For the love of Heaven, of justice, of generosity, of the honor of your noble name, I pray you, Monsieur heretofore the Marquis, to help and release me. My fault is that I have been true to you. Oh, Monsieur heretofore the Marquis, I pray you, be you true to me!

"From this prison here of horror, whence I every hour tend nearer and nearer to destruction, I send you, Monsieur heretofore the Marquis, the assurance of my unhappy service.

"Your afflicted
"GABELLE."

The uneasiness in Darnay's mind was roused by this letter. The peril of an old servant, whose only crime was faithfulness to himself and his family, stared him reproachfully in the face as he walked to and fro in the Temple garden considering what to do.

He knew very well that he had been careless in his arrangements regarding the estates which he had inherited in France. He had hurried from the land of tyranny without working out carefully a plan for bettering the lot of his tenants. Then his love for Lucie and the happiness of his new home, together with his need to work busily to make a living, had made him postpone the making of those plans, which always had been upon his conscience.

But he had oppressed no man. He had imprisoned no man. He had not harshly insisted on payment of his dues, but had sacrificed them of his own free will. Monsieur Gabelle had held written instructions to spare the people, to give them what little there was to give. No doubt Gabelle had stated this fact in his plea for his own safety. It would be sure to make Charles safe, if, as he had begun to resolve, he should go to Paris.

Every thought that occurred to his mind drew him in that direction. He had been troubled because bad aims were being worked out in his own unhappy land by bad leaders. He felt reproached because he was not there, trying to do something to stop bloodshed and assert the claims of mercy. This afternoon he had been distressed at comparing himself with the brave old gentleman in whom duty was so strong. Then had followed Gabelle's letter, the appeal of an innocent prisoner in danger of death, to his justice, honor, and good name.

His resolution was made. He must go to Paris.

He saw hardly any danger. He was sure that his good intention in giving up his income from the estates would be gratefully acknowledged in France as soon as he appeared to explain it. A glorious vision of doing good rose before him, and he even saw himself with power to guide this raging Revolution that was running so fearfully wild.

But neither Lucie nor her father must know of his

going until after he was gone. Lucie would thus be spared the pain of parting, and for Doctor Manette there would be no awakening of the old memories that brought him such distress.

He walked to and fro, with thoughts very busy, until it was time to return to Tellson's and take leave of Mr. Lorry. As soon as he arrived in Paris he would present himself to this old friend, but he must say nothing of his intention now.

A carriage with post horses was ready at the bank door, and Jerry was booted and equipped.

"I have delivered that letter," said Charles Darnay to Mr. Lorry. "I would not consent to your carrying written answers, but perhaps you will take one by word of mouth?"

"That I will, and readily," said Mr. Lorry, "if it is not dangerous."

"Not at all. It is to a prisoner in the Abbaye, named Gabelle."

"Gabelle," said Mr. Lorry, setting it down in his notebook. "And what is the message to the unfortunate Gabelle in prison?"

"Simply, 'He has received the letter, and will come.'"

"Any time mentioned?"

"He will start upon his journey tomorrow night."

He helped Mr. Lorry to wrap himself in a number of coats and cloaks, and went out with him from the warm atmosphere of the old bank, into the misty air of Fleet Street. "My love to Lucie, and to little Lucie," said Mr. Lorry at parting, "and take precious care of them till I come back." Charles Darnay shook his head and doubtfully smiled, as the carriage rolled away.

That night Charles sat up late and wrote two letters. One was to Lucie, explaining why he felt so earnestly that it was his duty to go to Paris, and why he was so certain that he would be in no danger. The other was to the doctor, entrusting the two Lucies to his care. Early next evening he kissed his wife and the little girl, pretending that he must meet an imaginary engagement. He had made ready and hidden a bag packed with his clothes. So he went out into the heavy mist of the heavy streets, with a heavier heart.

He left his two letters with a trusty porter, to be delivered half an hour before midnight, and no sooner; took horse for Dover; and began his journey. "For the love of Heaven, of justice, of generosity, of the honor of your noble name!" was the poor prisoner's cry with which he strengthened his sinking heart, as he left all that was dear on earth behind him and sailed away.

Book 3

The Track of a Storm

1 *In Secret*

The traveler in France, in the autumn of 1792, made slow progress. Not only was he delayed by bad roads, rickety vehicles, and poor horses. At every town and village he was stopped by bands of patriots, who questioned him, looked at his papers, talked him over among themselves, and decided whether or not it was safe to let him go on his way in the new Republic.

So Charles Darnay found himself delayed, as he made his slow and painful way along the road to Paris. He knew, very soon after landing in France, that there could be no turning back. Whatever befell him, he must go on to his journey's end. Every town gate that closed behind him was an iron door, barring him from England.

Twenty times a day he was stopped; so that it was almost the end of August when he went to bed tired out in a little town still a long way from Paris. His difficulty at the guardhouse here had been greater than usual. Even Gabelle's letter, which had helped him previously, did little good. The men who examined him were still not satisfied when they allowed him to rest until morning in the little inn. He was not surprised, therefore, to be awakened in the middle of the night.

A timid local official and three armed patriots in rough red caps sat down on the bed.

"Emigrant," said the official, "I am going to send you on to Paris under an escort."

"Citizen, I desire nothing more than to get to Paris, though I could do without the escort."

"Silence!" growled a redcap. "Peace, aristocrat!"

"It is as the good patriot says," said the timid official. "You are an aristocrat and must have an escort—and must pay for it."

"I have no choice," said Charles Darnay.

"Choice! Listen to him!" cried the scowling redcap. "As if it was not a favor to be protected!"

"It is always as the good patriot says," remarked the official. "Rise and dress yourself, emigrant."

Darnay obeyed, and was taken back to the guard-house, where other patriots in rough red caps were smoking, drinking, or sleeping by a fire. Here he paid a heavy price for his escort, and started with it on the wet roads at three o'clock in the morning, with the sharp rain driving in his face.

The escort were two mounted patriots in red caps with cockades of the red, white, and blue stripe known as the tricolor. Armed with guns and swords, they rode one on each side of him. A loose line was fastened to his bridle, with its end around the wrist of one of the patriots.

They traveled in the night, halting an hour or two after daybreak and lying by until the twilight fell. Most of the villages through which they passed were glittering with lights; the people seemed never to sleep, and often they were dancing round a Liberty tree or singing a Liberty song. The escort were so wretchedly clothed that they twisted straw round their bare legs and over their ragged shoulders to keep the wet off.

Apart from personal discomfort, Charles Darnay

did not allow the restraint in which he was kept to awaken in him any serious fears. He could not be under arrest, for his case was not yet known in Paris. When that case was stated, supported by Gabelle's testimony, he would be free to go and come.

But when they came at evening on September first to the town of Beauvais, the streets were filled with people whose manner was alarming. A threatening crowd gathered to see him dismount at the posting yard, and many voices called out loudly, "Down with the emigrant!"

Darnay, remaining in his saddle as the safest place, called to them, "Emigrant, my friends! Do you not see me here in France of my own free will?"

"You are a cursed emigrant," cried a blacksmith, coming toward him furiously with upraised hammer, "and you are a cursed aristocrat."

The postmaster thrust himself between this man and Darnay's bridle, saying soothingly, "Let him be. Let him be! He will be judged at Paris."

"Ay," shouted the smith, swinging his hammer, "and condemned as a traitor."

The crowd roared approval. As soon as he could make his voice heard, Darnay called again, "Friends, you deceive yourselves. I am not a traitor."

"He lies!" cried the smith. "He is a traitor since the decree. His life is forfeit to the people. His cursed life is not his own!"

Before the crowd could rush upon him, the postmaster turned the horse into the yard, the escort rode in close behind, and the gates were shut and barred. The smith struck a blow upon them with his hammer, and the crowd groaned, but in a few moments they went away.

"What is this decree that the smith spoke of?" inquired Darnay when he had dismounted.

"Truly, a decree for selling the property of emigrants."

"When passed?"

"On the fourteenth."

"The day I left England!"

"Everybody says it is but one of several, and that there will be others—if there are not already—banishing all emigrants, and condemning all to death who return. That is what he meant when he said your life was not your own."

"But there are no such decrees yet?"

"What do I know?" said the postmaster, shrugging his shoulders; "there may be, or there will be. It is all the same. What would you have?"

They rested on some straw in a loft until the middle of the night, and then rode forward again when all the town was asleep. Daylight at last found them before the walls of Paris. The gate was closed and strongly guarded when they rode up to it.

"Where are the papers of this prisoner?" demanded a resolute looking man in authority.

Struck by the disagreeable word, Charles Darnay requested the speaker to take notice that he was a free traveler and French citizen, in charge of an escort that had been forced upon him and that he had paid for.

"Where," repeated the same officer, without taking any heed of him, "are the papers of this prisoner?"

One of the escort had them in his cap and produced them. Casting his eyes over Gabelle's letter, the officer showed some surprise, and looked at Darnay with close attention. Then, without saying a word, he went into the guardroom, while Darnay and the escort sat upon their horses outside the gate, which was guarded by a mixed company of soldiers and patriots.

After half an hour, the same officer returned and ordered the guard to open the gate. Then he gave the escort a receipt for Darnay, and asked him to dismount. The two patriots, leading his tired horse, turned and rode away without entering the city.

Darnay went with his guide into the guardroom, where soldiers and patriots, asleep and awake, drunk or sober, were standing and lying about. Some registry books were lying open on a desk, in charge of a coarse, dark officer.

"Citizen Defarge," said he to the man with Darnay, "is this the emigrant Evrémonde?"

"This is the man."

"Your age, Evrémonde?"

"Thirty-seven."

"Married, Evrémonde?"

"Yes."

"Where married?"

"In England."

"Without doubt. Where is your wife, Evrémonde?"

"In England."

"Without doubt. You are consigned, Evrémonde, to the prison of La Force."

"Just Heaven!" exclaimed Darnay. "Under what law, and for what offence?"

"We have new laws, Evrémonde, and new offences, since you were here," said the officer with a hard smile.

"I entreat you to observe that I have come here of my own will, in response to that written appeal of a fellow countryman which lies before you. I ask no more than the opportunity to reach him without delay. Is not that my right?"

"Emigrants have no rights, Evrémonde," was the stolid reply. The officer wrote until he had finished and handed the paper to Defarge with the words, "In secret." Then Defarge, the prisoner, and a guard of two armed patriots went down the steps and entered Paris.

"It is you," said Defarge in a low voice, "who married the daughter of Doctor Manette, once a prisoner in the Bastille?"

"Yes," replied Darnay, looking at him with surprise.

"My name is Defarge, and I keep a wine shop in the Quarter Saint Antoine. Possibly you have heard of me."

"My wife came to your house to find her father? Yes!"

Defarge said with sudden impatience, "In the name of that sharp female newly born and called La Guillotine,* why did you come to France?"

"You heard me say why, a minute ago. That is the truth. But all here is so changed, so sudden and unfair, that I am quite lost. Will you help me a little?"

"No," said Defarge, looking straight before him.

"In this prison that I am going to so unjustly, shall I be able to communicate with the world outside?"

"You will see."

"I am not to be buried there, without any means of presenting my case?"

"You will see. But what then? Other people have been similarly buried in worse prisons, before now."

"But never by me, Citizen Defarge."

---

* The guillotine had just been invented by a French doctor for whom it was named. Since the guillotine beheaded instantly, the machine was considered a merciful invention. The execution was painless, not painful and uncertain like the ax or the rope.

Defarge glanced darkly at him, and walked on in silence.

"I must get in touch," Darnay went on, "with Mr. Lorry, the English gentleman who years ago took Doctor Manette from your house. He is now in Paris. I wish him merely to hear the fact that I have been sent to the prison of La Force. Will you have that done for me?"

"I will do nothing for you," Defarge doggedly replied. "My duty is to my country. I am the sworn servant of the people. I will do nothing for you."

Charles Darnay felt it hopeless to entreat him further, and his pride was touched besides. They walked on in silence. He knew now that he had fallen among far greater dangers than those he knew of when he left England. He might not have come, if he had known of these last decrees against emigrants. And yet, how could he have refused Gabelle's appeal?

Reaching the dreary courtyard of the gloomy prison of La Force, he was turned over to the jailer, who grumbled at receiving another prisoner. Darnay as yet did not know that every prison in Paris was crowded with the nobles who had been hunted down in the last few days.

"In secret, too," complained the jailer, looking at the written paper. "As if I was not already full to bursting!" He took up his keys. "Come with me, emigrant," he said, and strode ahead of Charles, cursing as he went.

Through the dismal prison twilight, by corridor and staircase, with doors clanging shut behind them, they went on. At last they came into a large, low, vaulted chamber, crowded with prisoners of both sexes. The women were seated at a long table, reading and writing, knitting, sewing, and embroidering. The men were for the most part standing behind their chairs, or lingering up and down the room.

To his surprise, they all rose at once to receive him, with every courtesy and grace of manner known to the time. Charles Darnay, though he knew that these must be the ladies and gentlemen of France, seemed to himself to stand amidst a company of the dead. Ghosts all! The ghost of beauty, the ghost of stateliness, the ghost of elegance, the ghost of pride, the ghost of wit, the ghost of youth, the ghost of age, all waiting their dismissal from that desolate place. It struck him motionless. It was as if the long, unreal journey had brought him to a land peopled by shadows.

He was not, however, permitted to remain in this company. He heard a murmur of pity as the jailer led him across the room to a grated door. Many voices gave him good wishes and encouragement. Then, as the grated door closed behind him, the gracious company vanished from his sight forever.

A stone staircase led upward. When they had climbed forty steps, the jailer opened a low black door and they entered a solitary cell. It was cold and damp, but not dark.

"Yours," said the jailer.

"Why am I confined alone?"

"How do I know!"

"I can buy pen, ink, and paper?"

"Such are not my orders. You will be visited, and can ask then. At present, you may buy your food, and nothing more."

There were in the cell a chair, a table, and a straw mattress. As Darnay looked about him after the jailer had gone, he thought in a wandering way, "Now am I left as if I were dead." He began to walk to and fro in the cell.

"Five paces by four and a half, five paces by four and a half," he counted aloud, remembering how a Bastille prisoner of long ago had paced a cell like this one.

From outside, the roar of the city arose like muffled drums with a wild swell of voices added to them.

"He made shoes, he made shoes, he made shoes." The prisoner counted the measurement again, and paced faster. He tried to think of something else, to keep himself from counting. "The ghosts that vanished when the grating closed. There was one among them, a lady˘ dressed in black, who had a light shining upon her golden hair, and she looked like Lucie. Let us ride on again, for God's sake, through the lighted villages with the people all awake! . . . He made shoes, he made shoes, he made shoes. . . . Five paces by four and a half."

With such scraps tossing and rolling upward from the depths of his mind, the prisoner walked faster and faster, counting and counting; and the roar of the city still rolled in like muffled drums, with the wail of voices that he knew in the swell that rose above them.

2 The Grindstone

Tellson's Bank in Paris was situated in the wing of a large house that had, before the Revolution, belonged to one of the higher nobility. The nobleman had fled, and his property, like that of other emigrants, had been given to a patriot who deserved special reward at the hands of the new Republic. The wing where the bank was faced a courtyard, and was shut off from the street by a high wall and a strong gate. So far the bank had not been disturbed, and the flag of the Republic over the main part of the building made it fairly safe.

In his faithfulness to Tellson's, however, Mr. Lorry was not considering the question of his personal safety. He occupied rooms in the bank, where there were trusty people on guard, Jerry among them. One of his rooms overlooked the courtyard.

On the night of September third, Mr. Lorry sat in this room beside a newly kindled wood fire, and on his honest and courageous face there was a deeper shadow than the hanging lamp could throw. It was a shade of horror. Rising to close the shutter and the window, he could see, by the light of two flaming torches fastened to the pillars of the courtyard, a large grindstone, roughly mounted. Looking at this harmless object, Mr. Lorry shivered. From the streets beyond the high wall, there came the usual night hum of the city, and

155

mingled with it the roll of drums and the sound of voices, howling or shrieking, weird and unearthly. It was the same sound that had come to the ears of Charles Darnay the night before.

Beside his warm fire, Mr. Lorry still shivered. "Thank God," he said, clasping his hands, "that no one near and dear to me is in this dreadful town tonight. May He have mercy on all who are in danger!"

Soon afterwards, the bell at the gate sounded. "They have come back!" he thought with dread. But there followed no noisy entrance of the crowd into the courtyard, and he heard the gate clash shut again. All was quiet until his door suddenly opened and two figures rushed in, at sight of whom he fell back in amazement.

Lucie and her father! Lucie, with her arms stretched out to him!

"What is this?" cried Mr. Lorry, breathless and confused. "What is the matter? Lucie! Manette! What has happened? What has brought you here?"

Pale and wild, she panted out in his arms, imploringly, "Oh, my dear friend—my husband!"

"Your husband, Lucie? What of him?"

"Here, in Paris. He has been here two days; we learned it at the gate of Paris. He left home on an errand of mercy—left without our knowing until too late. When the news came to London of the new decrees regarding emigrants, we started at once, knowing he was in danger."

"But why in danger, more than all of us?"

"My father knew his danger—knew what I did not know, his true name, and that he is a nobleman of France."

Mr. Lorry remembered the letter delivered to Darnay at the bank. He understood too clearly what had happened. "The name is Evrémonde?" he asked.

"Evrémonde," replied Doctor Manette. "He was stopped at the gate of Paris, so we have learned, and sent to prison."

Remembering the sights and sounds of the last two days and nights, the old man cried out in horror. At the same moment, the bell of the gate rang again, and a loud noise of feet and voices was heard in the courtyard.

"What is that noise?" said the doctor, turning towards the window.

"Don't look!" cried Mr. Lorry. "Don't look out! Manette, for your life, don't touch the blind!"

The doctor turned, with his hand upon the fastening of the window, and said, with a cool, bold smile:

"My dear friend, I have a charmed life in this city. I have been a Bastille prisoner. There is no patriot in Paris who, knowing me to have been a prisoner in the Bastille, would touch me, except to overwhelm me with embraces, or carry me in triumph. My old pain has given me a power that has brought us through all difficulties on the way, and gained us news of Charles, at the gate of Paris, and brought us here. I knew it would be so. I knew I could help Charles out of all danger. I told Lucie so. What is that noise?" His hand was again upon the window.

"Don't look!" cried Mr. Lorry. "No, Lucie, my dear, nor you!" He got his arm round her, and held her. "Don't be so terrified, my love. We must believe no harm has happened to Charles. What prison is he in?"

"La Force!"

"La Force! Lucie, my child, if ever you were brave in all your life, you will be so now. You must do exactly as I bid you. You can do nothing tonight to help; you cannot possibly stir out. You must go now into my bedroom, without delay, and leave your father and me alone."

"I will do as you say," she sighed. "I know that you are wise."

Miss Pross, with little Lucie in her charge, was standing inside the door, unnoticed until now. Mr. Lorry hurried them all into the inside room and turned the key. Then he joined the doctor beside the open window and looked out with him upon the courtyard.

A throng of men and women had rushed in to work at the grindstone, which had evidently been set up there for their use. But such awful workers, and such awful work!

The grindstone had a double handle, and turning at it madly were two men, whose faces, as their long hair flipped back, were more horrible and cruel than the faces of the wildest savages. As these ruffians turned and turned, women held wine to their mouths that they might drink, the stains of wine mingling with the stains of blood on their hands and garments. Not one creature in all the group was free from the smear of blood. Shouldering one another to get next at the stone to sharpen their weapons were men stripped to the waist, with the stain upon their limbs and bodies; men in all sorts of rags, with the stain upon those rags. Hatchets, knives, bayonets, swords, brought to be sharpened, all were red with it.

The two gentlemen drew back from the window, and the doctor looked at his friend for an explanation of the dreadful scene.

"They are murdering the prisoners," whispered Mr. Lorry. "Every aristocrat whom they could find in all Paris has been thrown into prison on one excuse or another. They go through a form of trial—a farce only —before the Revolutionary tribunal set up in each prison. Those who are found guilty—and that is all but a

very few—are thrown out at the prison door to the mercy of the mob. This has been going on for two days."

As he talked, he was urging the doctor toward the outer door. "If you are sure of what you say," he went on, "if you really have the power you think you have, make yourself known to these devils, and get taken to La Force. There is not a minute to lose—it may be too late already!"

Doctor Manette hastened bareheaded out of the room, and was in the courtyard by the time Mr. Lorry reached the window. The crowd made way for him, at sight of his streaming white hair and his strange, handsome face. Pushing the weapons out of his way, he reached the grindstone. For a moment there was a pause, then the faint sound of his voice, then a murmur of many voices. Amazed, Mr. Lorry saw his friend in the midst of a line twenty men long, linked shoulder to shoulder, hurrying out of the courtyard. Loud cries arose. "Live the Bastille prisoner! Help for the Bastille prisoner's kindred in La Force! Room for the Bastille prisoner! Save the prisoner Evrémonde at La Force!"

Mr. Lorry closed the lattice and hastened to tell Lucie that the people were friendly to her father and had gone with him in search of her husband. Miss Pross had laid little Lucie on the bed, and soon the good woman herself lay sleeping beside the child. The long hours wore away, with Mr. Lorry in his great armchair and Lucie on a footstool beside his knee, clinging to his hand. There at last she too fell asleep.

When the sun rose, and Mr. Lorry carefully detached himself from Lucie's clasping hand and went to the window to look out, the morning light sent a red glow over the courtyard. But the grindstone stood alone there, with a red upon it that the sun had never given and would never take away.

3 *The Shadow*

Whatever events took place in his personal life, Mr. Lorry never forgot the business with which he was entrusted. So he realized at once that it was dangerous for Tellson's Bank to shelter beneath its roof the wife of an emigrant prisoner. He would have risked his own life and possessions for Lucie and her child without hesitation; but the great trust he held was not his own.

At noon, when Doctor Manette had still not returned, the old gentleman spoke to Lucie of this matter of lodgings. She said at once that her father had suggested finding rooms for the family not far from the bank. He was quite certain that, even if Charles were at once released, they would not be able to leave the city for some time. So Mr. Lorry went to seek for such an apartment, and found one on an upper story of a dwelling in a side street, where the closed blinds in all the other houses showed deserted homes.

To this lodging Lucie and her child, with Miss Pross, were at once removed. Mr. Lorry left Jerry with them on guard at the door, and returned to his own occupations with a disturbed and doleful mind.

Late in the afternoon he was again alone in his room when he heard a foot upon the stair, and a man entered who addressed him by his name. He was a strongly built man with dark, curling hair, about fifty years of age.

"Your servant," said Mr. Lorry, looking puzzled.

"Do you not know me?" inquired the visitor.

"I have seen you somewhere."

"Perhaps at my wine shop?"

"Yes!" Mr. Lorry rose excitedly. "You come from Doctor Manette?" he cried, adding, when the visitor assented, "And what does he say? What word does he send?"

Defarge gave into his anxious hand an open scrap of paper. It bore the words:

"Charles is safe, but I cannot safely leave this place yet. I have obtained the favor that the bearer has a short note from Charles to his wife. Let the bearer see her."

The note was dated less than an hour ago at La Force.

"Will you go with me," said Mr. Lorry, joyfully relieved, "to where his wife lives?"

"Yes," said Defarge, in a curiously cold and mechanical way.

Mr. Lorry put on his hat and they went down into the courtyard. There they found a woman knitting. "Madame Defarge, surely!" said Mr. Lorry, who had left her in exactly the same attitude some seventeen years ago.

"It is she," answered her husband.

"Does Madame go with us?" inquired Mr. Lorry.

"Yes. In that way she will be able to recognize the faces of the persons we are to visit. It is for their safety."

Beginning to be struck by Defarge's stern manner, Mr. Lorry looked doubtfully at him and led the way to Lucie's lodging, where she was thrown into a rapture of happiness by the news Mr. Lorry brought. She clasped gratefully the hand that delivered to her the note from her husband.

"Dearest," the note read, "take courage. I am well, and your father has influence around me. You cannot answer this. Kiss our child for me."

Having read the precious words, Lucie turned from Defarge to his wife and kissed one of the hands that knitted. It was a loving, grateful, womanly action, but the hand made no response. It dropped, cold and heavy, and took to its knitting again. Checked by its touch, Lucie looked, terrified, at Madame Defarge, who met the look with a cold, hard stare.

"My dear," said Mr. Lorry, "there are frequent risings in the streets. Although it is not likely they will ever trouble you, Madame Defarge wishes to see those whom she has the power to protect at such times, to the end that she may know them—that she may identify them. I believe I state the case correctly, Citizen Defarge?"

Defarge looked gloomily at his wife and made a gruff sound of agreement.

"Is that his child?" asked Madame Defarge, pointing her knitting needle at little Lucie.

"Yes, madame," answered Mr. Lorry, "this is our poor prisoner's darling daughter and only child."

The shadow of Madame Defarge seemed to fall so threatening and dark on the child that her mother knelt on the ground beside her and held her to her breast. The shadow seemed then to fall, threatening and dark, on both the mother and the child.

"It is enough, my husband," said Madame Defarge. "I have seen them. We may go." But her manner was so threatening that Lucie, alarmed again, said,

"You will be good to my poor husband? You will do him no harm? You will help me to see him if you can?"

"Your husband is not my business here," returned Madame Defarge calmly. "It is the daughter of your father who is my business here."

"For my sake, then, be merciful to my husband. For my child's sake!"

Madame Defarge looked at her husband, who had moved uneasily, but who now collected his face into a sterner expression.

"What is it that your husband says in that little letter?" madame inquired with a smile. "Influence— something about influence."

"He says my father has much influence around him."

"Surely it will release him!" said Madame Defarge. "Let it do so."

She resumed her knitting and went out. Defarge followed and closed the door.

"Courage, my dear Lucie," said Mr. Lorry. "Courage, courage! So far all goes well with us—much, much better than it has of late gone with many poor souls. Cheer up, and have a thankful heart."

"I am not thankless, I hope, but that dreadful woman seems to throw a shadow on me and on all my hopes."

"Tut, tut!" said Mr. Lorry. "A shadow, indeed! No substance in it, Lucie."

But in his heart he was not so sure. The shadow of the manner of these Defarges was dark upon him, too, and in his secret mind it troubled him greatly, especially in the two days that still had to pass before Doctor Manette returned.

On the morning of the fourth day of his absence, the doctor appeared, with very little to say, in Lucie's hearing, of what he had seen and heard. Not until long afterward did she know that eleven hundred defenseless prisoners of both sexes and all ages had been killed by the people. She only knew that there had been an attack upon the prisons, that all political prisoners had been in danger, and that some had been dragged out by the crowd and murdered.

To Mr. Lorry, however, the doctor told his story. "They took me," he said, "to the prison of La Force and brought me before the tribunal. I told them that I had been for eighteen years a secret prisoner in the Bastille, thrust there without trial. Defarge, who was one of the tribunal, at once identified me.

"Then I found out from their records that Charles was still alive, and I succeeded in having him brought before the court and examined. He seemed on the point of being released, when the tide in his favor met with some check which I do not yet understand. The court whispered together, and then they told me that Charles must remain in prison, but would, for my sake, be kept safe. He was then sent back to his cell; but they allowed me to remain and see that no mistake was made about his safety. So I stayed in the courtroom until the danger was over, last evening, and the crowd ended its bloody work."

As Mr. Lorry listened to his friend, a fear arose in his mind that these dreadful scenes would revive the old danger of mental shock. Doctor Manette was no longer young; his age was sixty-two. But the anxiety was unnecessary. For the first time the doctor felt that the suffering he had passed through long ago had not been useless or in vain. "It all tended to a good end, my friend," he said. "It was not mere waste and ruin after all. Because of what I endured then, I shall be able now to help my beloved child." His eyes shone, and his face was calm.

He used his personal influence so wisely that he was soon the inspecting physician of three prisons, among them La Force. He brought it about that Charles was no longer confined alone, but was mixed with the general body of prisoners. He saw Darnay every week, and brought his messages to Lucie.

But though the doctor never ceased trying to get his son-in-law set at liberty, or at least to get him brought to trial, the feeling of the time would not allow him to succeed. In January of 1793, the king was tried, doomed, and beheaded. Eight months later his fair wife suffered the same fate. The Republic of Liberty, Equality, Fraternity, or Death declared war against the tyrants of the earth, and an army of three hundred thousand men gathered from all parts of France. New laws made it possible for any good and innocent person to be accused by any bad and guilty one who hated him, so that the prisons were crowded with people who had done no wrong and could obtain no hearing. Since the nobles who had not fled had already been put to death, the victims now were very few of them aristocrats. In their thirst for blood, the people had begun to turn upon one another. They were too ignorant of freedom to know how to use it wisely, now that they had it.

Above all, one hideous figure grew familiar—the figure called La Guillotine, erected in the heart of Paris, in what is now the Place de la Concorde. It sheared off so many heads, that it and the ground it stood on were a rotten red. It hushed the eloquent, struck down the powerful, destroyed the beautiful and good.

Among these terrors, while for fifteen months Charles lay in prison, the doctor walked with a steady head, never doubting that he would save Lucie's husband at last. In that wicked and maddened city, no man was better known than he. No man was in a stranger situation. Silent, kind, useful in hospital and prison, he was a man apart. He was not suspected or questioned, any more than if he had indeed been recalled to life some eighteen years before.

Yet over him, as over his dear ones, lay that lengthening shadow, stretching from the village in the west where Gaspard had been hanged above the fountain— the shadow of doom, as knitted twelve years before into the register of Madame Defarge.

4 The Woodsawyer

One year and three months! During all that time, Lucie was never sure, from hour to hour, but that the guillotine would strike off her husband's head next day. Every day, through the stony streets, the carts called tumbrils now jolted heavily, filled with condemned. Lovely girls; bright women; youths; strong men and old; gentle born and peasants—all poured red wine for La Guillotine.

But, like her father, Lucie walked steadily among her duties. In the new home, with the doctor busy in the routine of his calling, she arranged the little household exactly as if her husband had been there. Everything had its appointed place and time. She taught little Lucie as regularly as if they had been at home in England. Cheating herself into a belief that Charles would soon be with them, she made little preparations for his coming, setting aside his chair and his books, making ready a place where he might write.

She did not greatly alter in appearance. The plain, dark dresses which she and her child wore were as neat and dainty as the brighter clothes of happier days. She lost her color, and her expression was tense and strained; otherwise, she was still very pretty. Sometimes she burst into tears as she kissed her father good-night; but he always comforted her, saying, "Nothing can happen to him without my knowledge, and I know that I can save him, Lucie."

After a few weeks, the doctor said one evening, "My dear, there is an upper window in the prison where Charles can sometimes stand, at three in the afternoon. He thinks that from it he might see you in the street, if you stood in a certain place that I can show you. But you will not be able to see him, and even if you could, it would be unsafe for you to make any sign of recognition."

"Oh! show me the place, my father, and I will go there every day."

From that time, in all weathers, she waited there two hours. As the clock struck two, she was there, and at four she turned away. When it was not too wet for her child to be with her, they went together. At other times she was alone. But she never missed a single day. Her husband saw her, so her father said, once in five or six times; it might be two or three times together; it might be, not for a week or two. That did not matter, if her presence cheered him. As for any thought of danger to herself, it never entered her brave mind.

The place where she stood was the dark and dirty corner of a small winding street. The hut of a cutter of wood into lengths for burning was the only house at that end. All else was wall. On the third day of her being there he noticed her.

"Good day, citizeness."

"Good day, citizen."

This mode of address was now required by law.

"Walking here again, citizeness?"

"You see me, citizen!"

The woodsawyer, a little man who had once been a mender of roads, cast a glance at the prison, pointed at it, shook his head, and grinned. "But it's not my business," he said, and went on sawing his wood.

Next day he was looking out for her, and spoke to her the moment she appeared.

"What? Walking here again, citizeness?"

"Yes, citizen."

"Ah! A child, too! Your mother, is it not, my little citizeness?"

"Do I say yes, mamma?" whispered little Lucie, drawing close to her.

"Yes, dearest."

"Yes, citizen," said the little girl.

"Ah! But it's not my business. My work is my business. See my saw! I call it my little Guillotine." He resumed his sawing. "La, la, la! La, la, la! and off his head comes," he chuckled, as a piece of wood fell into his basket.

Lucie shuddered; but at the corner where she must stand, it was impossible to avoid his sight. She realized fully what harm he might do her, but that was a risk she must run, for Charles' sake. After that, she always spoke to him first. Sometimes, when she had quite forgotten him in gazing at the prison, she would find him looking at her, with his saw stopped in its work. "But it's not my business," he would say then, and briskly fall to his sawing again.

On a lightly snowing afternoon of December, 1793, Lucie arrived at the usual corner. It was for some reason a day of celebration, with all the houses decorated with liberty caps and tricolored streamers. She was relieved to find the miserable shop of the woodsawyer shut, so that she was quite alone. But presently she heard a sound of many feet and voices, which filled her with fear. In a moment a throng of people came

pouring around the corner of the prison, all dancing like demons to the music of their own singing. The tune was the popular Revolution song.

At first they were a mere storm of coarse red caps and coarser woollen rags; but as they filled the place and stopped to dance about Lucie, some likeness of a dance-figure gone mad appeared among them. They advanced, retreated, caught one another's hands, spun round alone or in couples. Then they linked hands in a ring and all spun round together, until the ring broke and in smaller rings of two and four they turned and turned. Suddenly they formed into lines the width of the street and, with their heads low down and their hands high up, swooped off screaming.

This was the Carmagnole, the Revolutionary dance as terrible as a battle. As it passed, leaving Lucie frightened and bewildered in the woodsawyer's doorway, the feathery snow fell quietly and lay white and soft.

Suddenly her father stood beside her, and she turned to him in relief. "Such a cruel, bad sight, my father," she whispered.

"I know, my dear, I know. I have seen it many times. Don't be frightened. Not one of them would harm you."

"I am not frightened for myself, my father. But when I think of my husband, left to the mercies of these people—"

"We will set him above their mercies very soon. I left him climbing to the window, and I came to tell you. There is no one here to see. You may kiss your hand toward that highest shelving roof."

"I do so, father, and I send him my soul with it!"

A footstep in the snow—Madame Defarge. "I salute you, citizeness," from the doctor. "I salute you, citizen." This in passing. Nothing more. Madame Defarge gone, like a shadow over the white road.

"Give me your arm, my love. Pass from here with an air of cheerfulness and courage, for his sake. That was well done. Charles is summoned for tomorrow."

"For tomorrow!"

"He has not received the notice yet, but I know that he will presently be summoned for trial tomorrow, and removed to the Conciergerie prison. You are not afraid?"

She could scarcely answer, "I trust in you."

"Your suspense is nearly ended, my darling. He will be with you inside a few hours. I have surrounded him with every protection. Now I must see Lorry."

The brave old gentleman was still at his post. He and his books were frequently needed for reference as to property seized by the Republic. What he could save for the owners, he saved.

It was dusk when Lucie and her father arrived at the bank. Mr. Lorry already had a visitor, it appeared. Someone who did not wish to be seen was in the inner room; his riding coat lay upon a chair. The old gentleman, excited and surprised, came out of the bedroom, leaving this unseen guest. But he turned back to call to his visitor, repeating Lucie's words, "Removed to the Conciergerie, and summoned for tomorrow."

5 A Knock at the Door

The dread tribunal of five judges, the public prosecutor, and the determined jury sat every day. Their lists went forth every evening, and were read out by the jailers of the various prisons to their prisoners.

"Charles Evrémonde, called Darnay!"

So at last began the list at La Force.

When a name was called, its owner stepped apart into a space reserved for those who were announced. There were twenty on the list tonight. The names were read in the vaulted chamber where Darnay had seen the assembled prisoners on the night of his arrival. Every one of those had perished in the massacre.

There were hurried words of farewell and kindness from the prisoners remaining, and the little group of twenty set out for the Conciergerie. The way to it was short and dark; the night in its cells long and cold. Next day, fifteen of the group were put to the bar and condemned quickly before Charles Darnay was at last summoned to his trial.

His judges sat upon the bench in feathered hats, but the rough red cap with the tricolored cockade was the headdress of the jury and audience. Of the men, the greater part were armed in various ways; of the women, some wore knives, some daggers and many knitted. Among these last was one in a front row, by the side of a man whom Charles at once remembered as

173

Defarge. The woman seemed to be his wife. He noticed that although they were posted as close to himself as possible, they never looked towards him, but always at the jury. They seemed to be waiting for something with a dogged determination. In a seat below that of the chief judge was Doctor Manette, in his usual quiet dress, and near him was Mr. Lorry.

Charles Evrémonde, called Darnay, was accused by the public prosecutor as an emigrant, whose life was forfeit to the Republic under the law which banished all emigrants on pain of death. It was nothing that the date of the law was a date since his return to France. There he was, and there was the law. He had been captured in France, and his head was demanded.

"Take off his head!" cried the audience. "An enemy to the Republic!"

The chief judge rang his bell to silence these cries, and asked the prisoner whether it was not true that he had lived for many years in England. Charles answered that it was.

"Are you not an emigrant, then? What else do you call yourself?"

"Not an emigrant, I think, within the meaning of the law."

The judge desired to know why not.

"Because," answered Charles, "I gave up of my own will a title and a position in which I was unhappy, and left my country before the word emigrant was in use. I went to live by my own industry in England, instead of living on the industry of the oppressed people of France."

Asked for proof, he handed in the names of two witnesses: Theophile Gabelle and Alexandre Manette.

The judge then reminded him that he had married in England.

"True, but not an Englishwoman."

"A citizeness of France?"

"Yes. By birth."

"Her name and family?"

"Lucie Manette, only daughter of Doctor Manette, the good physician who sits there."

This answer had a happy effect upon the audience. Loud cries arose in praise of the well-known good physician. Tears rolled down the faces of several fierce citizens who a moment ago had been demanding Darnay's head. The plan which Doctor Manette had outlined so carefully was working well.

"Why did you return to France when you did?" inquired the judge. "And why not before?"

"I did not return sooner because I had no means of living in France except the property which I had given up, and from which I wished no income. In England I could make a living by teaching the French language. I returned at the pressing entreaty of a French citizen, who wrote me that his life was in danger because of my absence. I came back to save a citizen's life and to bear witness to the truth. Is that criminal in the eyes of the Republic?"

The people cried enthusiastically, "No!" and the judge rang his bell to quiet them.

Asked for the citizen's name, Charles explained that the citizen was his first witness. "His letter," he went on, "which was taken from me, is no doubt among the papers now before you."

The doctor had made sure that it would be there, and it was produced and read. Citizen Gabelle, only just now released from the Abbaye prison on account of it, was called to swear to its genuineness, and did so. Then Doctor Manette was questioned.

His popularity and the clearness of his answers made a great impression on the court. He showed that the prisoner had been his first friend on his release from the Bastille. "He has remained in England, always faithful to my daughter and to me," declared the doctor. "And, so far from being in favor with the aristocrat government there, he was actually tried for his life by it, as the foe of England and friend of the United States and therefore of that country's ally, France."

By this time the jury and the people were one. When the doctor appealed by name to Monsieur Lorry, an English gentleman now present who had been a witness at the trial in England, the jury declared that they had heard enough and were ready with their votes. All their voices were in the prisoner's favor, and the chief judge pronounced him free. There was a great shout of joy. Only the Defarges seemed displeased, as if the thing they were waiting for had not happened.

When Charles and Doctor Manette went out at the gate, there was a great crowd about it. They surrounded Darnay, weeping, embracing, and shouting. They put him into a great chair they had among them, which was draped with a red flag and decorated with a pike and a liberty cap. In this car of triumph he was carried to his home on men's shoulders, with a sea of red caps heaving about him.

They carried him thus into the courtyard of the house where he lived. Lucie's father had gone ahead to prepare her, and she was at the door to meet him. As he was set down upon his feet and turned her beautiful head between his face and the brawling crowd, the people fell to dancing, and in a moment the courtyard overflowed with the Carmagnole. Swelling out into the streets and along the river's bank and over the bridge, the Carmagnole whirled them away.

Charles grasped the hand of the doctor, who stood victorious and proud before him, and the hand of Mr. Lorry, who came panting in, breathless. He kissed little Lucie and the good Miss Pross. Then he took his wife in his arms and carried her upstairs to the home he had never seen.

"Lucie, my own! I am safe," he said over and over as he held her close. "Do not weep any more. See, here is your father waiting for you to speak to him. No other man in all this France could have done what he has done for me."

Still shaking with sobs, weeping from relief as she had not done through all the long months of strain, now ended, she leaned against her father's shoulder. He was proud and happy in his strength. He was repaid now for all his suffering in the past. "Do not tremble so, my darling," he begged her. "All your trouble is over now. I have saved him."

She knew that this was true, but she could hardly believe it. It was not a dream. He was really here. Yet still she trembled, with a vague fear in her heart, that was not lightened of its load as she felt it ought to be. The shadows of the wintry afternoon were beginning to fall, and even now the dreadful carts were rolling through the streets to the guillotine. Her mind pursued them, and then she clung closer to her husband and trembled more.

At last, however, the little family settled down more peacefully. Miss Pross, escorted by Jerry Cruncher carrying the basket, went out to do the marketing for the next day. The two Lucies, Charles, and the doctor sat in the firelight; Mr. Lorry was expected back later. Doctor Manette began, in a low voice, to tell the little girl a fairy story. All was so peaceful that Lucie began to feel more at ease.

"What is that?" she cried suddenly.

"My dear," said her father, stopping in his story, "control yourself. How upset you are! The least thing —nothing—startles you."

"I thought, my father," faltered Lucie, "that I heard strange feet upon the stairs."

"My love, the staircase is as still as death."

As he spoke, a blow was struck upon the door.

"Oh, father, father! What can this be? Hide Charles. Save him!"

"My child," said the doctor, rising, "I *have* saved him. What weakness is this, my dear! Let me go to the door."

He crossed the two outer rooms, and opened it. A rude clattering of feet over the floor, and four rough men in red caps, armed with swords and pistols, entered the room.

"The Citizen Evrémonde, called Darnay," said the first.

"Who seeks him?" answered Darnay.

"I seek him. We seek him. I know you, Evrémonde, I saw you before the tribunal today. You are again the prisoner of the Republic."

The four surrounded him, where he stood with his wife and child clinging to him.

"How and why am I again a prisoner?"

"It is enough that you return straight to the Conciergerie and will know tomorrow. You are summoned for tomorrow."

Doctor Manette confronted the speaker.

"You know him, you have said. Do you know me?"

"Yes, I know you, Citizen Doctor."

"We all know you, Citizen Doctor," said the other three.

He looked from one to another, and said, in a lower voice, after a pause,

"Will you answer his question to me then? How does this happen?"

"Citizen Doctor," said the man unwillingly, "he has been accused by citizens in the section of Saint Antoine. This citizen is from Saint Antoine."

"Of what is he accused?"

"Citizen Doctor," said the man, "ask no more. If the Republic demands sacrifices from you, without doubt you as a good patriot will be happy to make them. The Republic goes before all. Evrémonde, we are in haste."

"One word," the doctor entreated. "Will you tell me who denounced him?"

"It is against the rule," answered the man. "But you can ask him of Saint Antoine here."

The doctor turned his eyes upon the second man, who moved uneasily, and at last said, "Well, truly it is against rule. But he is denounced—and gravely—by the Citizen and Citizeness Defarge. And by one other."

"What other?"

"Do *you* ask, Citizen Doctor?"

"Yes."

"Then," said he of Saint Antoine, with a strange look, "you will be answered tomorrow. Now, I am dumb!"

6 A Hand at Cards

Happily unconscious of the new trouble at home, Miss Pross made her way along the narrow streets, Jerry, with the basket, walking at her side. When she had finished buying her groceries, she remembered that wine was needed, and she chose, as the quietest place to buy it, a wine shop near the Tuileries where the few customers were either asleep or quietly talking. If she had looked more carefully, she might have seen that one solitary figure in a corner, who looked like an Englishman, was very wide awake.

As the wine was being measured, a man rose from a table and said goodbye to a companion with whom he had been talking earnestly. Their place was close beside that of the wakeful customer just mentioned. The departing person, in going, turned toward Miss Pross. No sooner did he face her than she uttered a scream and clapped her hands.

Everyone started up, but all they saw was a man with all the look of a Frenchman and a good Republican, with a woman, evidently English, staring at him.

"What is the matter?" said the man in English, speaking low in a vexed, abrupt way.

"Oh, Solomon, dear Solomon!" cried Miss Pross, clapping her hands again. "After not setting eyes upon you or hearing of you for so long, do I find you here!"

"Don't call me Solomon. Do you want to be the death of me?" asked the man.

"Brother, brother!" cried Miss Pross, bursting into tears. "Have I ever been so hard with you that you ask me such a cruel question?"

"Then hold your meddlesome tongue," said Solomon, "and come out, if you want to speak to me. Pay for your wine, and come out. Who's this man?"

Miss Pross said through her tears, "Mr. Cruncher."

"Let him come out too," said Solomon. "Does he think me a ghost?"

Apparently, Mr. Cruncher did, to judge from his looks. He said not a word, however, and Miss Pross paid for the wine. Solomon spoke a few words in French to the customers, and they all sat down again.

"Now," said Solomon, stopping at the dark street corner, "what do you want?"

"How dreadfully unkind in a brother nothing has

ever turned my love away from!" cried Miss Pross, "to give me such a greeting, and show me no love."

"There. Confound it! There," said Solomon, making a dab at Miss Pross's lips with his own. "Now are you happy?"

Miss Pross only shook her head and wept in silence.

"If you expect me to be surprised," said her brother Solomon, "I am not surprised; I knew you were here; I know of most people who are here. If you really don't want to put my life in danger, go your way and let me go mine. I am busy. I am an official."

"My English brother Solomon," mourned Miss Pross, "an official among foreigners, and such foreigners! I would almost sooner have seen the dear boy lying in his—"

"I said so!" cried her brother, interrupting. "I knew it! You want to be the death of me."

"The gracious and merciful Heavens forbid!" cried Miss Pross. "Far rather would I never see you again, dear Solomon, though I have ever loved you truly, and ever shall. Say but one kind word to me, and I will keep you no longer."

But before he could say the kind word, Mr. Cruncher, touching him on the shoulder, asked a strange question. "I say," he inquired, "is your name John Solomon or Solomon John?"

The official turned towards him with sudden distrust.

"Come," said Mr. Cruncher, "speak out. She calls you Solomon, and she must know, being your sister. And I know you're John, you know. Which of the two goes first? And regarding that name of Pross, likewise. That warn't your name over the water."

"What do you mean?"

"Well, I don't know all I mean, for I can't call to mind what your name was over the water. But I'll swear it was a name of two syllables."

"Indeed?"

"Yes, I know you. You was a spy witness at the Bailey. What in the name of old Nick was you called then?"

"Barsad," said another voice striking in.

"That's the name for a thousand pound!" cried Jerry.

The new speaker was Sydney Carton. He wore the riding coat that had been on the chair at Mr. Lorry's the night before; and he stood as carelessly as he had seemed to sit a few minutes before in the corner of the wine shop.

"Don't be alarmed, my dear Miss Pross. I arrived at Mr. Lorry's, to his surprise, yesterday evening. The reports of wholesale executions here had been growing so terrifying that I thought, as a lawyer, I might be of some use to Mr. and Mrs. Darnay—so I came. But it seemed wisest for me not to go to see them unless I could be useful, so my coming is a secret. Just now I should like a little talk with your brother. I wish you had a better employed brother than Mr. Barsad. I wish for your sake that Mr. Barsad was not a prison spy."

"How dare you—" began the spy, turning pale.

"I'll tell you," said Sydney. "I saw you, Mr. Barsad, coming out of the prison of the Conciergerie an hour or more ago. You have a face to be remembered, and I remember faces well. Made curious by seeing you here, I walked in your direction. I went into the wine shop after you and sat down near you. I understand French well. I had no difficulty in learning from your conversation what is the nature of your business. So I have formed a purpose, Mr. Barsad."

"What purpose?" the spy asked.

"It would be dangerous to explain in the street. Could you favor me with some minutes of your company at the office of Tellson's Bank?"

"Why should I go there?"

"Really, Mr. Barsad, I can't say, if you can't."

"Do you mean that you won't say, sir?"

"You understand me very clearly, Mr. Barsad. I won't. Do you go with me to the bank?"

"I'll hear what you've got to say. Yes, I'll go with you."

Carton's careless recklessness of manner came strongly to the aid of his quickness and skill in such a business as he had in mind and with such a man as he had to deal with.

"I propose," he went on, "that we first take your sister safely to the corner of her own street. Let me take your arm, Miss Pross. This is not a good city for you to be out in, unprotected. And as your escort knows Mr. Barsad, I will invite him to Mr. Lorry's with us."

When they left her at her corner, Carton led the way to Mr. Lorry's, only a few minutes' walk. Mr. Lorry had just finished his dinner and was sitting before a cheery little fire. He turned his head as they entered, surprised at seeing a stranger.

"Miss Pross's brother, sir," said Sydney. "Mr. Barsad."

"Barsad?" repeated the old gentleman, "Barsad? I have an association with the name—and with the face."

"I told you you had a remarkable face, Mr. Barsad," observed Carton, coolly. "Pray sit down."

As he took a chair himself, he supplied the link that

Mr. Lorry wanted, by saying to him with a frown, "Witness at that trial years ago." Mr. Lorry, remembering, gazed at his visitor with frank dislike.

"Mr. Barsad has been recognized by Miss Pross as the brother you have heard of," said Sydney, "and has admitted the relationship. I pass to worse news. Darnay has been arrested again."

"What do you tell me?" exclaimed the old gentleman. "I left him safe at home less than two hours ago, and am about to return there."

"Arrested, for all that. When was it done, Mr. Barsad?"

"Just now, if at all."

"Mr. Barsad is the best authority possible, sir," said Sydney. "I heard him tell another spy that the arrest has taken place. He said he had left the messengers at the gate and had seen them admitted by the porter. There is no earthly doubt that he is retaken. Now I hope," he went on, "that Doctor Manette's influence may help him as much tomorrow as today. But it may not be so. I am worried by the fact that he was not able to prevent this arrest."

"He may not have known of it beforehand," said Mr. Lorry.

"But that very fact would be alarming."

"That's true," admitted Mr. Lorry, with his troubled eyes on Carton.

"In short," said Sydney, "this is a dreadful time, when no one's life is safe. Anyone carried home by the people today may be condemned tomorrow. Let the doctor play the winning game. I will play the losing one. Now, the stake I have resolved to play for is a friend in the Conciergerie. And the friend I purpose to win is Mr. Barsad."

"You need have good cards, sir," said the spy.

"I'll run them over. I'll see what I hold."

He went on, in the tone of a player really looking over a hand at cards: "Mr. Barsad, spy and secret informer employed by the Republican government, poses to his employers under a false name. That's a very good card. Mr. Barsad, now in the employ of the Republican French government, was formerly in the employ of the aristocratic English government, which is the enemy of France and freedom. That's an excellent card. Knowing these two facts, good patriots here are sure to suspect Mr. Barsad of being the spy of Pitt and still in the employ of England, especially since it is proved that he is an Englishman. That's a card not to be beaten. They will say that Mr. Barsad is that English traitor who has plotted so much mischief against the Republic and who has not yet been found. Have you followed my hand, Mr. Barsad?"

"Not to understand your play," returned the spy uneasily.

"I play my ace, the winning card—accusation of Mr. Barsad to the nearest tribunal. Look over your hand, Mr. Barsad, and see what *you* have. Don't hurry."

The spy's hand was a poorer one than Sydney Carton suspected. He saw losing cards in it that the lawyer knew nothing of. Thrown out of employment in England, he had taken service under the royal government in France, first as a spy on his own countrymen there, later as a spy on the natives. He had been a spy in the suburb of Saint Antoine; had sought to get information from the Defarges and had broken down completely before that terrible woman. He remembered with fear that she had knitted steadily while she talked with him. He had since seen her over and over produce her knitted register and denounce people, whose lives were immediately ended at the guillotine.

He knew, like every spy, that he was never safe. Flight was impossible. He was tied fast under the shadow of the ax; a word might bring it down upon him. If he did not do the bidding of this English lawyer, the lawyer would speak that word, and the ax would fall. The dreadful woman would produce against him that fatal register, and he would be put to death as a foreigner plotting against the Republic.

"You do not seem to like your hand," said Sydney, calmly. "Do you play?"

"No," said the spy. "I give up. You told me you had a proposal. What is it? It is no use to ask too much of me. If you want me to put my head in danger, I might as well take the risk of having you denounce me. I should choose to do so. Now, what do you want with me?"

"Not very much. You are a jailer at the Conciergerie?"

"I am sometimes."

"You can be when you choose."

"I can pass in and out when I choose."

Sydney Carton rose. "So far we have spoken before these two," he said, "because it was best that we should have witnesses. Now come into the inner room, and let us have one final word alone."

7 *The Game Made*

Jerry Cruncher had left when Sydney Carton and the spy returned from the inside room. "Adieu, Mr. Barsad!" said the former. "Now that our arrangement is made, you have nothing to fear from me."

He sat down in a chair by the fire, opposite Mr. Lorry, who asked him what he had done.

"Not much. If it goes ill with Darnay, I have made sure of seeing him once. It is all I could do," he went on, seeing Mr. Lorry's disappointment. "To propose too much would only put this man's head under the ax, and then he would do nothing. There is no help for it."

"But seeing him," said Mr. Lorry, "will not save him."

"I never said it would."

Mr. Lorry was an old man, weighed down with anxiety. He looked at the fire, and his tears fell.

"You are a good man and a true friend," said Carton, in an altered voice. "Forgive me if I notice that you weep. I could not see my father weep and sit by careless, and I could not respect you more if you were my father."

There was a true feeling and respect in his tone that Mr. Lorry, who had never seen the better side of him, was wholly unprepared for.

"To return to poor Darnay," said Carton. "Don't tell his wife of this interview or this arrangement. It would

not enable her to go to see him, and she might think a
thousand things that would make her trouble greater in
the end. Don't speak of me to her. As I said last night, I
had better not see her. I can do any little helpful thing
I find to do, without that. Are you going to her now?"

"Yes, immediately."

"I am glad of that. She is so fond of you and trusts
you so much. How does she look?"

"Anxious and unhappy, but very beautiful."

"Ah!" It was a long, grieving sound, like a sigh—
almost like a sob. It drew Mr. Lorry's eyes to Carton's
face. A light, or a shade, passed from it as swiftly as a
change will sweep over a hillside on a wild bright day.
The old gentleman realized what he had not thought
of before—that this man, on the surface so hard and
careless, loved Lucie deeply. He wore the white riding
coat and top boots then in fashion; the light of the fire
made him look very pale, and his long brown hair hung
loose.

"And your duties here have come to an end, sir?"
said Carton, after a pause.

"Yes. As I was telling you last night when Lucie
came in so unexpectedly, I have at length done all that
I can do here. I hoped to have left them in perfect
safety. I have my passport and am ready to go."

They were both silent.

"Yours is a long life to look back upon, sir?" said
Carton wistfully.

"I am in my seventy-eighth year."

"You have been useful all your life; steadily and
constantly occupied; trusted, respected, and looked up
to?"

"I have been a man of business ever since I was
a boy."

"See what a place you fill at seventy-eight. How many people will miss you when you leave it empty!"

"A solitary old bachelor," answered Mr. Lorry, shaking his head. "There is nobody to weep for me."

"How can you say that? Wouldn't she weep for you? Wouldn't her child?"

"Yes, yes, thank God. I didn't quite mean what I said."

"It *is* a thing to thank God for; is it not?"

"Surely, surely."

"If you could say, with truth, to your own heart, tonight, 'I have not won for myself the love, the gratitude, the respect of any human creature; I have done nothing good to be remembered by,' your seventy-eight years would be seventy-eight heavy curses, would they not?"

"You say truly, Mr. Carton; I think they would be."

Sydney again looked at the fire. His words had expressed his thought of what his own old age would be. In a moment he rose, to help the old gentleman with his outer coat. "I'll walk with you to her gate," he said. "You know my restless habits. If I should prowl about the streets a long time, don't be uneasy; I shall be here in the morning. You go to the trial tomorrow?"

"Yes, unhappily."

"I shall be there, as one of the crowd. My spy will find a place for me."

They went downstairs and out into the street. Carton left Mr. Lorry at Lucie's door. Then he lingered, and turned back to touch the gate when it was shut. He had heard of her going to the prison every day. "She came out here," he said, looking about him, "turned this way, must have trod these stones often. Let me follow in her steps."

It was ten o'clock when he stood before the prison of La Force. A little woodsawyer was smoking his pipe at his shop door.

"Good night, citizen," said Sydney Carton, pausing, for the man eyed him inquisitively.

"Good night, citizen."

"How goes the Republic?"

"You mean the guillotine. Not ill. Sixty-three today. We shall mount to a hundred soon. You have seen La Guillotine at work?"

"Never." Carton turned away.

"But you are not English," said the woodsawyer, "though you wear English dress?"

"Yes," said Carton, over his shoulder.

"You speak like a Frenchman."

"I am an old student here."

"Aha, a perfect Frenchman! Good night, Englishman."

"Good night, citizen."

Sydney had not gone far out of his sight, when he stopped under a lamp and wrote with his pencil on a scrap of paper. Then, passing through several dark and dirty streets, he stopped at a chemist's shop—a small, dim, crooked shop, kept by a small, dim, crooked man. Before him Sydney laid the scrap of paper.

"Whew!" the chemist whistled softly as he read it. "For you, citizen?"

"For me."

"You will be careful to keep them separate, citizen? You know the consequences of mixing them?"

"Perfectly."

Certain small packets were made and given to him. He put them, one by one, in the breast of his inner coat, counted out the money for them, and left the shop.

"There is nothing more to do," said he, glancing upward at the moon, "until tomorrow. I can't sleep."

It was not a reckless manner in which he said these words aloud under the fast-sailing clouds. It was the settled manner of a tired man, who had wandered, and struggled, and got lost, but who at length struck into his road and saw its end.

Long ago, when he had been talked of as a youth of great promise, he had followed his father to the grave. His mother had died, years before. These solemn words, which had been read at his father's grave, arose in his mind as he went down the dark streets, among the heavy shadows, with the moon and the clouds sailing on high above him: "I am the resurrection and the life, saith the Lord; he that believeth in me, though he were dead, yet shall he live; and whosoever liveth and believeth in me, shall never die."

In a city ruled by the ax, the chain of memory that brought the words to mind might have been easily found. He did not seek it, but repeated them and went on, crossing the river into the lighter streets.

"I am the resurrection and the life, saith the Lord; he that believeth in me, though he were dead, yet shall he live; and whosoever liveth and believeth in me, shall never die."

Now, that the streets were quiet, and the night wore on, the words were in the echoes of his feet, and were in the air. Perfectly calm and steady, he sometimes repeated them to himself as he walked; but he heard them always.

The night wore out, and, as he stood upon the bridge listening to the water, the day came coldly. The night, with the moon and the stars, turned pale and died, and the glorious sun, rising, seemed to strike those words, the burden of the night, straight and warm to his heart in its long, bright rays. A bridge of light appeared to span the air between him and the sun, while the river sparkled under it.

He walked by the stream, far from the houses, and in the light and warmth of the sun fell asleep on the bank. When he awoke, he lingered there yet a little longer, watching an eddy that turned and turned purposeless, until the stream absorbed it, and carried it on to the sea.—"Like me!"

A trading boat, with a sail of the softened color of a dead leaf, then glided into his view, floated by him, and died away. As its silent track in the water disappeared, the prayer that had broken up out of his heart ended in the words, "I am the resurrection and the life."

Mr. Lorry was already out when he got back, and it was easy to guess where the good old man was gone. Sydney Carton drank nothing but a little coffee, ate some bread, and, having washed and changed to refresh himself, went out to the place of trial.

The court was all astir and abuzz when the spy pressed him into a hidden corner among the crowd. Mr. Lorry was there, and Doctor Manette. Lucie was there, sitting beside her father. When her husband was brought in, she turned upon him a look so brave and loving that it warmed his heart and stirred his soul to courage.

There was no favorable leaning toward the prisoner in audience or jury today. They looked at him like a pack of hounds held in leash before they set out to chase the deer. A murderous meaning lit the eyes of the judges and the public prosecutor, as the latter rose to read the accusation.

"Charles Evrémonde, called Darnay. Released yesterday; reaccused and retaken yesterday. Enemy of the Republic, aristocrat, one of a family of tyrants, who have used their privileges to oppress the people."

The chief judge asked by whom the prisoner was accused.

"By three voices: Ernest Defarge, wine seller of Saint Antoine; Thérèse Defarge, his wife; and Alexandre Manette, physician."

There was a great uproar in the court. Doctor Manette was seen, pale and trembling, standing where he had been seated.

"I indignantly protest," he cried, "that this is a forgery and a fraud. You know the accused to be my daughter's husband. My daughter and those dear to her are dearer to me than my life. Who dares to say that I denounce the husband of my child?"

"Citizen Manette, be calm. Nothing, not even the sacrifice of his child, can be so dear to a good citizen as the Republic. Listen to what will follow. In the meantime, be silent."

Frantic shouts were again raised. The doctor sat down, with his lips trembling. His daughter drew closer to him.

Defarge was produced and rapidly told the story of the doctor's imprisonment and release, and of his state when delivered to Defarge's care. He was then asked to tell the court what he did within the Bastille on the day of its fall.

"I knew," said Defarge, "that the prisoner whom I had received into my house had been confined in a cell known as One Hundred and Five, North Tower. When the place fell, I resolved to examine that cell. Directed by a jailer, I mounted to the cell, together with a fellow citizen. We examined the cell very closely. In a hole in the chimney I found a written paper. This is that paper. I have examined some specimens of the writing of Doctor Manette. This paper is in his hand. I give this paper, therefore, into the care of the court."

"Let it be read."

In a dead silence the paper was read, as follows.

8 The Substance of the Shadow

"I, Alexandre Manette, unfortunate physician, write this paper in my doleful cell in the Bastille, during the last month of the year 1767. I write it at stolen moments, under every difficulty. I shall hide it in the wall of the chimney, where some pitying hand may find it when I and my sorrows are dust.

"I write with difficulty in scrapings of soot and charcoal from the chimney, mixed with blood, in the last month of the tenth year of my captivity. Hope has quite left me. I know that my reason will not long remain sound, but I solemnly declare that I am now in my right mind. I write the truth since I shall answer at the Day of Judgment for these my last recorded words.

"One cloudy moonlit night in December, 1757, I was walking by the river at an hour's distance from my home, when a carriage came along behind me, driven very fast. As I stood aside to let it pass, a head was put out at the window, and a voice told the driver to stop and called to me by my name. I answered. Two gentlemen alighted from the carriage, both wrapped in cloaks. They were of about my own age, and they were greatly alike in figure, manner, voice, and face. In answer to their question, I said that I was Doctor Manette, formerly of Beauvais. They explained that, having heard of me as a rising young physician and expert surgeon, they had been to my house, and had been told that I might be found in this direction.

"'Will you please enter the carriage?' said one. Their manner was commanding. They stood so as to place me between them and the carriage door. They were armed. I was not.

"'Gentlemen,' I said, 'pardon me, but I usually ask who does me the honor to seek my aid, and what is the nature of the case to which I am called.'

"'Doctor,' was the reply, 'your clients are people of position. As for the case, your skill will enable you to see for yourself. Will you please enter the carriage?'

"I could do nothing else but enter. They got in after me, and the carriage turned and drove on at its former speed, leaving the city by the north gate. At no great distance from the gate, we left the main road, and presently stopped at a lonely house. We walked, by a damp, soft footpath in a garden where a neglected fountain had overflowed, to the door of the house. By the light of the lamp in the hall, the two gentlemen looked so exactly alike that I saw them to be twin brothers.

"As soon as we had left the carriage, I had heard cries coming from an upper room. To this room I was now taken, and found there, lying on a bed, a patient in a high fever. She was a young woman of great beauty, of perhaps twenty years. Her hair was torn and ragged, and her arms were bound to her sides with sashes and handkerchiefs. In her restlessness she had turned over on her face on the edge of the bed, and was almost choking on a scarf. As I moved the scarf aside, I saw embroidered in its corner the crest of a nobleman and the letter E.

"I turned the girl gently over. Her eyes were dilated and wild, and between fits of shrieking she would repeat the words, 'My husband, my father, and my brother!' Then she would count up to twelve and say 'Hush!' For an instant she would pause to listen, and then would burst into piercing shrieks again. Over and over the words and the counting were repeated, always punctuated by shrieks.

"I asked how long this had been going on. The brother who seemed to have more authority (I will call him the elder and the other the younger) answered, 'Since about this hour last night.'

" 'She has a husband, a father, and a brother?'

" 'A brother.'

" 'She has some recent association with the number twelve?'

"The younger brother impatiently replied, 'With twelve o'clock.'

" 'See, gentlemen,' said I, 'how useless I am, as you have brought me! If I had known what I was coming to see, I could have come provided.'

"The younger brother said haughtily, 'There is a case of medicines here.' He brought it from a closet and set it on the table. I found among them something that I could use to quiet the patient, and with great difficulty made her swallow it. Then I sat down beside the bed to wait until it was time to repeat the dose. In a corner there was a timid servant woman.

"The house was damp and decayed, poorly furnished, and evidently only temporarily used. Some thick old hangings had been nailed up before the windows, to deaden the sound of the shrieks. They continued to be uttered in their regular succession.

"I had sat there for half an hour when the elder brother said, 'There is another patient.'

"I was startled, and asked, 'Is it a pressing case?'

" 'You had better see,' he carelessly answered, and took up a light.

"The other patient lay in a back room, which was a sort of loft over a stable. There was a low plastered ceiling to part of it; the rest was open to the roof. On some hay, with a cushion thrown under his head, lay a handsome peasant boy of about seventeen years of age. He lay on his back, with his teeth set and his right hand clenched over a wound in his chest.

" 'I am a doctor, my poor fellow,' said I. 'Let me examine your wound.'

" 'I do not want it examined,' he said. 'Let it be.'

"I soothed him to let me move his hand away. The wound was a sword thrust, received some twenty-four hours before; but even if it had been looked to at once, no skill could have saved him. He was dying fast. I turned my eyes to the elder brother.

" 'How has this been done, monsieur?' said I.

" 'The crazed young common dog forced my brother to draw upon him, and has fallen by my brother's sword—like a gentleman!'

"There was no touch of pity or regret in his voice.

"The boy's eyes had been fixed upon him; now they moved to look at me. 'Doctor,' he said, 'they are very proud, these nobles. But we common dogs are proud too, sometimes. They plunder us, outrage us, beat us, kill us. But we have a little pride left, sometimes. She— have you seen my sister, doctor?'

"When I said that I had, he told me the story of what had happened. The gentleman who stood by did not interrupt him, evidently not caring how much I knew of his treatment of this boy and girl, whose family, it appeared, had been his tenants. They had been taxed, oppressed, and ground into the earth. Finally the girl, recently married, had been seen and admired by the younger brother, who had then so overworked her husband as to drive him to his death. By day he was harnessed to a cart and driven; by night he was kept out in the dampness of a swamp to quiet the frogs, so that the sleep of these nobles might not be disturbed. Taken out of harness one day at noon, he sobbed twelve times, once for every stroke of the clock, and died on her bosom.

" 'Then,' the boy went on, growing fainter but determined to finish his story, 'with the aid of that man who stands here, his brother took her away, though she hated him with a deadly hatred. I saw her pass me on the road in his carriage. When I took the news home, my father died of shock. I took my other young sister to a place beyond the reach of this man. Then I tracked the brother here, and last night climbed in—a common dog, but sword in hand.'

"I glanced about me, and saw that the hay and straw were trampled over the floor as if there had been a struggle.

" 'She heard me, and ran in. I told her not to come near us till he was dead. He came in and first tossed me some pieces of money; then struck at me with a whip. But I, though a common dog, so struck at him as to make him draw his sword. Yes, I, the peasant, made the gentleman draw his sword to defend himself. I made him thrust at me with all his skill for his life.

" 'Now lift me up, doctor, lift me up. Turn my face to him.'

"I did so, raising the boy's head against my knee. 'Marquis,' said the boy, with his right hand raised, 'in the days when all these things are to be answered for, I summon you and yours, to the last of your bad race, to answer for them. I mark this cross of blood upon you, as a sign that I summon you.' With his forefinger stained with blood from his wound, he drew a cross in the air. Then his hand dropped and his head fell back. I laid him down dead.

"When I returned to the younger woman, I found her raving as before. I repeated the medicine, and sat beside her bed till far into the night. The condition lasted until the next evening. By that time I had come and gone twice. On the second evening she at last sank into a stupor and lay like the dead.

" 'Is she dead?' asked the Marquis, coming into the room.

" 'Not dead,' said I, 'but like to die.'

" 'What strength there is in these common bodies!' he said, looking down at her with some curiosity.

" 'There is great strength,' I answered him, 'in sorrow and despair.'

"He first laughed at my words, then frowned at them, and then proceeded to warn me not to speak of what I had seen. I had been chosen as a young man with his way to make, who would therefore be discreet.

" 'Monsieur,' I said, 'in my profession, the words of patients are always received in confidence.' I was guarded in my answer, for I was troubled in my mind by what I had heard and seen.

"I knew that they would not have troubled themselves with a doctor except for the embarrassment of the poor woman's screams. The boy's death in a quarrel could cause them no danger; such events were usual. But there were servants in the house who would wonder and talk if the sick woman were not cared for.

"I write with so much difficulty, the cold is so severe, I am so fearful of being caught and removed to an underground cell and total darkness, that I must cut short this story. There is no confusion or failure in my memory. I remember many details that I do not write.

"The girl lingered for a week. Towards the last, she asked where she was, and I told her; asked who I was, and I told her. It was in vain that I asked her for her family name. She shook her head upon the pillow and kept her secret.

"It seemed strange to me at the time that the brothers did not seem to mind how much I learned from either boy or girl of the story of their wrongs. The only thing that seemed to trouble them was that the younger brother had crossed swords with a peasant. This they thought was a disgrace.

"I was alone with my patient when she died, two hours before midnight. The brothers were waiting in a room downstairs, impatient to ride away. The Marquis handed me a purse of gold. I took it from his hand, but laid it on the table. I had resolved to accept nothing.

" 'Pray excuse me,' said I. 'Under the circumstances, no.'

"They exchanged looks, but bent their heads to me as I bent mine to them, and we parted without another word on either side.

"I am weary, weary, weary—worn down by misery. I cannot read what I have written.

"Early in the morning, the gold was left at my door in a little box, with my name on the outside. From the first, I had anxiously considered what I ought to do. I decided, that day, to write privately to the Minister of Police, stating all the circumstances of the two cases to which I had been called. I knew that no nobleman was likely to be brought to justice, no matter what he did; but I wished to relieve my own mind. I stated in my letter that I had kept the matter a secret even from my wife. I had no fear of any danger to myself. I was fearless in those days.

"I rose early next morning to finish my letter. It was the last day of the year. The letter was lying before me, just completed, when I was told that a lady wished to see me. She was young, beautiful, and charming. She introduced herself as the wife of the Marquis de St. Evrémonde. I connected the title with which the peasant boy had addressed the older brother with the initial on the scarf, and knew that I had seen the lady's husband very lately.

"She had discovered the main facts of the cruel story, but she did not know that the girl was dead. Her hope had been, she said in great distress, to show her, in secret, a woman's sympathy. She thought also that there was a younger sister living, whom she would like to help. The reason she had come to me was to find out the name and dwelling of the family. Alas, I knew neither.

"These scraps of paper fail me. One was taken from me with a warning yesterday. I must finish my record today.

"She was a good, kind lady, and not happy in her marriage. How could she be! When I handed her down to the door, there was a child, a pretty boy from two to three years old, in her carriage.

" 'For his sake, doctor,' she said, pointing to him in tears, 'I would do all I can to make what poor amends I can.'

"She kissed the boy, and said, 'Thou wilt help me, little Charles? Thou wilt be faithful?' The child answered her bravely, 'Yes!' She took him in her arms and they drove away.

"I added no mention of her husband's name to the

letter. The two brothers described there were nameless. I sealed the letter and delivered it myself that day.

"That night, towards nine o'clock, a man in black clothes rang at my gate, asked to see me, and followed my servant, the boy Ernest Defarge, upstairs, to the room where I sat with my wife—O my wife, beloved of my heart! My fair young English wife!

"There was an urgent case in the Rue St. Honoré, he said. He had a coach waiting.

"It brought me here. It brought me to my grave. When I was clear of the house, a black muffler was drawn tightly over my mouth and my arms were bound. The two brothers crossed the road from a dark corner and identified me with a single gesture. The Marquis took from his pocket the letter I had written, showed it to me, and burnt it in the flame of a lantern that was held. Not a word was spoken. I was brought here; I was brought to my living grave.

"If either of the brothers, in these frightful years, had granted me any news about my dearest wife, I might have thought that God had not quite abandoned them. But now I believe that the mark of the red cross is fatal to them, and that they have no part in His mercies. And them and their descendants, to the last of their race, I, Alexandre Manette, unhappy prisoner, do this last night of the year 1767, in my unbearable agony, denounce. I denounce them to Heaven and to earth."

A terrible sound arose in the court when the reading of this document was done, a sound of eagerness for blood. The story called up the most revengeful passions of the time, and there was not a head in the nation that would not have dropped before it.

There was little need to show how the Defarges

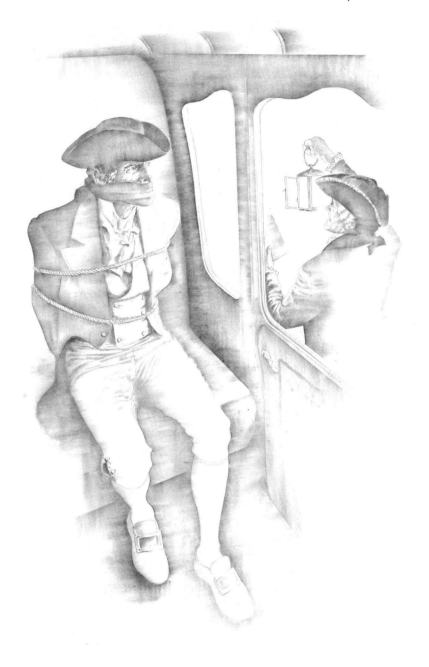

had not made the paper public, but had kept it, biding their time. Little need to show that this detested family name had long since been knitted into the fatal register in vengeance for Gaspard's death. The man never trod ground whose virtues would have saved him that day from the storm of excitement and patriotic fervor.

"Much influence around him, has that doctor?" murmured Madame Defarge. "Save him now, my doctor, save him!"

At every juryman's vote there was a roar, another and another, roar on roar; for every vote was the same, finding Charles Darnay guilty. At heart and by birth an aristocrat, an enemy of the Republic, an oppressor of the people, he was to be sent back to the Conciergerie, and was doomed to death within twenty-four hours.

9 *Farewell in the Darkness*

The tribunal adjourned. The crowd departed. Lucie stood in the deserted courtroom stretching out her arms to her husband, with love and consolation in her face.

"If I might touch him! If I might embrace him once! Oh, good citizens, if you would have so much pity on us!"

There was but one jailer left, along with two of the four men who had taken him last night, and Barsad. He proposed to the rest, "Let her embrace him, then. It is but for a moment." They passed her over the seats in the hall to a raised place, where he, by leaning over the dock, could fold her in his arms.

"Farewell, dear darling of my soul. My parting blessing on my love. We shall meet again, where the weary are at rest!"

They were her husband's words, as he held her close.

"I can bear it, dear Charles. Don't suffer for me. A parting blessing for our child."

"I send it to her by you. I kiss her by you. I say farewell to her by you."

Her father had followed her, and would have fallen on his knees to both of them, but that Darnay put out a hand and seized him, crying,

"No, no! What have you done, that you should kneel to us! We know, now, what a struggle you made of old. We know, now, how you felt when you suspected my descent, and when you knew it. We thank you with all our hearts, and with all our love and duty."

The doctor's only answer was to draw his hands through his white hair and wring them in anguish.

"It could not be otherwise," said Charles. "All things have worked together as they have fallen out. Good could never come of such evil. Be comforted, and forgive me for the misery I and my family have brought upon you."

As he was drawn away, his wife released him, and stood looking after him with a comforting smile. As he went out at the prisoners' door, she turned, tried to speak to her father, and fell fainting.

Then from his hidden corner Sydney Carton came and took her up. His arm trembled as it raised her. "Shall I take her to a coach?" he asked. "I shall never feel her weight."

He carried her to the door and laid her tenderly down in a coach. Her father and Mr. Lorry got into it, while Sydney took his seat beside the driver. When they arrived at her door, he lifted her again and carried her up the staircase to their rooms. There he laid her down on a couch.

"Don't recall her to herself," he said to Miss Pross. "She is better so."

"Oh, Carton, Carton, dear Carton!" cried little Lucie, springing up and throwing her arms round him, in a burst of grief. "Now that you have come, I think you will do something to help mamma, something to save papa! O, look at her, dear Carton!"

He bent over the child, and laid her blooming cheek

against his face. He put her gently from him, and looked at her unconscious mother.

"Before I go," he said, "I may kiss her?"

It was remembered afterwards that when he bent down and touched her face with his lips, he murmured some words. The child, who was nearest to him, told them afterwards that she heard him say, "A life you love."

When he had gone out into the next room, he turned suddenly on Mr. Lorry and her father, and said to the latter,

"You had great influence yesterday, Doctor Manette; let it at least be tried. These judges, and all the men in power, are very friendly to you. Try them again."

"I intend to try. I will not rest a moment."

"That's well. I have known such energy as yours do great things before now."

"I will go," said Doctor Manette, "to the prosecutor and the chief judge, and to others whom it is better not to name."

"When are you likely to have seen these dread powers, Doctor Manette?" asked Sydney.

"Immediately after dark, I should hope. Within an hour or two from this."

"It will be dark soon after four. Let us stretch the hour or two. If I go to Mr. Lorry's at nine, shall I hear what you have done, either from our friend or from yourself?"

"Yes."

"May you prosper!"

Mr. Lorry followed Sydney to the outer door. "I have no hope," said he in a low and sorrowful whisper.

"Nor have I. But don't despair," said Carton very gently. "Don't grieve. I encouraged Doctor Manette in this idea, because I felt that it might sometime be a comfort to her. Otherwise, she might think, 'His life was carelessly thrown away,' and that would trouble her."

"Yes, yes," said Mr. Lorry. "You are right. But he will perish; there is no real hope."

"Yes. He will perish; there is no real hope," echoed Carton, and walked with a settled step downstairs.

He paused in the street, not quite decided where to go. "At Tellson's Bank at nine," he thought. "Shall I do well, in the meantime, to show myself? I think so. It is best that these people should know that such a man as I is here." He turned in the direction of Saint Antoine, stopping on the way for dinner and for a sleep with his head on the restaurant table.

Awaking at seven o'clock refreshed, he inquired the way to Defarge's wine shop. As he passed along the streets, he stopped before a mirror in a shop window, and straightened his disordered coat collar and neckcloth, smoothing his wild hair into an arrangement more like Darnay's. Entering Defarge's shop, he took his seat and asked for a small glass of wine. He was careful to speak in very poor French, for he wanted these people to have no doubt that he was English, and he remembered that the woodsawyer had thought him French. Moreover, he wanted them to continue their conversation without fear of his understanding it; for he saw that husband and wife were deep in talk with one of that day's jurymen, the man known as Jacques Three.

Madame Defarge, as she took Carton's order, cast a careless glance at him, and then a keener one. Then she asked him to repeat his request. He did so.

"English?" she asked, raising her dark eyebrows.

He looked at her as if even one French word were

hard for him to understand; then he replied in a strong foreign accent, "Yes, madame; yes, I am English."

Madame Defarge returned to her counter to get the wine. Sydney took up a newspaper, pretending to be puzzled over its meaning. He heard her say, "I swear to you, he looks like Evrémonde!"

Defarge brought the wine and said good evening.

"What is that? Oh, yes; good evening, citizen." He tasted the wine. "Ah, and good wine. I drink to the Republic."

Defarge went back to the counter. "Certainly a little like," he said.

"I tell you, a good deal like," madame retorted sternly.

Behind his paper, Sydney drew a breath of satisfaction. He had accomplished one of his purposes. They knew that there was in Paris an Englishman who looked like Darnay. He went on reading, apparently with difficulty, following the lines of print with his forefinger. The three at the counter picked up their interrupted conversation, which he was near enough to hear.

"It is true what madame says," said Jacques Three. "Why stop?"

"Well, well," reasoned Defarge, "but one must stop somewhere. The question is where?"

"At utter destruction," said madame.

"Destruction is good doctrine, my wife," said Defarge, rather troubled. "In general, I say nothing against it. But this doctor has suffered much. You saw his face today when the paper was read."

"Yes, I saw his face," agreed madame angrily. "I saw his face to be not the face of a true friend of the Republic."

"And you saw the grief of his daughter, which must be a dreadful grief to him!"

"I saw his daughter," repeated the madame. "Yes, I have seen his daughter more times than one. I saw her today in the court, and I have seen her in the street by the prison. Let me but lift my finger—!"

"The citizeness is superb!" croaked Jacques Three.

"As for you," went on madame to her husband, "if it depended on you, you would rescue this man even now."

"No!" protested Defarge. "Not if to lift this glass would do it. But I would leave the matter there. I say, stop there."

"See you then, Jacques," said Madame Defarge. "For other crimes as tyrants and oppressors, I have this family a long time on my register, doomed to destruction. Then in the beginning of the great days, when the Bastille falls, my husband finds this paper of today, and he brings it home, and in the middle of the night when this place is shut, we read it, here on this spot, by the light of this lamp. Is this so, Defarge?"

He assented.

"Then do I tell him a secret which always I have kept. When first he knew me, I lived among the fishermen of the seashore, by whom I was brought up. But they were not my people. My family was that peasant family so injured by the two Evrémonde brothers. That dying boy and his sister were my brother and my sister, their father was my father, those dead are my dead, and that call to take vengeance for their wrongs is a call to me! Tell wind and fire where to stop. But to me say no word of stopping."

The conversation was interrupted by the entrance of customers. The Englishman paid for his wine, puzzled over his change, and asked to be directed to the National Palace. Madame Defarge took him to the door and pointed out the road. He knew now the reason for her bitter personal hatred of Darnay.

At nine o'clock he found Mr. Lorry walking up and down in restless anxiety. He had just left Lucie. Her father had not been seen since he left them at four o'clock.

He had been more than five hours gone. They waited until ten; then Mr. Lorry went back to Lucie for two hours, leaving Carton to wait for the doctor.

The clock struck twelve, but Doctor Manette did not come back. Mr. Lorry returned without news of him. Where could he be?

They were discussing this question when they heard him on the stairs. The instant he entered the room, it was plain that all was lost.

Whether he had really been to anyone, or whether he had been all that time wandering the streets, was never known. As he stood staring at them, they asked him no question, for his face told them everything.

"I cannot find it," said he, "and I must have it. Where is it?"

His head and throat were bare, and, as he spoke with a helpless look straying all around, he took his coat off, and let it drop on the floor.

"Where is my bench? I have been looking everywhere for my bench, and I can't find it. What have they done with my work? Time presses. I must finish those shoes."

They looked at one another, and their hearts died within them.

"Come, come!" said he, in a whimpering miserable way; "let me get to work. Give me my work."

Receiving no answer, he tore his hair, and beat his feet upon the ground.

Lost, utterly lost!

They each put a hand upon his shoulder, and soothed him to sit down before the fire, with a promise that he should have his work presently. He sank into the chair and sat brooding and moaning, rocking himself to and fro.

Carton was the first to break the despairing silence.

"The last chance is gone," he said. "It was not much. He had better be taken to Lucie. But before you go, will you listen to me carefully? Don't ask me why I say what I shall say. I have a reason—a good one."

"I do not doubt it," answered Mr. Lorry. "Say on."

Carton stooped to pick up the doctor's coat, which lay at his feet. As he did so, a small wallet fell on the floor. In it Carton found a folded paper, opened it, and exclaimed, "Thank God!"

"What is it?" asked Mr. Lorry eagerly.

"Let me speak of it in its place." He took another paper from his pocket. "Here is my passport, letting me go from Paris. You see—'Sydney Carton, Englishman'?"

Mr. Lorry held it open in his hand.

"Keep it for me until tomorrow. I shall see Darnay tomorrow, and I had better not take it into the prison. Now, take this paper of Doctor Manette's. It too is a passport, enabling him and his daughter and her child to leave Paris and France at any time. Perhaps he obtained it as his last precaution against evil, yesterday. Put it up carefully with mine and your own. It is good until recalled, but I have reason to think that it soon will be recalled."

"They are not in danger?"

"They are in great danger, of being accused by Madame Defarge. I overheard words of hers tonight which have shown me their danger. Since then, I have seen the spy. He knows that a woodsawyer, living by the prison wall, is under the control of the Defarges. He will say that he has seen Lucie making signals to prisoners. The charge will be the common one, a prison plot, and it will cost her life and perhaps her child's and her father's, for both have been seen with her at that place. Don't look so horrified. You will save them all."

"Heaven grant I may, Carton! But how?"

"I am going to tell you how. It will depend on you. This new attack will certainly not take place until after tomorrow; probably not for two or three days afterwards. You have money, and can buy the means of traveling to the coast quickly. You say you are all ready to return to England. Early tomorrow, have a coach and horses here in the courtyard, with all the luggage, so that you may start at two o'clock."

"It shall be done!"

Carton's manner was so eager and inspiring that Mr. Lorry had caught the flame.

"You are a noble heart. We could depend upon no better man. Tell her tonight what you know of the danger to her child and her father. Dwell upon that, for she would lay her own fair head beside her husband's cheerfully. Press upon her the need to leave Paris, with them and you, tomorrow at two. Tell her that it was her husband's last wish. Tell her that more depends upon it than she dare hope. Will her father, in this sad state, obey her?"

"I am sure of it."

"Very well. Make all these arrangements quietly; put them all into the coach, and even take your own seat there. The moment I come to you, take me in and drive away."

"You mean that I am to wait for you under all circumstances?"

"You have my passport in your hand with the rest, you know. Wait for nothing but to have my place filled, and then for England!"

"Why, then," said Mr. Lorry, grasping his hand, "it does not all depend on one old man, but I shall have a young and able man at my side."

"By the help of Heaven you shall! Promise me solemnly that nothing will make you change this course."

"Nothing, Carton."

"Remember: alter this course, or delay in it for any reason, and no life can possibly be saved. Above all, I am not selfish when I tell you again not to go until my place is filled."

"I will remember. I hope to do my part faithfully."

"And I hope to do mine. Now, goodbye!" He said it with a grave smile, and put the old man's hand to his lips.

But they did not part at once. Together they roused the rocking figure before the dying fire, put a cloak and hat upon it, and tempted it forth to find where the bench and work were hidden that it still begged to have. Together they led Lucie's poor father to the courtyard of the house where she waited through the awful night. There in the courtyard Sydney lingered for a while alone, looking up at the light in the window of her room. Before he went away, he breathed blessing toward it, and a farewell.

10 *Fifty-two*

In the black prison of the Conciergerie, the doomed of the day awaited their fate. They were in number as the weeks of the year—fifty-two. Among them, Charles Darnay, alone in a cell, fully understood that nothing now could possibly save him. In every line of the story that had been read, he had heard his fate.

Yet it was not easy, remembering his beloved wife, to compose his mind to what it must bear. For hours he strove to resign himself to death, and as evening fell he grew calmer. He had been allowed to purchase pen, ink, and paper, as well as a lamp. So he sat down to write until the prison lights should be put out.

He wrote a long letter to Lucie, showing her that he had known nothing of her father's imprisonment until he had heard of it from herself. "Even then," he wrote, "I was as ignorant as you of my father's and uncle's responsibility for those years of misery. I knew nothing of it till the story was read today. As you know, I kept my name a secret from you because your father made me promise it before he would consent to our marriage. We know now his reason. He wanted nothing to come between us. If he remembered that he had written the paper—as perhaps he did, for you remember how upset he was when I told that story of the prisoner in the Tower of London—he probably thought it was destroyed with the Bastille. Do not distress him by asking about this. Tell him that he has done nothing for which he can justly blame himself." He closed the letter with farewell words of love and blessing.

To Doctor Manette he wrote entrusting his wife and child to his care. To Mr. Lorry he explained his worldly affairs, asking him to attend to them. He never thought of Carton. He did not even know he was in Paris.

He had time to finish these letters before the lights were put out. When he lay down on his straw bed, he thought he was done with the world.

He awoke in the gloomy morning, not realizing where he was or what had happened, until it flashed upon his mind, "This is the day of my death!" But he was conscious of no fear.

Walking to and fro in his cell, he heard the clocks of the city strike away the numbers he would never hear again. Nine gone forever, ten gone forever, eleven gone forever, twelve coming on to pass away. The worst of the strife was over. As he walked up and down, he prayed for himself and his loved ones.

Twelve gone forever.

He had been told that the final hour was three, and he knew he would be sent for some time earlier. He resolved to keep two in his mind as the hour. He heard one struck away from him without surprise. He thought, "There is but one more hour now." Then he stopped in his pacing, as he heard footsteps in the stone passage outside the door.

The key was put in the lock and turned. As the door opened, a man said in a low voice, in English, "He has never seen me here; I have kept out of his way. Go you in alone; I wait near. Lose no time!"

The door was quickly closed, and there stood before

him face to face, quiet, intent upon him, with the light of a smile on his features, and a finger on his lip, Sydney Carton. There was something so bright and remarkable in his look that until he spoke Darnay doubted his own eyes.

"Of all the people upon earth, you least expected to see me?" said the visitor.

"I can scarcely believe it. You are not a prisoner?"

"No. I chanced to gain a power over one of the keepers here by something I knew of his past. By that means I stand before you. I come from your wife, dear Darnay. I bring you a request from her."

"What is it?"

"You have no time to ask me why I bring it or what it means; I have no time to tell you. You must obey it. Take off those boots you wear, and draw on these of mine."

He had already pushed Charles into a chair that stood against the wall behind him. He stood over the prisoner barefoot.

"Draw on these boots of mine. Put your hands to them; put your will to them. Quick!"

"Carton, there is no escaping from this place; it never can be done. You will only die with me. It is madness."

"It would be madness if I asked you to escape; but do I? When I ask you to pass out at that door, tell me it is madness and remain here. Change that neckcloth for this of mine, that coat for this of mine. While you do it, let me take this ribbon from your hair, and shake out your hair like this of mine!"

With wonderful quickness, he forced all these changes upon Darnay.

"Carton! Dear Carton! It is madness. It never can

be done. It has been attempted, and has always failed. I implore you not to add your death to the bitterness of mine."

"Do I ask you, my dear Darnay, to pass the door? When I ask that, refuse. There are pen and ink and paper on this table. Is your hand steady enough to write?"

"It was, when you came in."

"Steady it again, and write what I shall dictate. Quick, friend, quick!"

Pressing his hand to his bewildered head, Darnay sat down at the table. Carton, with his right hand inside the pocket of his waistcoat, stood close beside him.

"Write exactly as I speak."

"To whom do I address it?"

"To no one." Carton, still standing over him with his hand in his pocket, began to dictate. "'If you remember,'" he said, "'the words that passed between us long ago, you will readily understand this when you see it. You do remember them, I know. It is not in your nature to forget them.'"

He was drawing his hand from his pocket; the prisoner chancing to look up as he wrote, the hand stopped, closing upon something.

"Is that a weapon in your hand?" Darnay asked.

"No. I am not armed."

"What is it in your hand?"

"You shall know directly. Write on. There are but a few words more." He dictated again. "'I am thankful that the time has come when I can keep my promise. That I do so is no reason for regret or grief.'" As he said these words, his hand slowly and softly moved down close to the writer's face.

The pen dropped from Darnay's fingers on the table and he looked about him vacantly.

"What vapor is that?" he asked.

"I am conscious of nothing. Take up the pen and finish. Hurry, hurry!"

As if his memory were failing or his sense dulled, Darnay made an effort. He looked at Carton with clouded eyes and altered breathing; then he bent over the paper once more.

"'If it had been otherwise,'" Carton dictated, while his hand again softly stole down, "'I never should have used the opportunity that longer life would have given me. If it had been otherwise, I should only have had so much the more to answer for.'" The hand was at the writer's face. " 'If it had been otherwise—' " Carton looked at the pen, and saw that it was trailing off into meaningless signs.

Carton's hand moved back to his pocket no more. The prisoner sprang up with a reproachful look, but Carton's hand was close and firm at his nostrils, and Carton's left arm caught him round the waist. For a few seconds he faintly struggled with the man who had come to take his place and lay down his life for him. In a minute or so he was stretched unconscious on the floor. The drug which Carton had purchased from the chemist had done its work, and he could carry out the plan which Darnay would never consciously have permitted.

Quickly Carton dressed himself in the clothes the prisoner had laid aside, combed back his hair, and tied it with the ribbon the prisoner had worn. He signed his name on the written paper, folded it, and addressed it to Lucie. Then he softly called, "Enter there!" and the spy came in.

"You see?" said Carton, looking up as he kneeled on one knee beside the unconscious figure, putting the paper in the breast of the coat. "Is your risk very great?"

"Mr. Carton," the spy answered, with a timid snap of his fingers, "my risk is not *that*, in the thick of the business here, if you are true to the whole of your bargain."

"Don't fear me. I will be true to the death. Now get assistance, and take me to the coach at Tellson's Bank."

"Take *you*?" asked the spy nervously.

"Him, man, with whom I have exchanged. You go out at the gate by which you brought me in?"

"Of course."

"The guards noticed that I was weak and faint when I came, and I am fainter now you take me out. The parting interview has brought on a heart attack. Such a thing has happened here often, and too often. Your life is in your own hands. Quick! Call assistance!"

"You swear not to betray me?" said the trembling spy, as he paused for a last moment.

"Man, man!" returned Carton, stamping his foot; "have I sworn by no solemn vow already, to go through with this, that you waste the precious moments now? Take him yourself to the courtyard you know of, place him yourself in the carriage. Tell Mr. Lorry to give him no medicine but air, and bid him remember his promise of last night and drive away!"

The spy withdrew, and Carton seated himself at the table, resting his head in his hands. Barsad returned immediately with two men, who glanced unmoved at the unconscious figure in the conspicuous white coat and riding boots. They placed it on a litter and bent to carry it away.

"The time is short, Evrémonde," said the spy in a warning voice.

"I know it well," answered Carton. "Be careful of my friend, I entreat you, and leave me."

The door closed, and Carton was left alone. Straining his ears, he listened for any sound that might mean suspicion or alarm. There was none. Keys turned, doors clashed, footsteps passed along distant passages; no cry was raised or hurry made. Breathing more freely in a little while, he sat down at the table and listened again until the clock struck two.

Sounds that he was not afraid of, for he knew their meaning, then began. Several doors were opened, and finally his own. A jailer with a list in his hand looked in, merely saying, "Follow me, Evrémonde!" and he followed into a large dark room, at a distance.

It was a dark winter day, and he could see only dimly the other prisoners there. He was aware that among these prisoners must be some who knew Darnay. Would they recognize that he was not Darnay? If any did, it would show that there was danger of recognition at the last moment by the Defarges. He had let himself be seen in the shop, in order that there might be no suspicion when a man who looked like Darnay departed from Paris. But if she knew him at the guillotine, the coach might be stopped and Darnay and the others brought back to their death.

As he stood by the wall in a dim corner, one man stopped in passing to embrace him as a friend. It thrilled him with a great dread of discovery, but the man saw no difference. A few moments later, a young woman with a slight, girlish form, a sweet, pale face, and large, patient eyes rose from her seat and came to speak to him.

"Citizen Evrémonde," she said, touching him with her cold hand. "I am a poor little seamstress, who was with you in La Force."

He murmured for answer, "True. I forget what you were accused of?"

"Plots. Though the just Heaven knows I am innocent of any. Is it likely? Who would think of plotting with a poor little weak creature like me?" She smiled forlornly and went on, "I am not afraid to die, Citizen Evrémonde, but I have done nothing. I am not unwilling to die, if the Republic, which is to do so much good to us poor, will profit by my death; but I do not know how that can be, Citizen Evrémonde."

As the last thing on earth that his heart was to

warm and soften to, it warmed and softened to this piti-able girl.

"I heard you were freed, Citizen Evrémonde. I hoped it was true."

"It was. But I was again taken and condemned."

"If I ride with you, Citizen Evrémonde, will you let me hold your hand? I am not afraid, but I am little and weak, and it will give me more courage."

As the patient eyes were lifted to his face, he saw a sudden doubt in them, and then astonishment. He pressed the work-worn, hunger-worn young fingers, and touched his lips.

"Are you dying for him?" she whispered.

"And his wife and child. Hush! Yes."

"Oh, you will let me hold your brave hand, stranger?"

"Hush! Yes, my poor sister, to the last."

It was Lucie that he thought of as he soothed her—Lucie, who was now, please God, in a coach speeding away from Paris. God grant that his plan move now to its conclusion, that no one else recognize him and ride after the coach.

The same shadows that are falling on the prison are falling, in the same hour of early afternoon, on the gate of Paris. The usual crowd stands about, when a coach going out of the city drives up to be examined.

"Who goes here? Whom have we within? Papers!"

The papers are handed out, and read.

"Alexandre Manette. Physician. French. Which is he?"

This is he; this helpless, wandering old man pointed out.

"Apparently the Citizen-Doctor is not in his right

mind? The Revolution fever will have been too much for him?"

Greatly too much for him.

"Hah! Many suffer with it. Lucie. His daughter. French. Which is she?"

This is she.

"Apparently it must be. Lucie, the wife of Evrémonde, is it not?"

It is.

"Hah! Evrémonde has an appointment elsewhere. Lucie, her child. English. This is she?"

She and no other.

Kiss me, child of Evrémonde. Now, you have kissed a good Republican; something new in your family. Remember it! Sydney Carton. Lawyer. English. Which is he?"

He is pointed out, lying in the corner of the carriage.

"Apparently the English lawyer is ill? He seems to have fainted."

It is hoped he will recover in the fresher air. His health is poor, and he has parted sadly from a friend who has displeased the Republic.

"Is that all? It is not a great deal, that! Jarvis Lorry. Banker. English. Which is he?"

"I am he, necessarily, being the last."

It is Jarvis Lorry who has replied to all the questions. It is Jarvis Lorry who has alighted and stands with his hand on the coach door, replying to a group of officials. They leisurely walk round the carriage and leisurely mount the box, to look at what little luggage it carries on the roof; the country people press nearer to the coach doors and stare in.

"Behold your papers, Jarvis Lorry, countersigned."

"One can depart, citizen?"

"One can depart. Forward, my postilions! * A good journey!"

"I salute you, citizens.—And the first danger passed!"

These are again the words of Jarvis Lorry. There is terror in the carriage, there is weeping, there is the heavy breathing of the unconscious Darnay, there is grief over the letter Lucie has found in his coat.

"Are we not going too slowly? Can they not be induced to go faster?" asks Lucie, clinging to the old man.

"It would seem like flight, my darling. I must not urge them too much; it would rouse suspicion."

"Look back, look back, and see if we are pursued!"

"The road is clear, my dearest. So far, we are not pursued."

Houses in twos and threes pass by us, solitary farms, ruinous buildings, open country, avenues of leafless trees. The hard, uneven pavement is under us; the soft deep mud is on either side. Sometimes we strike into the skirting mud, to avoid the stones that clatter us and shake us. Sometimes we stick in ruts there. The agony of our impatience is then so great, that in our wild alarm and hurry we are for getting out and running.

Out of the open country, in again among ruinous buildings, solitary farms, cottages in twos and threes, avenues of leafless trees. Have these men deceived us, and taken us back by another road? Is not this the same place twice over? Thank Heaven, no. A village. Look back, look back, and see if we are pursued! Hush! the posting house.

* A postilion was a driver of a very fast coach who sat upon the back of one of the horses instead of on the driver's seat of the coach.

Leisurely, our four horses are taken out; leisurely, the coach stands in the little street; leisurely, the new horses appear; leisurely, the new postilions follow. All the time our hearts are beating at a rate that would outstrip the fastest horses.

At length the new postilions are in their saddles. We are through the village, over a hill, on low, watery ground. Suddenly the horses are pulled up almost on their haunches. We are pursued!

"Ho! Within the carriage there. Speak, then!"

"What is it?" asks Mr. Lorry, looking out at window.

"How many did they say?"

"I do not understand you."

"—At the last post. How many to the guillotine today?"

"Fifty-two."

"I said so! A brave number! The guillotine goes handsomely. Hi, forward, then!"

The night comes on dark. Charles moves more; he is beginning to revive and to speak clearly. He thinks he and Carton are still together; he asks him what he has in his hand. Oh, pity us, kind Heaven, and help us! Look out, look out, and see if we are pursued.

The wind is rushing after us, and the clouds are flying after us, and the moon is plunging after us, and the whole wild night is in pursuit of us. But, so far, we are pursued by nothing else.

11 The Knitting Done

At about the same time when Sydney Carton came to the cell of Darnay, Madame Defarge was in the shed of the woodsawyer. She had come there for a private talk, away from her husband and the shop, with Jacques Three and with her closest friend among the savage women of the Revolution, one known as "the Vengeance." The woodsawyer was permitted to listen.

"But our Defarge," Jacques Three was saying, "is certainly a good Republican, is he not?"

"My husband, fellow citizen," said Madame Defarge, "is a good Republican and a bold man. He has worked well for the people. But he has his weaknesses, and one of them is sympathy for this doctor."

"It is a great pity," croaked Jacques Three, shaking his head. "It is not quite like a good citizen."

"See you," said madame. "I care nothing for this doctor, I. He may wear his head or lose it, for any interest I have in him. It is all one to me. But the Evrémondes are to be destroyed, and the wife and child must follow the husband and father."

"She has a fine head for it," croaked Jacques Three. "I have seen blue eyes and golden hair at the guillotine, and they looked charming."

"In a word," said madame, after further thought, "I cannot trust my husband in this matter. I dare not tell him the details of my plans, and I feel that if I delay, he may give the doctor warning, and then they might escape."

"That must never be," croaked Jacques Three. "No one must escape."

"It is settled, then," said madame. "I must act for myself. Come hither, little citizen."

The woodsawyer, to whom she spoke, and who was in mortal fear of her, stepped forward with his hand to his red cap.

"About those signals that she made to the prisoners," said Madame Defarge sternly. "You will bear witness that you saw them?"

"Yes, yes. Why not?" cried the woodsawyer. "Every day, in all weathers, always signalling; sometimes with the child, sometimes without. I have seen with my eyes."

"Clearly, plots," said Jacques Three.

"Now let me see," went on Madame Defarge. "Can I spare this doctor to my husband? But he was with her when I saw her, and I cannot accuse one without the other. No. He must take his chance," she finished. "I cannot spare him."

She then directed the woodsawyer to come at eight that night to the wine shop, so as to go with her to tell the story to the authorities. She herself would go immediately to the home of Lucie, where she would find her mourning for an enemy of the Republic, and likely to say bitter things about the injustice done her husband. This would give another reason for accusing her.

"Take you my knitting," she said to the Vengeance, "and have it ready for me in my usual seat beside the guillotine. Keep me my usual chair."

"I willingly obey the orders of my chief," said the

Vengeance, kissing her cheek. "You will not be late? It is a special day."

"I will be there before three, before the tumbrils arrive. Have no fear." And madame departed.

There were many cruel women at that time in Paris, but no one of them was more to be dreaded than this woman now taking her way along the streets. She was absolutely without pity. It was nothing to her that an innocent man was to die for the sins of his forefathers. She saw not him, but them. To appeal to her was hopeless. She had no sense of pity even for herself.

With a loaded pistol lying hidden in her dress, and a sharp dagger lying hidden at her waist, she took her way along the streets in the direction of Lucie's lodgings. Her tread was strong and free. Her dark hair looked rich under the coarse red cap.

The rooms toward which she moved were not altogether deserted, though the coach had departed some ten minutes before, at two o'clock. There had been no room for Miss Pross and Jerry, who were therefore to follow in a light, fast chaise, without luggage. They were under no suspicion, and no one would interfere with their movements. Starting at three o'clock, they would overtake the coach, pass it, and be helpful on the road by engaging horses in advance of the fugitives.

The two were making their last preparations to leave, even as Madame Defarge, taking her way through the streets, now drew nearer and nearer.

"Now what do you think, Mr. Cruncher," said the much upset Miss Pross, "of our not starting from Tellson's courtyard? Folks might suspect something, if they saw a second carriage start from there the same day."

"My opinion, miss," returned Mr. Cruncher, "is as you're right."

And still Madame Defarge, on her way along the streets, came nearer and nearer.

"If you were to go ahead," said Miss Pross, "and stop the chaise from coming here, and were to wait with it somewhere for me—wouldn't that be best?"

Mr. Cruncher thought it might. Still Madame Defarge came nearer and nearer.

"By the cathedral door, then—would it be much out of the way to take me in by the cathedral?"

"No, miss," said Jerry. "But I am doubtful about leaving of you. We don't know what may happen."

"Heaven knows we don't," returned Miss Pross, "but have no fear for me. Go now, and get the chaise and horses, and take me in at the cathedral at three o'clock."

As Jerry went out at the door, Madame Defarge was drawing very near indeed.

Miss Pross looked at her watch. It was twenty minutes past two, and she had no time to lose. She must get ready at once. She poured a basin of cold water and began to bathe her eyes, which were swollen from crying. Nervous at the stillness, she kept looking round to see that no one was behind her. Finally, as she so turned, she screamed, for she saw a figure standing in the room.

Madame Defarge looked coldly at her, and said, "The wife of Evrémonde; where is she?"

It flashed upon Miss Pross's mind that the doors were all standing open, and would suggest the flight. Her first act was to shut them. There were four in the room, and she shut them all. She then placed herself before the door of the room which Lucie had occupied.

Madame Defarge's dark eyes followed her through this rapid movement and rested on her when it was finished. Miss Pross had nothing beautiful about her; years had not softened the grimness of her appearance. But she was as determined a woman as Madame Defarge.

"You might, from the look of you, be the wife of Satan," said Miss Pross to herself. "However, you shall not get the better of me. I am an Englishwoman."

Madame Defarge looked at her scornfully. "On my way yonder," she said, "where they reserve my chair and my knitting for me, I come to visit the wife of Evrémonde. I wish to see her."

"I know you mean ill," said Miss Pross, "though I cannot understand a word you say. Depend upon it, I can hold my own against you."

Each spoke in her own language. Neither understood the other's words.

"It will do her no good to keep herself hidden," said Madame Defarge. "Go tell her that I wish to see her; do you hear?"

"You needn't try to frighten me with those eyes of yours," returned Miss Pross. "No, you wicked foreign woman; I am your match."

Madame Defarge understood enough, from look and manner, to know that she was set at naught.

"I take no answer from you," she said. "Either tell her that I demand to see her, or stand out of the way and let me go to her!"

"I little thought," said Miss Pross, "that I should ever want to understand your nonsensical language; but I would give all I have, except the clothes I wear, to know whether you suspect the truth, or any part of it."

Madame Defarge had not moved from the spot where she stood when Miss Pross first became aware of her; but she now advanced one step.

"I am a Briton," said Miss Pross; "I am desperate. I don't care an English twopence for myself. I know that the longer I keep you here, the greater hope there is for my Ladybird. I'll not leave a handful of that dark hair upon your head, if you lay a finger on me!"

Thus spoke Miss Pross, who had never struck a blow in her life. But her very courage so upset her that tears filled her eyes. This Madame Defarge mistook for a sign of weakness. "Ha, ha!" she laughed, "you poor wretch! What are you worth? I address myself to that doctor." Then she raised her voice and called out, "Citizen Doctor! Wife of Evrémonde! Child of Evrémonde! Any person but this miserable fool, answer the Citizeness Defarge!"

Perhaps the following silence, perhaps something in Miss Pross's expression, whispered to Madame Defarge that they were gone. Three of the doors she opened swiftly and looked in.

"Those rooms are all in disorder, there has been hurried packing, there are odds and ends upon the ground. There is no one in that room behind you! Let me look."

"Never!" said Miss Pross, who understood the request as perfectly as Madame Defarge understood the answer.

"If they are not in that room, they are gone, and can be pursued and brought back," said Madame Defarge.

"As long as you don't know whether they are in that room or not, you are uncertain what to do," said Miss Pross; "and you shall not know that, if I can prevent your knowing it."

"I will have you from that door if I have to tear you to pieces," said Madame Defarge.

"I pray for strength to keep you here, while every

minute you are here is helping to save my darling," said Miss Pross.

Madame Defarge made for the door. Miss Pross seized her round the waist in both her arms and held her tight. It was in vain for Madame Defarge to struggle and to strike. Miss Pross with the strength of love, always so much stronger than hate, clasped her tight. Madame's hands struck and tore at her face; but Miss Pross, with her head down, held her round the waist and clung to her.

Soon Madame Defarge's hands ceased to strike, and felt at her waist for her dagger. "It is here, under my arm," said Miss Pross. "You shall not draw it. I am stronger than you, thank Heaven."

Madame Defarge's hands moved to her bosom. Miss Pross looked up, saw the pistol, struck at it, struck out a flash and a crash, and stood alone, blinded with smoke. As the smoke cleared, leaving an awful stillness, the body of the furious woman lay lifeless on the floor.

After the first fright and horror left her, Miss Pross passed the body as far from it as she could, and went to get her bonnet and outdoor clothing. Then she shut and locked the door, putting the key in her pocket. She sat on the stairs a few moments to get her breath; then she hurried away.

In crossing the bridge, she dropped the door key in the river. With hair and dress disordered, and with nerves shocked and shaken, she took up her stand at the cathedral door. She had not long to wait before Jerry appeared with the post chaise, and they drove away from the horrors of Paris. There was no fear now, though the fugitives did not know it till next day, that the coach would be pursued and stopped. There would be no one to recognize Sydney Carton at the guillotine.

12 "Greater Love Hath No Man"

Along the Paris streets the tumbrils rumble, hollow and harsh, six in number. On either side the street is lined with faces, eager and curious, of people who have come to see the sight.

Some of the riders in the tumbrils watch all things on their last roadside with a blank stare. Others still show a lingering interest in what they see. Some, seated with drooping heads, are sunk in silent despair. Others are heedful of their looks. Several close their eyes and think. Not one of the whole number appeals, by look or gesture, to the pity of the people.

A guard of horsemen rides beside the tumbrils, and onlookers often look up at them to ask some question. It seems to be always the same question, for it is always followed by a crowding of people toward the third cart. The horsemen frequently point out one man in it. He stands at the back of the tumbril with his head bent down, talking with a girl who sits on the side of the cart and holds fast to his hand. He has no interest in the scene about him, and always speaks to the girl. Sometimes cries are raised against him. If they move him at all, it is only to a quiet smile, as he shakes his hair a little more loosely about his face, hiding it from the crowd.

On the steps of a church, awaiting the coming of the tumbrils, stands Barsad, the spy. He looks into the first cart; not there. He looks into the second; not there. He is asking himself, "Has he betrayed me?" when his face clears, as he looks into the third.

"Which is Evrémonde?" asks a man behind him.

"That. At the back there."

"With his hand in the girl's?"

"Yes."

The man cries, "Down, Evrémonde! To the guillotine all aristocrats! Down, Evrémonde!"

"Hush, hush!" the spy entreats him timidly.

"And why not, citizen?"

"He is going to pay the price. It will be paid in five minutes more. Let him be at peace."

But as the man continues to cry out, the face of Evrémonde is for a moment turned towards him. Evrémonde then sees the spy, and looks attentively at him, and goes his way.

The clocks are on the stroke of three. In front of the guillotine, seated in chairs as in a place of public entertainment, are a number of women, knitting. On one of the front row of chairs stands the Vengeance, looking about for her friend.

"Thérèse!" she cries shrilly. "Who has seen her? Thérèse Defarge!"

"She never missed before," says another knitting woman.

"No. Nor will she miss now," cries the Vengeance. "Thérèse!"

"Louder," the other woman recommends.

Yes, louder, Vengeance, much louder, and still she will scarcely hear.

"Bad fortune!" cries the Vengeance, stamping her foot. "Here are the tumbrils. And Evrémonde will be beheaded in a wink, and she not here! See her knitting in my hand, and her empty chair ready for her. I cry with vexation and disappointment!"

The tumbrils begin to discharge their loads. The headsmen are ready. Crash!—The knife falls, and a head is held up. The knitting women, who scarcely lifted their eyes to look at it a moment ago when it could think and speak, count One.

The second tumbril empties and moves on; the third comes up. Crash!—And the knitting women, never pausing in their work, count Two.

The supposed Evrémonde descends, and the seamstress is lifted out next after him. He has not let go of her patient hand in getting out, but still holds it as he promised. He gently places her with her back to the crashing engine that constantly whirrs up and falls, and she looks into his face and thanks him.

"But for you, dear stranger, I should not be so calm, for I am naturally a poor little thing, faint of heart; nor should I have been able to raise my thoughts to God. I think you were sent to me by Heaven."

"Or you to me," says Sydney Carton. "Keep your eyes upon me, dear child, and mind no other object."

"I mind nothing, while I hold your hand."

The two stand in the fast thinning throng of victims, but they speak as if they were alone. Even while he gives comfort to the girl who has brought him a last friendly touch with life, Carton's thoughts are on a traveling coach speeding on its way to England. If the start was made at two, Lucie must be well outside the city walls.

The girl speaks again. "Brave and generous friend, will you let me ask you one last question? I am very ignorant, and it troubles me."

"Tell me what it is."

"I have a cousin, an only relative and an orphan like myself, whom I love very dearly. She is five years younger than I, and she lives in a farmer's house in the south country. Poverty parted us, and she knows nothing of my fate—for I cannot write—and if I could, how should I tell her! It is better as it is."

"Yes, yes; better as it is."

"What I have been thinking as we came along, is this: If the Republic really does good to the poor, and they come to be less hungry and in all ways to suffer less, she may live a long time; she may even live to be old."

"What then, my gentle sister?"

"Do you think that it will seem long to me, while I wait for her in the better land?"

"It cannot be, my child. There is no time there, and no trouble there."

"You comfort me so much! I am so ignorant. Am I to leave you now? Is the moment come?"

"Yes."

The thin hand does not tremble as he releases it; nothing worse than a sweet, bright constancy is in the patient face. She goes next before him—is gone; the knitting women count Twenty-Two.

"I am the resurrection and the life, saith the Lord: he that believeth in me, though he were dead, yet shall he live: and whosoever liveth and believeth in me, shall never die."

The murmuring of many voices, the upturning of many faces, the pressing on of many footsteps, all flash away. Twenty-Three.

———

They said of him about the city that night that his was the most peaceful man's face ever beheld at the guillotine.

Not long before, a famous woman, Madame Roland, had asked to be allowed to write down the thoughts that filled her mind on her way to her death. If Sydney Carton could have written his, they would have been these, could he have looked into the future.

"I see Barsad and the Defarges, the knitting women, the jurymen, the judges, long ranks of the new tyrants who have taken the places of the old, perishing by this instrument of death. I see a beautiful city and a brilliant people rising from this horror. I see their struggles to be truly free. I see the evil of this time, and of the centuries before which brought about this evil, gradually making atonement for itself and wearing out.

"I see the lives for which I lay down my life, peaceful, useful, prosperous, and happy, in that England which I shall see no more. I see her with a child in her arms who bears my name. I see her father, aged and bent, but otherwise restored, and faithful to all men in his healing office, and at peace. I see the good old man, so long their friend, in ten years' time enriching them with all he has, and passing tranquilly to his reward.

"I see that I am held sacred in their hearts, and in the hearts of their descendants, generations hence. I see her, an old woman, weeping for me on the anniversary of this day.

"I see her child, Sidney Carton Darnay, winning his way up in that profession which once was mine. I see him winning it so well, that my name is made famous by the light of his. I see the blots I threw upon it faded away. I see him, foremost of just judges and honored men, bringing a boy of my name, with a forehead that I know and golden hair, to this place—then fair to look upon, with not a trace of this day's evil work. And I hear him tell the child my story.

"It is a far, far better thing that I do, than I have ever done; it is a far, far better rest that I go to, than I have ever known."

REVIEWING YOUR READING

Book 1—CHAPTER 1

FINDING THE MAIN IDEA

1. This chapter is mostly about a
   (A) highway robbery   (B) rough night   (C) chance meeting
   (D) bank officer's mysterious business trip

REMEMBERING DETAIL

2. This story begins in the year
   (A) 1577   (B) 1875   (C) 1775   (D) 1975
3. What is Mr. Jarvis Lorry's occupation?
   (A) Secret agent   (B) Bank president   (C) Bank officer
   (D) Bank messenger
4. Who is Jerry?
   (A) Mr. Lorry's son   (B) A highwayman   (C) A bank
   messenger   (D) A secret agent
5. Mr. Lorry receives a message that says
   (A) RECALLED TO LIFE   (B) PROCEED TO PARIS
   (C) RETURN IMMEDIATELY   (D) WAIT AT DOVER
6. The offices of Tellson's Bank are located in
   (A) New York and London   (B) New York and Paris
   (C) London and Paris   (D) London and Dover
7. Who has been "buried alive for eighteen years"?
   (A) Mr. Jarvis Lorry   (B) Jerry   (C) Ma'mselle   (D) A
   45-year-old man with white hair

DRAWING CONCLUSIONS

8. At the beginning of the story, you can tell that the weather is
   (A) warm and pleasant   (B) hot and dry   (C) cold and
   damp   (D) cool and comfortable

IDENTIFYING THE MOOD

9. When Jerry received Mr. Lorry's reply he was
   (A) sad   (B) very happy   (C) very surprised   (D) bored

THINKING IT OVER

1. Where do you think the person Mr. Lorry dreams about was
   buried? Explain your answer.

CHAPTER 2

FINDING THE MAIN IDEA
1. In this chapter, the author is mostly interested in telling how (A) Miss Manette learns that her father is alive (B) Mr. Lorry waits for Miss Manette to arrive (C) Miss Manette travels to Dover (D) Mr. Lorry likes Miss Manette

REMEMBERING DETAIL
2. Mr. Lorry and Miss Manette were meeting in a (A) house in London (B) hotel in Dover (C) park in Paris (D) hotel in Paris
3. Where is Monsieur Manette? (A) Dover (B) New York (C) London (D) Paris
4. Monsieur Manette has just been (A) released from a long prison term (B) cured of a terrible disease (C) away searching for his daughter (D) found in London
5. Mr. Lorry tells Miss Manette that her father's job is that of a (A) lawyer (B) doctor (C) banker (D) spy

DRAWING CONCLUSIONS
6. You can tell from the story that Miss Manette's mother was (A) English (B) French (C) American (D) Spanish
7. You can figure out from the story that Miss Manette always thought that her father had (A) remarried (B) become a businessman (C) moved to America (D) died many years ago
8. When Mr. Lorry ends his story, you can tell that Miss Manette (A) cries (B) faints (C) runs away (D) smiles

USING YOUR REASON
9. Mr. Lorry tells Miss Manette about her father in an indirect way because he (A) doesn't like her (B) wants to tease (C) is afraid the story may upset her (D) doesn't want her to know about her father

IDENTIFYING THE MOOD
10. Mr. Lorry's way of talking and his repeated references to "business " show that he is feeling (A) nervous (B) angry (C) silly (D) greedy

THINKING IT OVER

1. How would you have told Miss Manette this story? Why would you have told it to her that way?

CHAPTER 3

FINDING THE MAIN IDEA

1. The author is most interested in telling how
   (A) Mr. Lorry and Miss Manette meet Monsieur Manette
   (B) Monsieur and Madame Defarge run their wine shop
   (C) Monsieur and Madame Defarge attract customers to their shop   (D) Mr. Lorry and Miss Manette find the wine shop

REMEMBERING DETAIL

2. Which word best describes the look on the faces of the poor children and adults?
   (A) Dirty   (B) Bloody   (C) Hungry   (D) Tired
3. Who is Gaspard?
   (A) The owner of the wine shop   (B) The man who wrote the word "BLOOD" on the wall   (C) The hungriest man in the city   (D) The village fool
4. Which of these people were strangers to Monsieur and Madame Defarge?
   (A) Two men playing cards   (B) Two men playing dominoes   (C) Three men drinking at the counter
   (D) An elderly gentleman and a young lady

DRAWING CONCLUSIONS

5. You can tell from the story that the man making shoes is
   (A) an old shoemaker   (B) Monsieur Defarge's father
   (C) Monsieur Manette   (D) Jacques

USING YOUR REASON

6. Monsieur Defarge and the three men at the counter call each other "Jacques" because they
   (A) all have the same name   (B) are relatives   (C) use the name "Jacques" as a password   (D) don't want Madame Defarge to know their real names
7. Monsieur Defarge keeps Monsieur Manette's door locked because he
   (A) is keeping Monsieur Manette a prisoner   (B) is afraid

that Monsieur Manette will hurt someone   (C) fears that
Monsieur Manette will run away   (D) knows that Monsieur
Manette has grown used to a locked door

IDENTIFYING THE MOOD

8. How does Miss Manette feel when she enters her father's
   room?
   (A) Afraid   (B) Glad   (C) Sad   (D) Curious

THINKING IT OVER

1. How would you feel if you were in Miss Manette's place? in
   Mr. Lorry's place? in Defarge's place? in Monsieur Manette's
   place? Explain your answers.

CHAPTER 4

FINDING THE MAIN IDEA

1. This chapter is mostly about
   (A) Monsieur Defarge's wine shop   (B) Mr. Lorry's
   courage   (C) the reunion of Monsieur Manette and his
   daughter   (D) the meeting between Monsieur Manette and
   Mr. Lorry

REMEMBERING DETAIL

2. Through all the years of his imprisonment, Monsieur Manette
   kept a rag tied on a string around his neck. What was in it?
   (A) A cross   (B) Two strands of his wife's hair   (C) Two
   ticket stubs   (D) A rabbit's foot

DRAWING CONCLUSIONS

3. From the way Monsieur Manette reacts you can tell that, for
   a while, he thinks his daughter is his
   (A) enemy   (B) wife   (C) nurse   (D) jailer
4. You can tell from the story that the Manettes are on their
   way to
   (A) America   (B) England   (C) Italy   (D) Spain

USING YOUR REASON

5. When asked to tell his name, Monsieur Manette says, "One
   Hundred and Five, North Tower," because he is
   (A) insane   (B) telling a joke   (C) in the habit of giving
   his prison identity   (D) lonely

IDENTIFYING THE MOOD

6. When Monsieur Manette sees his daughter, he feels
   (A) happy and overjoyed   (B) angry and annoyed
   (C) tired and sleepy   (D) frightened and confused

Book 2—CHAPTER 1

FINDING THE MAIN IDEA

1. The main idea of this chapter is that
   (A) Mr. Lorry is well known in Fleet Street   (B) Charles
   Darnay is being tried for treason   (C) Jerry Cruncher is
   well known in Fleet Street   (D) the prisoner is a quiet man

REMEMBERING DETAIL

2. The year is now
   (A) 1780   (B) 1870   (C) 1788   (D) 1776
3. For the last five years, the Manettes have been living in
   (A) Boston   (B) London   (C) Paris   (D) Dover
4. The last time Jerry Cruncher appeared, he was
   (A) writing a letter to his father   (B) in love with Miss
   Manette   (C) studying to be a lawyer   (D) bringing a
   message for Mr. Lorry to the stagecoach
5. Old Bailey is
   (A) an old man who used to be a lawyer   (B) an old judge
   (C) a prison and criminal court   (D) a tavern
6. The two kings referred to in this chapter are King Louis XVI
   of France and King George III of
   (A) the United States   (B) England   (C) Ireland
   (D) Holland
7. In the England of 1780, a person found guilty of treason was
   (A) sentenced to life in prison   (B) banished from England
   (C) electrocuted   (D) hanged, drawn and quartered
8. Charles Darnay has been accused of treason for being
   (A) an American spy   (B) an English spy   (C) a French
   spy   (D) a hardened criminal
9. Which of the following describes Charles Darnay?
   (A) Fat, bald, about 40   (B) Short, blond, about 60
   (C) Tall, short hair, about 18   (D) Handsome, long hair,
   about 25

DRAWING CONCLUSIONS

10. You can tell from the story that the two people Charles

Darnay saw in the mirror are
(A) Mr. Lorry and Jerry Cruncher   (B) King George and
King Louis   (C) Monsieur Manette and Lucie (D) George
Washington and Benedict Arnold

IDENTIFYING THE MOOD
11. As the trial is about to begin Charles Darnay feels
(A) nervous and fearful   (B) sick and tired   (C) jolly and
amused   (D) calm and self-assured

CHAPTER 2

FINDING THE MAIN IDEA
1. In this chapter, the author is mostly interested in telling how
Charles Darnay is
(A) stabbed in the back   (B) sent to Virginia   (C) found
guilty   (D) found not guilty

REMEMBERING DETAIL
2. The Attorney General is
(A) the lawyer for Charles Darnay   (B) the highest-ranking
lawyer in England   (C) a general in the English army
(D) the lawyer for the government
3. Who is Mr. Stryver?
(A) A bank clerk   (B) The lawyer for Charles Darnay
(C) An English spy   (D) The Attorney General
4. Mr. Barsad is
(A) an English spy   (B) a bank president   (C) a
highwayman   (D) a lawyer
5. Who has Mr. Cly known for seven or eight years?
(A) Mr. Lorry   (B) Monsieur Manette   (C) Mr. Barsad
(D) Lucie
6. Mr. Carton works as
(A) a lawyer for the prosecution   (B) a bank messenger
(C) the Attorney General   (D) an assistant lawyer for the
defense
7. The two people in the courtroom who look very much alike
are
(A) Lucie and Monsieur Manette   (B) Mr. Lorry and
Jerry Cruncher   (C) Mr. Stryver and the Attorney General
(D) Charles Darnay and Mr. Carton

DRAWING CONCLUSIONS

8. You can figure out that five years ago Charles Darnay was
(A) in a tavern   (B) on a boat to America   (C) in the Old
Bailey   (D) on the same boat from France to England with
Mr. Lorry and the Manettes

USING YOUR REASON

9. Instead of saying "ACQUITTED," the author would have
meant the same thing if he had said
(A) GUILTY   (B) NOT GUILTY   (C) NO DECISION
(D) THE JURY QUITS

IDENTIFYING THE MOOD

10. In the story, Mr. Carton seems to care about
(A) Mr. Stryver   (B) Miss Manette   (C) Mr. Lorry
(D) Monsieur Manette

CHAPTER 3

FINDING THE MAIN IDEA

1. This chapter is mostly about which of these characters?
(A) Sydney Carton   (B) Lucie Manette   (C) Mr. Stryver
(D) Charles Darnay

REMEMBERING DETAIL

2. Who does Monsieur Manette stare at with a look of fear and
distrust?
(A) Mr. Stryver   (B) Charles Darnay   (C) Mr. Carton
(D) Mr. Lorry

3. Charles Darnay may have been the only person to see and
realize the importance of
(A) the note that Sydney Carton passed to Mr. Stryver
(B) the mirror in the courtroom   (C) the presence of Dr.
Manette at the trial   (D) the judge's wig

DRAWING CONCLUSIONS

4. You can tell from the story that Sydney Carton's feelings
toward Charles Darnay include
(A) hate   (B) jealousy   (C) curiosity   (D) joy

USING YOUR REASON

5. When the author says that Sydney Carton has finished the
"brief for that case," he is talking about

(A) a briefcase   (B) a short letter to Lucie Manette
(C) a plan of an argument, in behalf of a client   (D) an
expense account

6. Sydney Carton drinks because he

(A) has been told to stay on a liquid diet   (B) wishes to
forget the trial   (C) doesn't like people   (D) has wasted
his talents

THINKING IT OVER

1. Which character would you rather be like: Sydney Carton or
Mr. Stryver? Why?

CHAPTER 4

FINDING THE MAIN IDEA

1. This chapter is mostly about

(A) the rivalry between Sydney Carton and Charles Darnay

(B) the illness of Monsieur Manette   (C) the weather

(D) the friendship among the Manettes and Mr. Lorry

REMEMBERING DETAIL

2. Dr. Manette is getting to be known as

(A) an old grouch   (B) a kind gentleman   (C) a rich man
(D) a skilled physician

3. Dr. Manette is made comfortable by the presence of

(A) Lucie   (B) Sydney Carton   (C) Mr. Lorry
(D) Miss Pross

4. Lucie is called "Ladybird" by

(A) Sydney Carton   (B) Dr. Manette   (C) Miss Pross
(D) Charles Darnay

5. During the night, there is a

(A) storm   (B) tornado   (C) hurricane   (D) tidal wave

6. How long has it been since the trial?

(A) Four years   (B) Three weeks   (C) Four months
(D) Eight days

DRAWING CONCLUSIONS

7. You can tell that Dr. Manette gets dizzy and upset for a while
because of

(A) food poisoning   (B) Sydney Carton's laziness
(C) the rain   (D) Charles Darnay's story about the prisoner
in the tower

USING YOUR REASON

8. Another word for "fidelity" would be

(A) selfishness   (B) indifference   (C) faithfulness
(D) falseheartedness

IDENTIFYING THE MOOD

9. How did Sydney Carton feel when he heard Lucie's "foolish fancy"?

(A) Sympathetic   (B) Uncomfortable   (C) Suspicious
(D) Uncaring

THINKING IT OVER

1. Why do you think Dr. Manette still keeps his shoemaking tools? Why do you think Mr. Lorry might find the sight of the bench and tools upsetting? Why doesn't Miss Pross seem to mind?

CHAPTER 5

FINDING THE MAIN IDEA

1. This chapter is mostly about

(A) the accident in the road   (B) the Duke's palace
(C) the Marquis' handsome face   (D) Monsieur Defarge's philosophy

REMEMBERING DETAIL

2. The date is now

(A) July, 1790   (B) July, 1780   (C) July, 1800
(D) July, 1870

3. The action of this chapter is set in

(A) London   (B) Dover   (C) Los Angeles   (D) Paris

4. The Marquis is about how old?

(A) 30   (B) 40   (C) 50   (D) 60

DRAWING CONCLUSIONS

5. We can tell that the meeting between the Duke and the Marquis

(A) was a great success   (B) did not take place   (C) did not go well for the Marquis   (D) ended in bloodshed

6. From the story, you can tell that the Marquis' carriage has

(A) run over a child   (B) lost a wheel   (C) run over a dog   (D) gotten stuck in a ditch

7. You can tell that the child's father is
(A) Monsieur Defarge   (B) the Marquis   (C) the Duke
(D) Gaspard
8. You can figure out from the story that the tall, thin figure who follows the Marquis' carriage is
(A) Gaspard   (B) the Duke   (C) Monsieur Defarge
(D) Charles Darnay

IDENTIFYING THE MOOD

9. Which of the following words best describes the mood of the Marquis after having run over the child?
(A) Fear   (B) Sadness   (C) Indifference   (D) Horror
10. When one of his gold coins is thrown back at him, the mood of the Marquis changes to
(A) anger   (B) sadness   (C) fear   (D) horror

THINKING IT OVER

1. What kind of a person is the Marquis? Why do you think his greatest concern seems to be for his horses?
2. Who do you suppose threw the gold coin at the Marquis' carriage? Explain your answer.

CHAPTER 6

FINDING THE MAIN IDEA

1. This chapter is mostly about
(A) Charles Darnay   (B) the roadmender   (C) the Marquis   (D) Gaspard

REMEMBERING DETAIL

2. The people who live on the Marquis' land are
(A) poor   (B) well-off   (C) happy   (D) lazy
3. The people are burdened by too
(A) much work   (B) many children   (C) many bosses
(D) many taxes
4. The Marquis stops to question a
(A) carriage driver   (B) well digger   (C) tax collector
(D) road mender
6. Monsieur Gabelle is the
(A) road mender   (B) Marquis   (C) Duke
(D) Marquis' caretaker

7. Charles has decided that he will support himself by
   (A) working in England (B) working in France
   (C) living off his savings (D) living off the Manettes

DRAWING CONCLUSIONS

8. You can figure out from the story that the Marquis has seen
   (A) a bird (B) a bear (C) Monsieur Gabelle
   (D) Gaspard
9. You can tell from the story that Charles Darnay is the nephew of
   (A) Monsieur Gabelle (B) Monsieur Manette
   (C) Monsieur Defarge (D) the Marquis
10. You can figure out from the story that Charles thinks his uncle would like to
   (A) be friends with him (B) get rid of him (C) reward him (D) understand him

USING YOUR REASON

11. Charles Darnay seeks to correct the wrongs done by his family because it had been the wish of his
   (A) father (B) grandfather (C) mother (D) aunt

IDENTIFYING THE MOOD

12. What do the French peasants feel toward the Marquis and his family?
   (A) Respect and favor (B) Love and admiration
   (C) Hate and fear (D) Interest and curiosity

THINKING IT OVER

1. What do you suppose the author means when he says, "A stone face had been added, during the night, for which the castle had waited through about two hundred years"?

CHAPTER 7

FINDING THE MAIN IDEA

1. The main idea of this chapter is that
   (A) Charles Darnay and Dr. Manette have an understanding
   (B) Charles Darnay and Sydney Carton love Lucie
   (C) Sydney Carton and Lucie have a secret (D) Charles Darnay and Sydney Carton are bitter enemies

REMEMBERING DETAIL

2. Back in England, Charles Darnay supports himself by
(A) becoming a doctor   (B) working as a banker
(C) working as a teacher and translator   (D) working for a lawyer

3. Charles Darnay asks Dr. Manette for permission to
(A) leave England   (B) borrow a lot of money
(C) remain in England   (D) marry Lucie

4. Charles will tell Dr. Manette his real name
(A) in two weeks   (B) when the moon is full   (C) on his marriage morning   (D) in two days

5. Lucie discovers that her father has made use of his
(A) snuffbox   (B) shaving brush   (C) shoemaking tools
(D) stethoscope

6. Lucie was surprised by Sydney Carton's call because
(A) he hadn't visited her in a long time   (B) it came right after her marriage   (C) it came in the daytime   (D) she didn't care for Sydney Carton

7. Lucie had never been quite at ease with
(A) her father   (B) Mr. Lorry   (C) Sydney Carton
(D) Charles Darnay

DRAWING CONCLUSIONS

8. You can tell from the story that Sydney Carton thinks of himself as a
(A) great success   (B) very handsome man   (C) liar
(D) failure

IDENTIFYING THE MOOD

9. What does Lucie feel for Sydney Carton?
(A) Compassion and pity   (B) Love and adoration
(C) Boredom and impatience   (D) Hate and fear

THINKING IT OVER

1. In this chapter, Sydney Carton tells Lucie, "there is a man who would give his life, to keep a life you love beside you."
Do you find this realistic? Do you think that, if Sydney's words were put to the test some day, he would actually give up his life? Explain your answers.

2. If Sydney Carton is one of the TWO UNSELFISH LOVERS referred to in the chapter title, who is the other one? Might this chapter have been entitled THREE UNSELFISH LOVERS? Why?

256

CHAPTER 8

FINDING THE MAIN IDEA

1. The main idea of this chapter is that the family of the
Marquis, and of John Barsad, are
(A) coming into their inheritances   (B) related
(C) woven into Madame Defarge's knitting   (D) not on
speaking terms

REMEMBERING DETAIL

2. Who tells the story of Gaspard's last days?
(A) Jacques   (B) The road mender   (C) Madame Defarge
(D) Ernest Defarge

3. Who attempted to present the King with a petition asking
pardon for Gaspard?
(A) The road mender   (B) Madame Defarge   (C) Sydney
Carton   (D) Ernest Defarge

4. What was Gaspard's fate?
(A) He escaped.   (B) He was exiled.   (C) He died in
prison.   (D) He was hanged.

5. The Defarges and their friends record the names of their
enemies—in code—in Madame Defarge's knitting. Whose
name is woven into the knitting in revenge for the death of
Gaspard?
(A) John Barsad   (B) Sydney Carton   (C) Dr. Manette
(D) The family of the Marquis

6. What was the name of Charles Darnay's mother?
(A) Darnay   (B) Dorsey   (C) Dufais   (D) D'Aulnais

7. The Defarges learn from John Barsad that
(A) Dr. Manette is living in London   (B) Lucie Manette is
going to marry Sydney Carton   (C) Dr. Manette is returning
to Paris   (D) Lucie is engaged to Charles Darnay

DRAWING CONCLUSIONS

8. You can tell from the story that the people at the wine shop
know that a rose in Madame Defarge's hair is a signal to
(A) call the police   (B) leave the shop   (C) be on the
lookout for a suspicious person   (D) arm themselves

9. You can figure out from the story that the Defarges know
that the spy is
(A) Charles Darnay   (B) Jacques   (C) John Barsad
(D) the road mender

THINKING IT OVER

1. What sort of information do you suppose John Barsad hoped to get from the Defarges? If you were in his place, as an English spy in France, would you have asked the same questions, or different ones? Why?

CHAPTER 9

FINDING THE MAIN IDEA

1. The main idea of this chapter is that
   (A) Dr. Manette wishes to remarry   (B) Mr. Lorry is a wonderful friend   (C) Dr. Manette suffers a relapse
   (D) Mr. Lorry wishes to marry Miss Pross

REMEMBERING DETAIL

2. For the second time since his arrival in England, Dr. Manette is
   (A) making house calls   (B) delivering a baby
   (C) making shoes   (D) studying surgery
3. The people who kept watch over Dr. Manette are
   (A) Miss Pross and Lucie Manette   (B) Mr. Lorry and Sydney Carton   (C) Charles Darnay and Miss Pross
   (D) Mr. Lorry and Miss Pross
4. Dr. Manette was ill for
   (A) two days   (B) three weeks   (C) nine hours
   (D) nine days
5. Dr. Manette says his relapse is due to
   (A) distressing memories   (B) food poisoning   (C) a dislike for Charles Darnay   (D) worries about money
6. Dr. Manette and Mr. Lorry agree that Mr. Lorry will
   (A) vacation in Paris   (B) write to Lucie   (C) see Dr. Manette's patients   (D) destroy Dr. Manette's shoemaking bench
7. Miss Pross tells Lucie about
   (A) Mr. Lorry's good manners   (B) Sydney Carton's stories   (C) Dr. Manette's patients   (D) Dr. Manette's relapse
8. Lucie's two children have a strong affection for
   (A) Sydney Carton   (B) Mr. Lorry   (C) Miss Pross
   (D) Dr. Manette

9. Little Lucie is six years old in the year
   (A) 1799   (B) 1809   (C) 1779   (D) 1789

DRAWING CONCLUSIONS

10. You can figure out from the story that Dr. Manette suffers his relapse after the shock of
    (A) learning Charles Darnay's real name   (B) realizing that his only child is married   (C) learning Sydney Carton's real name   (D) discovering that he is getting old
11. You can tell from the story that the "friend" of Mr. Lorry is
    (A) Sydney Carton   (B) Dr. Manette   (C) Lucie
    (D) Charles Darnay

THINKING IT OVER

1. In this chapter, Mr. Lorry decides that he must remove Dr. Manette's shoemaking materials. Do you think that this was the best thing to do? If you were Mr. Lorry, would you have done the same thing? Explain.

CHAPTER 10

FINDING THE MAIN IDEA

1. The main idea of this chapter is that
   (A) the Defarges are wicked   (B) the Manettes were smart to leave France   (C) the poor people of Paris have revolted
   (D) Dr. Manette had been a prisoner in the Bastille

REMEMBERING DETAIL

2. The Bastille, in Paris, is a
   (A) street   (B) castle   (C) prison   (D) statue
3. The Defarges lead the assault on the
   (A) King's palace   (B) Marquis' castle   (C) Bastille
   (D) Eiffel Tower

DRAWING CONCLUSIONS

4. You can figure out from the story that Ernest Defarge is looking in Dr. Manette's old jail cell for a
   (A) purse   (B) hammer   (C) photograph   (D) note
5. You can tell from the story that the governor of the prison was
   (A) put on trial   (B) killed   (C) put in jail   (D) exiled

6. From reading the story, you can tell that one of the prison guards has been
(A) made a hero   (B) called a spy   (C) hung from a lamppost   (D) a prince in disguise

USING YOUR REASON
7. The people storm the Bastille because it is a symbol of
(A) justice, freedom, and good government   (B) tyranny, injustice, and oppression   (C) cannons, muskets, and smoke
(D) wealth, taxes, and property

THINKING IT OVER
1. How do you think the author feels about the attack on the Bastille? How do you feel about it? Explain your answers.

CHAPTER 11

FINDING THE MAIN IDEA
1. The main idea of this chapter is that the poor are
(A) challenging the old laws   (B) creating a new, fair government   (C) demanding revenge   (D) building statues of Ernest and Madame Defarge

REMEMBERING DETAIL
2. When do the events in this chapter take place?
(A) A year after the marriage of Charles Darnay and Lucie Manette   (B) The day after the capture of the Bastille
(C) A week after the capture of the Bastille   (D) A month after the capture of the Bastille
3. Who is Foulon?
(A) The old Prime Minister of France   (B) The Duke of Burgundy   (C) A friend of Charles Darnay   (D) A man who told the starving people that they could eat grass
4. What did the people seize that "they had never had before, for which they were not educated, and which, therefore, they often misused to unjust and cruel ends"?
(A) Power   (B) Freedom   (C) Wealth   (D) Land

IDENTIFYING THE MOOD
5. The mood of the people has changed from quiet to
(A) peaceful   (B) violent   (C) exhausted   (D) hungry

DRAWING CONCLUSIONS

6. You can figure out from the story that the
   (A) revolutionaries have set fire to the Marquis' castle
   (B) road mender has been taken prisoner   (C) people have
   forgotten all about Gaspard   (D) Defarges have forgotten
   all about Dr. Manette

7. You can tell from the story that Monsieur Gabelle saves his
   own life by
   (A) running away   (B) hiding at the top of his house
   (C) giving the people all his money   (D) hiding in the cellar

THINKING IT OVER

1. In this chapter we learn that the nobleman who owned the
   castle paid the villagers for working. He got very little rent or
   taxes. Yet the villagers burned the castle. Why do you think
   they did this?

CHAPTER 12

FINDING THE MAIN IDEA

1. In this chapter, the author is mostly interested in telling how
   Charles Darnay decides to
   (A) go to America   (B) bring his family to France
   (C) go to Paris to save Monsieur Gabelle   (D) leave
   Monsieur Gabelle to his fate

REMEMBERING DETAIL

2. The year is now
   (A) 1790   (B) 1791   (C) 1792   (D) 1793

3. During the past three years, most of the wealthy people of
   France have
   (A) fled the country   (B) fought for their lives and property
   (C) lived in Italy   (D) tried to become friendly with the
   people in power

4. The meeting place in London of the nobles who fled from
   France was
   (A) Buckingham Palace   (B) Hyde Park   (C) London
   Bridge   (D) Tellson's Bank

5. Despite the danger, Mr. Lorry has decided to go to Paris with
   Jerry because
   (A) Paris is beautiful   (B) the Tellson's Bank branch in

Paris has been burned to the ground   (C) he wants to save the books and papers that Tellson's Bank in Paris is holding for its clients   (D) Jerry has never been to Paris
6. In this chapter, we learn that Darnay's real name is
   (A) St. Everest   (B) Everready   (C) St. Eventide   (D) St. Evrémonde
7. That night, Charles Darnay wrote letters to
   (A) Mr. Lorry and Sydney Carton   (B) Dr. Manette and Miss Pross   (C) Lucie and Dr. Manette   (D) Lucie and Mr. Lorry

DRAWING CONCLUSIONS
8. You can figure out from the story that Mr. Lorry does not think Charles Darnay will go to Paris because
   (A) Charles Darnay has a family to look after   (B) Mr. Lorry is too busy preparing his own trip   (C) Mr. Lorry still does not know Charles Darnay's real name   (D) Darnay takes special measures so Mr. Lorry will not discover the truth

THINKING IT OVER
1. In this chapter, Charles decides to go to Paris to try to save the life of a trusty servant. Do you find it realistic that he would leave his family, and put his own life in danger, for the sake of a man he hardly knows? What would you have done? Explain.

Book 3—CHAPTER 1

FINDING THE MAIN IDEA
1. The main idea of this chapter is that, after a long, difficult trip to Paris, Charles Darnay is
   (A) cheered as a hero   (B) asked to leave the country   (C) given a medal   (D) put in jail

REMEMBERING DETAIL
2. Charles Darnay makes very slow progress because of the poor traveling conditions and because he was
   (A) sick with a fever   (B) homesick for his wife and child   (C) unsure of whether or not to continue   (D) stopped twenty times a day
3. In the town of Beauvais, the people curse Darnay for being

(A) an oppressor of the people   (B) a tyrant   (C) an aristocrat   (D) a writer
4. The revolutionaries may have passed a law that condemns to death all
(A) emigrants who return   (B) emigrants living outside of France   (C) peasants who wish to be aristocrats
(D) foreigners who visit France
5. When Darnay arrives in Paris he is immediately called a
(A) gentleman   (B) traitor   (C) prisoner   (D) scholar
6. When Darnay and Ernest Defarge speak together, Defarge
(A) promises to do what he can   (B) pretends that he does not know who Darnay is   (C) refuses to help Darnay
(D) tells Darnay to say his prayers
7. Darnay is taken to a prison called
(A) the Tower   (B) La Force   (C) the Bastille   (D) the Abbaye
8. When Darnay is led to his cell, he passes by
(A) pickpockets   (B) murderers   (C) peasants
(D) nobles

IDENTIFYING THE MOOD
9. When Darnay finds himself locked in his cell, he
(A) rants and raves   (B) tries to remain calm   (C) smiles at his rotten luck   (D) asks for a lawyer

THINKING IT OVER
1. What do you think Darnay would have done if he had known about the laws against emigrants before he left England? What would you have done, in Darnay's place? Explain.

CHAPTER 2

FINDING THE MAIN IDEA
1. This chapter is mainly about
(A) Mr. Lorry's financial worries   (B) Dr. Manette's charmed life   (C) Darnay's courage   (D) the arrival in Paris of Dr. Manette and Lucie

REMEMBERING DETAIL
2. In his faithfulness to Tellson's, Mr. Lorry did not think about
(A) personal safety   (B) financial security   (C) bank loyalty   (D) friendly relations

3. What could Mr. Lorry see through his window?
   (A) A church steeple   (B) La Guillotine   (C) A
   shoemaker's shop   (D) A large grindstone
4. Mr. Lorry is amazed to receive two visitors. They are
   (A) Charles and Lucie   (B) Lucie and Miss Pross
   (C) Dr. Manette and Lucie   (D) Dr. Manette and Jerry
   Cruncher
5. Dr. Manette believes that he is free from all danger because
   he has been a
   (A) close friend of the Defarges   (B) doctor in Beauvais
   (C) prisoner in the Bastille   (D) supporter of charities
6. Dr. Manette believes that he will be able to
   (A) speak to Charles   (B) help Charles out of all danger
   (C) steal Madame Defarge's knitting   (D) bribe Ernest
   Defarge

USING YOUR REASON
7. Dr. Manette and Lucie come to Paris because they
   (A) feel Charles must be lonely   (B) want to see Mr. Lorry
   (C) realize Charles's danger   (D) need a vacation

IDENTIFYING THE MOOD
8. How does Dr. Manette feel amidst the terrible dangers in
   Paris?
   (A) Timid and fearful   (B) Hot and bothered   (C) Calm
   and brave   (D) Sick and tired

THINKING IT OVER
1. What do you think about Mr. Lorry's suggestion that Dr.
   Manette speak to the crowd? What would you have done if
   you had been in Dr. Manette's place? Explain your answers.

CHAPTER 3

FINDING THE MAIN IDEA
1. The main idea of this chapter is that Dr. Manette's efforts to
   free Charles are being prevented by
   (A) Tellson's Bank   (B) unknown causes   (C) little
   Lucie's homesickness   (D) Darnay's stubborness

REMEMBERING DETAIL
2. Lucie and little Lucie do not stay with Mr. Lorry at the bank
   because

(A) Lucie wants her own apartment   (B) Lucie is the wife of an emigrant   (C) Lucie wants to get to know another part of the city   (D) there isn't enough room

3. Who finds Lucie's new apartment?
   (A) Lucie   (B) Miss Pross   (C) Mr. Lorry
   (D) Dr. Manette

4. Who gives Mr. Lorry the note from Dr. Manette which tells him that Charles is alive and well?
   (A) Madame Defarge   (B) Lucie   (C) Ernest Defarge
   (D) The road mender

5. Mr. Lorry is afraid that all the horrors Dr. Manette has just seen will
   (A) make him return to England   (B) shock Lucie
   (C) bring back the old illness   (D) give him a heart attack

DRAWING CONCLUSIONS

6. You can figure out from the story that, compared to his wife, Ernest Defarge is
   (A) more courageous   (B) less hardhearted   (C) more suspicious   (D) less friendly

7. You can tell from the story that the new government in France
   (A) is doing an excellent job   (B) has lost control of things   (C) is not interested in forming an army   (D) will last forever

IDENTIFYING THE MOOD

8. After kissing Madame Defarge's hand, Lucie's feelings toward her change from
   (A) fear to hate   (B) love to respect   (C) anger to surprise   (D) gratitude to alarm

THINKING IT OVER

1. Do you trust the Defarges? Do you believe that they are concerned for the welfare and safety of Charles and his family? Explain your answers.

CHAPTER 4

FINDING THE MAIN IDEA

1. The main idea of this chapter is that Lucie stands where Charles may be able to see her, and she is seen there by

(A) Jerry Cruncher and Miss Pross   (B) Sidney Carton and
John Barsad   (C) the woodsawyer and Madame Defarge
(D) Ernest Defarge and the road mender

REMEMBERING DETAIL

2. The date is now about
   (A) December, 1777   (B) June, 1799   (C) May, 1788
   (D) December, 1793
3. Lucie arranged her household as if
   (A) she were in New York   (B) her father had died
   (C) she had a very large family   (D) her husband had been
   there
4. Lucie's appearance
   (A) changes greatly   (B) stays the same   (C) does not
   change greatly   (D) changes for the better
5. Who tells Lucie about the place in the street where Charles
   may be able to see her?
   (A) Mr. Lorry   (B) John Barsad   (C) Miss Pross
   (D) Dr. Manette
6. The woodsawyer has a habit of saying
   (A) "I wonder who that could be?"   (B) "Go to the devil!"
   (C) "But it's none of my business"   (D) "It's business as
   usual"
7. The Carmagnole is a
   (A) kind of cheesecake   (B) song of freedom   (C) secret
   Revolutionary language   (D) frightening Revolutionary
   dance
8. Charles is about to be moved from La Force to
   (A) Lucie's home   (B) the bank office   (C) an
   underground hiding place   (D) the Conciergerie prison

USING YOUR REASON

10. When the author says "all poured red wine for La Guillotine,"
    he means that
    (A) the French did not drink white wine   (B) beer was
    never fashionable in France   (C) everyone who went to
    watch the beheadings drank wine   (D) the blood of victims
    of the Guillotine looked like red wine

IDENTIFYING THE MOOD

11. When Lucie saw the Revolutionary dance, she probably felt
    (A) happy   (B) curious   (C) afraid   (D) bored

266

CHAPTER 5

FINDING THE MAIN IDEA

1. In this chapter, the author is mostly interested in telling how
(A) Lucie takes care of her household   (B) Mr. Lorry
manages the bank   (C) Dr. Manette discovers Darnay's
enemies   (D) Charles is tried, released, and recaptured

REMEMBERING DETAIL

2. Monsieur Gabelle has just been released from
(A) the Bastille   (B) the Conciergerie   (C) La Force
(D) the Abbaye

3. After a few hours with his family, Charles is
(A) ready for bed   (B) upset by noise on the staircase
(C) again taken prisoner   (D) taught to dance the
Carmagnole

4. According to one of his captors, how many people have
accused Charles?
(A) One   (B) Two   (C) Three   (D) Four

5. Two of Darnay's accusers are
(A) Ernest and Madame Defarge   (B) the road mender and
the woodsawyer   (C) the woodsawyer and John Barsad
(D) Jerry Cruncher and Miss Pross

DRAWING CONCLUSIONS

6. You can figure out from the story that after Darnay's release
Lucie is still uncertain about his safety because she
(A) has been having nightmares   (B) is afraid of Madame
Defarge   (C) has heard rumors   (D) doesn't trust Mr.
Lorry

IDENTIFYING THE MOOD

7. When Lucie sees Charles, she
(A) laughs   (B) smiles   (C) frowns   (D) weeps

8. After the trial the mood of the people who surround Charles
and Dr. Manette is
(A) hostile   (B) quiet   (C) triumphant   (D) worried

THINKING IT OVER

1. In this chapter, Charles finally wins his release, only to be
taken prisoner again the very same day. Dr. Manette thought
that he had finally accomplished what he had been planning
for so long.

Have you ever had the experience of thinking that you had finally completed or achieved something, only to have it taken away before you could enjoy it? Describe your experience.

CHAPTER 6

FINDING THE MAIN IDEA
1. This chapter is mostly about
   (A) Lucie   (B) Dr. Manette   (C) Charles   (D) John Barsad

REMEMBERING DETAIL
2. In a wine shop, Miss Pross recognizes her
   (A) uncle   (B) sister   (C) brother   (D) mother
3. Solomon has been going under the name of
   (A) Sydney Carton   (B) Charles Evrémonde   (C) John Barsad   (D) Jerry Cruncher
4. Sydney Carton informs Mr. Lorry that
   (A) John Barsad is his brother   (B) Charles has been arrested again   (C) Jerry Cruncher wants to return to England   (D) Miss Pross is sick

DRAWING CONCLUSIONS
5. You can tell from the story that John Barsad is particularly afraid of
   (A) Dr. Manette   (B) Ernest Defarge   (C) Charles Darnay   (D) Madame Defarge

USING YOUR REASON
6. Sydney Carton has secretly come to Paris to help
   (A) Miss Pross   (B) Dr. Manette   (C) Mr. and Mrs. Darnay   (D) Mr. Lorry

IDENTIFYING THE MOOD
7. When John Barsad is recognized by Miss Pross he feels
   (A) delighted   (B) moved   (C) annoyed   (D) flattered
8. When Mr. Lorry remembers where he has seen Mr. Barsad before, he looks at him with
   (A) open dislike   (B) a friendly smile   (C) an understanding heart   (D) undisguised fear

THINKING IT OVER

1. Why is the title of this chapter A HAND AT CARDS? Why does Sydney Carton say, "Let the doctor play the winning game; I will play the losing one"? Throughout the last portion of the chapter, the situation is described in terms of a card game. Do you find the card game comparison interesting? Silly? Confusing? Explain.

CHAPTER 7

FINDING THE MAIN IDEA

1. This chapter is mostly about
   (A) Charles Darnay's second trial (B) Mr. Lorry's fatigue
   (C) John Barsad's spying tricks (D) Lucie's courage

REMEMBERING DETAIL

2. Sydney Carton tells Mr. Lorry that with Barsad's aid, Carton will be able to
   (A) free Charles (B) save Lucie (C) see Charles
   (D) help Mr. Lorry return to England
3. Mr. Lorry had never seen the better side of
   (A) Jerry Cruncher (B) Sydney Carton (C) Miss Pross
   (D) John Barsad
4. Mr. Lorry realizes that Sydney Carton is
   (A) no longer young (B) in love with Lucie (C) an
   excellent lawyer (D) a bit odd
5. Who is ready to leave Paris for London?
   (A) Mr. Lorry (B) Dr. Manette (C) Sydney Carton
   (D) Jerry Cruncher
6. How old is Mr. Lorry?
   (A) 45 (B) 56 (C) 67 (D) 78
7. The third accuser of Charles Darnay is
   (A) Sydney Carton (B) Dr. Manette (C) Mr. Lorry
   (D) the woodsawyer
8. Sydney Carton goes into the shop of a
   (A) chemist (B) butcher (C) grocer (D) tailor

IDENTIFYING THE MOOD

9. When Sydney Carton notices that Mr. Lorry is weeping for Charles Darnay, Carton feels
   (A) angry (B) sympathetic (C) proud (D) confused

THINKING IT OVER

1. Sydney Carton repeats to himself, "I am the resurrection and the life, saith the Lord." And the author tells us that "in a city ruled by the ax, the chain of memory that brought the words to mind might have been easily found."

   What do you think the author means by this statement? Explain your answer.

CHAPTER 8

FINDING THE MAIN IDEA

1. This chapter is mostly about
   (A) Sydney Carton's plans   (B) Mr. Lorry's wish to leave France   (C) Dr. Manette's paper   (D) Madame Defarge's knitting

REMEMBERING DETAIL

2. Dr. Manette wrote while he was in
   (A) the courtroom   (B) his home   (C) his office
   (D) prison

3. The story occurred in
   (A) December, 1757   (B) June, 1875   (C) July, 1752
   (D) October, 1775

4. The two patients that Dr. Manette visits are
   (A) 2 men, both 20 years old   (B) a young woman of 20 and a boy of 17   (C) an old man of 80 and a young man of 21   (D) a woman of 40 and a young woman of 19

5. What does the woman keep secret from Dr. Manette?
   (A) Her home town   (B) Her family name   (C) Her date of birth   (D) Her last wish

6. What does Dr. Manette refuse to take from the brothers Evrémonde?
   (A) A horse   (B) A gold watch   (C) A silk tie   (D) A purse of gold

7. Dr. Manette is visited at his home by
   (A) the brothers Evrémonde   (B) Lucie Manette   (C) the wife of the Marquis and her son Charles   (D) Sydney Carton

8. Dr. Manette resents the fact that the brothers Evrémonde have never brought him any news about
   (A) the world   (B) the stock market   (C) his wife
   (D) his patients

9. In his paper, Dr. Manette denounces
(A) the King and Queen   (B) Ernest Defarge   (C) the
brothers Evrémonde and their descendants   (D) the
Governor of the Bastille

10. As a result of the final trial, Darnay is
(A) found innocent and released   (B) sentenced to death
within 24 hours   (C) found guilty and fined $5,000
(D) sentenced to life in prison

DRAWING CONCLUSIONS

11. You can tell from the story that as a young man Dr. Manette
had been known as
(A) a lady-killer   (B) an excellent actor   (C) a man
without honor   (D) an able doctor

USING YOUR REASON

12. Instead of describing his cell as "doleful," Dr. Manette would
have meant the same thing if he had said it was
(A) filthy   (B) freezing   (C) sorrowful   (D) dark

THINKING IT OVER

1. Think about the behavior of the girl's brother. What do you
think of his actions? Was he heroic? Was he foolish? Explain
your answers.

CHAPTER 9

FINDING THE MAIN IDEA

1. The main idea of this chapter is that
(A) Mr. Lorry is in a hurry to get home   (B) Dr. Manette
is worried about Lucie   (C) Sydney Carton has a plan to
save Dr. Manette, Lucie and her daughter   (D) Ernest
Defarge has a soft spot in his heart for Lucie

REMEMBERING DETAIL

2. In the courtroom after the trial Lucie
(A) saw a ghost   (B) tripped   (C) fainted   (D) witnessed
a murder

3. While Lucie is still unconscious, Sydney kisses her and
whispers,
(A) I love you   (B) Get well soon   (C) I'll see you
tomorrow   (D) A life you love

271

4. When Carton enters the wine shop, Madame Defarge notices that he
(A) seems ill   (B) has a limp   (C) speaks excellent French
(D) looks like Darnay

5. When Dr. Manette finally comes back, he asks for his
(A) stethoscope   (B) pipe and slippers   (C) bench
(D) granddaughter

6. Carton has figured out that the Defarges are going to accuse Lucie and her father of
(A) stealing Revolutionary coins   (B) robbing Tellson's bank   (C) fleeing from Paris   (D) plotting a prison escape

USING YOUR REASON

7. At the wine shop, Carton learns why
(A) Madame Defarge hates Darnay   (B) Ernest Defarge has so many friends   (C) the Defarges are poor   (D) John Barsad became a spy

IDENTIFYING THE MOOD

8. When Ernest Defarge suggests that Dr. Manette should be spared, Madame Defarge replies
(A) meekly   (B) angrily   (C) sympathetically
(D) quietly

THINKING IT OVER

1. Has Sydney Carton changed since he was first introduced in the book? If you think that he has changed, do you find the change believable? Explain your answers.

CHAPTER 10

FINDING THE MAIN IDEA

1. This chapter is mostly about the
(A) failure of Carton's plan   (B) success of Carton's plan
(C) little seamstress's fear   (D) courage of Mr. Barsad

REMEMBERING DETAIL

2. Fifty-two is mentioned because it is
(A) Lucie's lucky number   (B) Dr. Manette's age
(C) the number of prisoners awaiting their fate   (D) the number of hours Darnay has left to live

3. Resigned to his fate, Darnay writes letters to Lucie, Dr. Manette, and
   (A) Sydney Carton   (B) Mr. Lorry   (C) Ernest Defarge
   (D) Jerry Cruncher
4. When Carton was at the chemist's shop, he bought a
   (A) bottle of aspirins for Lucie   (B) can of tobacco
   (C) bottle of smelling salts   (D) drug to make Darnay unconscious
5. Which of the following represents a final danger to the success of Sydney Carton's plan?
   (A) Dr. Manette may try to rescue him.   (B) Mr. Lorry may want to remain in Paris.   (C) Madame Defarge may recognize Carton.   (D) Lucie may recognize her husband.

DRAWING CONCLUSIONS

6. You can figure out from the story that Darnay's cell door is opened at
   (A) 3 A.M.   (B) 5 P.M.   (C) 12 A.M.   (D) 1 P.M.
7. You can figure out from the story that the first voice Darnay hears as his cell door is opened is that of
   A) Sydney Carton   (B) Mr. Barsad   (C) Ernest Defarge
   (D) the woodsawyer

IDENTIFYING THE MOOD

8. When Mr. Barsad is taking Darnay from the prison, Mr. Barsad feels
   (A) guilty   (B) sorrowful   (C) joyful   (D) nervous
9. After the coach is examined at the city gates, the people feel
   (A) joy and excitement   (B) terror and grief   (C) hatred and anger   (D) confidence and satisfaction

THINKING IT OVER

1. Why do you think Carton made sure that the Defarges saw him in Paris? How did this fit into his plan? Explain.
2. Why did Carton drug Darnay? Was this necessary? Explain.

CHAPTER 11

FINDING THE MAIN IDEA

1. In this chapter, the author is mainly interested in telling how
   (A) Miss Pross and Jerry Cruncher escape from Paris

(B) Miss Pross wins a battle to the death with Madame Defarge   (C) the woodsawyer has seen Lucie signalling to Charles   (D) Jacques Three plans to prevent Dr. Manette's escape

REMEMBERING DETAIL

2. Madame Defarge was in the woodsawyer's shed at about the same time that
   (A) Carton came to the cell of Darnay   (B) Ernest Defarge was speaking to Jacques Two   (C) Miss Pross and Jerry Cruncher had arranged to meet   (D) Dr. Manette, Lucie, and Mr. Lorry had reached Beauvais
3. Miss Pross and Jerry agree to meet at the
   (A) guillotine   (B) Tuileries   (C) cathedral
   (D) woodsawyer's shed
4. Miss Pross and Madame Defarge are both very
   (A) beautiful   (B) determined   (C) hysterical
   (D) tender
5. Miss Pross would give anything to know whether
   (A) Madame Defarge suspects that Lucie has already fled
   (B) Jerry Cruncher is waiting for her   (C) Madame Defarge is armed   (D) Madame Defarge understands Italian

USING YOUR REASON

6. Miss Pross did not want to start out from Tellson's Bank because
   (A) the bank was destroyed   (B) soldiers have surrounded the bank   (C) people might be suspicious   (D) she never liked Mr. Lorry
7. Miss Pross throws the door key into the river because she
   (A) doesn't want anyone else to rent the apartment
   (B) wants to make it hard for the patriots to discover that the others have fled   (C) thinks it will bring her good luck
   (D) doesn't need it anymore

THINKING IT OVER

1. Does the author increase the suspense of his story by telling about the flight of the others in the coach *before* telling about Miss Pross and Madame Defarge? Explain your answer.

CHAPTER 12

FINDING THE MAIN IDEA

1. The main idea of this chapter is that
(A) the seamstress falls in love with Carton   (B) Lucie and the others are back in England   (C) Miss Pross is caught trying to escape   (D) Sydney Carton dies at the guillotine

REMEMBERING DETAIL

2. As the tumbrils rumble toward the guillotine, the clocks strike
(A) six   (B) three   (C) seven   (D) eight
3. Chairs are set up in front of the guillotine and a number of the women sit
(A) gossiping   (B) reading   (C) drawing   (D) knitting
4. The Vengeance is the
(A) guillotine   (B) anger of the people   (C) friend of Ernest Defarge   (D) friend of Madame Defarge
5. What advice does Carton give to the frightened seamstress?
(A) Close your eyes and count to one hundred.   (B) Keep your eyes on me and pay no attention to anything else.
(C) Keep your eyes on the guillotine.   (D) Close your eyes and make your mind a blank.
6. While Carton tries to comfort the seamstress, his thoughts are on
(A) his approaching death   (B) the seamstress   (C) his chances of escape   (D) Lucie and the others
7. The "tumbrils" in this chapter are also called
(A) cages   (B) jail cells   (C) carts   (D) sleds

USING YOUR REASON

8. Barsad says to himself, "Has he betrayed me?" because he
(A) suspects that Carton is plotting with the seamstress
(B) never trusted Carton in the first place   (C) looks into two of the three tumbrils and does not see Carton   (D) fears that Carton will escape

IDENTIFYING THE MOOD

9. The people who had witnessed Carton's death said that his mood had been
(A) hostile   (B) pitiable   (C) peaceful   (D) horrible

THINKING IT OVER

1. Why was it necessary for Lucie and the others to leave Paris
at exactly two o'clock? Why did Carton plan the escape for
the last possible moment? Explain.